"YOU DAMNED YOUNG FOOL!"

Lefty Dunlin screamed in rage. "I told you to quit while you still could.
You ain't made for this life. And now you've killed a man!"

Danny Crossett was too numb to speak as the outlaw went on. "And you might at least have killed some bully or gun-fightin' swine. But a straight one like Tolliver—"

Dunlin seemed to choke with fury and disgust. "Now you're with me forever, I guess. But kid—they'll kill you in less than three months!"

Books by Max Brand

Ambush at Torture Canyon
The Bandit of the Black Hills
The Bells of San Filipo
Black Jack
Blood on the Trail
The Blue Jay
The Border Kid
Danger Trail
Dead or Alive
Destry Rides Again
The False Rider
Fightin' Fool
Fightin' Four
Flaming Irons
Ghost Rider (Original title: Clung)
The Gun Tamer
Gunman's Reckoning
Harrigan
Hired Guns
Hunted Riders
The Jackson Trail
Larromee's Ranch
The Longhorn Feud
The Longhorn's Ranch
The Long, Long Trail
The Man from Mustang
On the Trail of Four

The Outlaw of Buffalo Flat
The Phantom Spy
Pillar Mountain
Pleasant Jim
The Reward
Ride the Wild Trail
Riders of the Plains
Rippon Rides Double
Rustlers of Beacon Creek
The Seven of Diamonds
Seven Trails
Shotgun Law
Silvertip's Search
Silvertip's Trap
Singing Guns
Steve Train's Ordeal
The Stingaree
The Stolen Stallion
The Streak
The Tenderfoot
Thunder Moon
Tragedy Trail
Trouble Kid
The Untamed
Valley of the Vanishing Men
Valley of Thieves
Vengeance Trail

Published by POCKET BOOKS

Max Brand

HUNTED RIDERS

PUBLISHED BY POCKET BOOKS NEW YORK

POCKET BOOKS, a Simon & Schuster division of
GULF & WESTERN CORPORATION
1230 Avenue of the Americas, New York, N.Y. 10020

ISBN: 0-671-82894-0

First Pocket Books printing December, 1950

12   11   10   9   8   7

Trademarks registered in the United States and other countries.

Printed in the U.S.A.

Contents

1. THE BLACK THIRTEENTH 1
2. LEFTY DUNLIN 5
3. HARD TO BEAR 11
4. HIS OWN PEOPLE 17
5. IN JAIL 21
6. "NEVER RUSH A DUNLIN" 26
7. THROUGH THE TREES 32
8. FOR FREEDOM 37
9. BULLDOGGING THROUGH 42
10. A VERY GOOD GIRL 47
11. LEFTY'S COUNTRY 52
12. TOLLIVER TAKES THE TRAIL 60
13. WHAT'S YOUR NAME? 64
14. A COOL RECEPTION 67
15. HERE'S A FRIEND 72
16. IN FOR IT NOW 77
17. THE GRIP OF FATE 82
18. THROUGH THE DOORWAY 87
19. FISHING FOR WHALES 91
20. A GOLDEN MOMENT 99
21. SCHEMES AND DREAMS 103
22. QUESTIONS AND ANSWERS 108
23. INTO THE WILDERNESS 113
24. A GHOST TRAILING 118
25. ONE CHANCE IN THREE 123

26. IT'S ME HE WANTS 128
27. THE HOLDUP 133
28. FUGITIVES 138
29. THREE HUNGRY WOLVES 144
30. IN THE SHADOWS 150
31. ANOTHER OMEN 154
32. A MESSAGE DELIVERED 159
33. A PLEASANT MESSENGER 164
34. A DECISION 169
35. WHAT NEXT? 174
36. OUT OF THE NIGHT 180
37. FIFTY ON THEIR HEELS 185
38. MANY AGAINST THEM 190
39. A PAINFUL PASSAGE 195
40. THE FOLLOWING PHANTOM 201
41. TYSON QUITS 206
42. A MEETING 212
    POSTSCRIPT 216

1. The Black Thirteenth

FROM LAMMER FALLS one can get into the mountains in ten minutes at a moderate walking pace, and in ten minutes more one may have a chance to take a shot at deer, at wolf, at bear, at some skulking puma, at a stone-yellow coyote, at lofty elk, or mountain sheep and goats which sometimes may venture down from their preferred region against the sky. That was why Jeremy Crossett brought his son West, and why he picked out Lammer Falls. They were only one easy stage from a railroad, and yet they were in the wilderness.

That was what Crossett wanted—to get out of the old civilized skin, so to speak, and slip into a new and rougher exterior, a new and rougher nature. But something altogether different from the old environment was what he wished for, so that like water the new would close over the head of his son and make him forget all that had gone before.

In his heart, Crossett knew that he would fail, and that his boy stood even now on the pale and uncertain horizon between death and life; but what brought him West with the youngster, what kept him here, what made him decide on the voyage through the mountains was the grim determination to keep struggling on.

The youth who sat at the other window in the same room with his father did not appear to be in the slightest danger. He was somewhat slender, but it was an athletic slightness; his eye and his skin were clear, and he had neither the fallen head nor the rounded shoulders of an invalid.

Now he stood up and leaned out the window.

"There's excitement coming our way," he declared with a sort of boyish enthusiasm. "Noise of something coming up the valley road, and every one in town is running that way! What's up, I wonder?"

"A new pack train is coming—that's all," suggested the older Crossett.

"No, they're taking their guns with them as they go to look!"

The father said nothing, but let his glance roam through the window and across the roofs of the blacksmith's shop and bakery across the street, and on up the mountainside beyond. He could see the great fir and spruce forest on the lower slopes, and the thinner growth of pines and lodgepole pines above, like a beard on the face of a giant, and the white streak of the Lammer River looking like a narrow ridge of snow in the distance; and then there was the timber line, and the beginning of the bald region of rocks above. That was as high as he could look, from where his chair stood, and the big peak crowded the window from top to bottom.

It had a voice, too, which caused every voice in Lammer Falls to be raised a little in speaking; that was the thunder of the cataract in which the course of the river ended down the mountainside, before it turned at sharp right angles to speed down the valley. Crossett, listening to the roar and beat of that thundering water, felt his heart expand with a desire to harness the wasted power. With it, he could turn how many mills, and draw how many trains straight up the gulch until they had tapped the vast resources of this lumber center.

He had the money, the imagination, and the practical experience for the execution of that task, but he could not more than give it a glance, now. A vaster problem lay before him, and that had to do with Daniel Crossett, his only son, his only child, and he now wifeless, fatherless, brotherless, sisterless in this world.

Could he keep Danny alive? he asked himself by day and by night. And though he had optimistic moments, yet he knew in his heart that he could not unless some inspiration were placed in his brain. Otherwise, his son was no better than a dead man!

Which needs some explanation.

There were two elements in the Crossett blood. If one turned back to the oldest family portraits one could see at a glance that the family had been divided in blood at that time, as it had remained ever since. There were the fair Crossetts and the black Crossetts, and there were none between. The vast majority of the family were blondes. Jeremy himself had had almost foolishly yellow hair and blue eyes when he was a child. How vastly he had detested himself and his appearance in those far-off days! After the blondes, there was no appearance in the family of brown-haired or gray-eyed people; but here and there appeared a Crossett with glistening black hair and gleaming black eyes. They were called in family history the "black Crossetts."

And Danny was black!

There was also this peculiarity about them—that every black Crossett in the memory of man had had an unlucky life. There were so few of them, and they appeared at such a distance one from the other, that no one had noticed this peculiarity connected with the Crossetts of the darker complexion until Jeremy began to delve into family history and examine the thing for himself.

He found plenty of records, and plenty of details, but in four centuries there were only twelve black Crossetts— in the direct line of descent, that is to say.

Not one of them had lived to forty. And Jeremy knew their names and all their fortunes by heart.

Edward Crossett was killed in a duel in Paris, in his twenty-second year. Sir Gerald Crossett was lost in his thirtieth year trying to find a Northwest Passage. Octavius Crossett, baronet, took his own life when his king died on the scaffold.

Oliver Crossett, a younger son, who was a brilliant captain in Marlborough's army, was found hanging from a rafter in his attic.

William Carney Crossett, baronet, in his twenty-fourth year, was found drowned in a swimming pool.

Charles Carney Crossett, Lord Windhurst, fell in a duel when he was hardly more than a boy.

Albert Crossett, Lord Windhurst, having followed Wellington in the Peninsular Campaign, one evening after dinner put a bullet through his head!

Then Sidney Crossett came to the States, the first of the family to make the step. His hair was black, also. He founded a great plantation in Virginia and lived to his thirty-ninth year when he was found dead in his bed, his face distorted by the effect of poison.

Henry Oswald Crossett, his son, at the age of eighteen, shot himself through the head in his room at college.

Andrew and Dickinson Crossett, twin brothers, fought for the Lost Cause together until, after Chancellorsville, they walked out one evening, and their bodies were found dead, side by side.

Denmen Crossett, a hero in the Indian Wars, in his twenty-second year, was drowned in a rapids on the upper Missouri.

These were the histories, in brief, of the last twelve Crossetts, black-haired and black-eyed, of whom Jeremy could be sure. And every one of them had died young. All had been brilliant, adventurous, successful. Three fell in duels, and the remaining nine had died in such circumstances that it seemed most likely they had taken their own lives.

For his own part, Jeremy Crossett was sure of it. A strange plague had followed that dark strain in the Crossett blood. No doubt it was caused, very largely, by a difference in the physical composition of all these men— all slender, tall, supple, alert fellows, with hair-trigger nerves, and with eyes that blazed from their portraits. Such men, consuming themselves by their own ardor, might well burn to the ashes of life before more normal people had fairly begun to live.

For in not a single instance was there a reasonable explanation of why these young men had chosen to end their lives. But a world of pain, a deep melancholy, had swept over them, and so they had fallen by their own hands.

Now, his own son, the thirteenth black Crossett, was of exactly the same type. For whether in his childhood or in his college days, Dan Crossett had been a leader, a burning brand among his fellows, gay, reckless, headlong in all his ways.

So he finished his college work, and there lay before him every prospect of a brilliant career. He had the great fortune of his father to look forward to. But there was one fatal blow—he was a black Crossett. Worst of all, Daniel himself knew all about the odd history of his predecessors. For, with his father during a summer vacation, he had wandered through picture galleries in England and examined the portraits; together they had delved into the family records.

And now, whether the defect really existed or not in the character of Daniel, certain it was that he felt himself foredoomed to take his life by his own hand!

2. Lefty Dunlin

HOW FAR SUGGESTION would work in that keen, nervous, highly sensitive soul, Jeremy Crossett could only guess, and all his forecast of the future was gloomy in the extreme. It was as though a hand were thrusting Daniel forward to a dark and unhappy fate. With him would go the last of the line. And those thoughts, in fact, were simply so much more fuel to the boy's natural impulse.

What we feel is foredoomed is apt to be hurried in execution. One grows tired of waiting for manifest destiny to overtake one. And every time the father saw the son with head bowed in gloom, his heart turned cold with expectancy; and whenever, in the night, he heard the restless foot of his boy pacing his room, Jeremy Crossett sat up in his bed and groaned in an agony of fear.

Then, in desperation, he thought of the West.

There would be a new environment; there would be a rough and sufficiently headlong life to fill the mind of Danny; and it was only in the lulls between campaigns— at the end of the day's work, so to speak—that the black Crossetts fell into despondency and felt the worthlessness of life.

So far, Jeremy was delighted with his plan, for the

boy had showed the greatest interest in it. He had loved hunting. He had grown up with a rifle in his hands, and whether at a target or a deer he was equally keen, equally accurate. He could barely wait in Lammer Falls until their outfit was ready, so keen was he to get into the uplands and at the game which awaited them there. Every detail of their equipment had been a joy to the youth, whether in the selection of the pack mules, or the hiring of the guides, or the engagement of a camp cook, or the picking out of the rifles, the revolvers, the shotguns. There were several saddle horses to buy; and the best were hardly good enough for the fat purse of Jeremy Crossett.

All this had filled the mind of Daniel, but still, from time to time, the dark humor came upon him, and the father felt that the danger was postponed, not actually overcome.

In the meantime, that noise was swelling at the lower end of the street, and Jeremy stood up to look from the window, not that such matters could interest him, but because he felt it his duty to encourage the interest of his son in all external things, in all that might keep his gloomy eyes from turning inward.

They saw that every one in Lammer Falls, apparently, had turned out of houses and shops and now were flocking into the street, with eager eyes all turned in one direction and now, around the lower bend, came a group of riders, and a dense mass of men around them.

When they drew nearer, Jeremy saw that the central figure in the cluster was a youth whose hands were bound to the pommel of his saddle, a darkly handsome rascal, who looked boldly and carelessly around him on the hostile faces in the crowd.

Even in spite of those bonds, it seemed that the guards feared this fellow, for they watched him, catlike. One on either side had a lariat over the head of the captive's horse, and guns were drawn in their hands.

As the cavalcade came under the windows of the hotel, a girl started out into the street and shook her fist at the prisoner.

"You'll hang, Lefty Dunlin!" she screamed. "You'll hang, and I'll watch it, and laugh—and laugh, Lefty!"

The prisoner turned in his saddle. His smile was bright as though he were acknowledging a cheer instead of an imprecation.

"No Dunlin ever was hanged, honey," said he.

The riders moved slowly on, halting at the little squat jail that stood on the next corner.

"Looked like my twin brother," said Daniel Crossett.

"Twin brother? Yours? I hope not, Dan," said the father. "That's a young scoundrel, I'll swear. I've heard that name before, though."

"It's not a rare name, is it?" asked the son. "We had some Dunlins at home, didn't we?"

He turned suddenly from the window, picked up some fishing tackle, and began to adjust it, with a frown. The father, watching, bit his lip, for he saw that the dark fit had fallen again on this boy.

When the rod was dropped, he was not surprised; nor when Daniel stood up suddenly and announced that he would go for a walk.

"It's a bare half hour till dinner time; you'd better wait," suggested Jeremy Crossett.

Daniel paused, then shrugged his shoulders, and slumped into a chair again, and his dull, blank eyes wandered to the window. So it was, day after day, that the fit seized him, and the terror seized his father.

They went down to dinner together and sat at a table covered with oilcloth, frayed by scrubbing until its pattern had disappeared. The room was well filled and at every corner there was only one topic of conversation, and that was the capture of Lefty Dunlin. They overheard enough to draw the sketch of Lefty's character; and what more they needed to know, the waitress paused to tell them, after staring at people who had not heard of the Dunlins.

For they were a famous lot, it appeared, and since they never had worked for a living and never would work, they had supported themselves by their wits for many generations. The Dunlins, it seemed, possessed various talents—they could turn their hand to confidence work, or to counterfeiting, or to shoving the queer, or to rustling, or to sneak-thieving, or to safe-cracking, or to crooked gambling, or to the clever sale of green goods, or to the salting of mines and the disposal of the same—in short, there was hardly a phase of illegitimate art to which they were not attached, and of which they were not the complete masters.

These gentlemen from time to time produced a man of more fiery blood, who battled for the sake of battle. There usually was a Dunlin somewhere in any large-sized shooting scrape among those mountains, and now and again there rode forth from the Dunlin clan a super-killer, a natural desperado.

Lefty Dunlin was of that type. He had roamed freely back and forth across the range, sometimes holding up a stage to make a bit of honest money, and sometimes cracking a safe in a bank, but doing all things single-handed, for it was said that he would trust no man in the entire world.

"But how long has this fellow been at large?" asked Daniel Crossett curiously.

"Him? Oh, he killed his first man when he was thirteen, and——"

"At thirteen!" cried Daniel.

"It was only a greaser," said the waitress dispassionately. "But still, the sheriff had to go through the motions of making an arrest, y'understand? And when he did it, Lefty Dunlin shot him down and left him near dead. That was just a beginning for Lefty, and he's kept on improvin' ever since."

"You speak," said Daniel, more curiously than before, "as though he's been slaughtering men ever since!"

"Oh, no," said the waitress, "I wouldn't give you the idea that Lefty is such a bad fellow. He ain't. And he ain't been so real bloodthirsty either. I suppose maybe he's killed not more than nine or ten—not known to have killed more, I mean. You don't bother Lefty and he don't bother you. Y'understand?"

"Nine men!" exclaimed Daniel, his eyes on fire. "To take the lives of nine men—and over a course of years?"

"He's thirty, I suppose," said the girl, "but he looks a lot younger, account of him having such an easy life!"

"An easy life!" exclaimed Daniel, more amazed than before.

"Well, what would you call it?" asked the waitress. "I mean, just sloping around the country taking what you want and dropping them that try to stop you? What would you call it? Easy, I'd say, and they never would've caught poor Lefty if it hadn't been for a wicked devil of a woman that betrayed him, bad luck to her!" She added with conviction. "But they'll never have the hanging of him, much as they'd like to have it!"

"Will the governor pardon him, then?"

"How long would he be governor if he did, now I ask you? But something will happen. They've had a dozen of the Dunlins waiting in jail to be hanged, one time or other. But have they ever got a rope on the neck of any of 'em? I guess I never heard about it nor nobody else around here. They ain't made to be hanged!"

"They live to ripe old age, then, the rascals?" asked Jeremy Crossett.

"They do that," said the girl. "They do that, just! They wither up and they get smaller, and finally they dry up and blow away, and no more is heard of 'em."

"Living almost forever in this manner," said Jeremy Crossett, "I suppose that they're beginning to swarm?"

"There never was many of them," said the girl. "They don't take very kind to married life, you see, but they just wander about, mostly, living on the fat of the land an' never worrying about nothing. Oh, nobody lives no fatter than a Dunlin, I can tell you!"

Jeremy Crossett fell into a brown study.

"To think that this fellow came from our own city, Danny," said he.

"From our city?" cried Daniel. "Is he really one of our own Dunlin tribe?"

Jeremy Crossett seemed a great deal disturbed. He started in his chair and frowned nervously at his son.

"Did I say from our own city?" he muttered. "Did I say that? I didn't mean it, Danny. I—it slipped from the tongue—I meant to say that perhaps he came from our own city."

Jeremy Crossett grew confused and took shelter behind his coffee cup. His son looked straight into his face and said nothing; after all, it was hardly a matter worth further inquiry.

After dinner, they went up from the dining room, and Danny went straight to his own chamber beside that of his father, while Jeremy Crossett sat before his window and watched Lammer Mountain rising dimly among the stars. He had many thoughts and wild ones, now, and as he leaned from the window to study the cause of a rising murmur in the street, he hardly noticed the little groups of men who were gathering at the street corners, talking excitedly.

The waitress, now the chambermaid, came in to turn down his bed.

"They'll be makin' trouble before the morning," said she.

Jeremy Crossett, deep in speculations, returned no answer.

"And maybe they'll be giving our town a black eye for the rest of the world!" said she. "Do you think so, sir?"

"I?" said Crossett hastily. "A black eye?"

"If they do it, I mean," she said.

"If they do what, please?"

"What they're aiming to do," said the girl darkly, and paused to pat the pillow into shape.

Mr. Crossett, mildly interested, waited.

"But if they hang him, they'll have no luck," said the girl fiercely. "The rest of the Dunlins will mark 'em down, and there'll be such a slaughter around here as no man ever heard of before! They'll mark down all the ringleaders and murder 'em one by one."

"Is a mob rising to lynch Lefty Dunlin?" asked Crossett.

"There's talk," said the girl. "I dunno what'll come

of it. But there's a lot of talk in the street about not waiting for the law to miss him!"

She left the room and, a moment later, Mr. Crossett became aware of a rapid, nervous, and uneven footfall that went up and down in the next chamber. He hurried to the wall and pressed his ear close to a crack. There was no doubt about it; his son had fallen deep into one of his fits of melancholy. That restless pacing might continue half the night, or if it were ended suddenly—

Mr. Crossett started up, covered with cold perspiration.

3.   Hard to Bear

AFTER THAT, Jeremy Crossett stood irresolute, like one drawn in two ways by a double purpose.

Finally, he turned sharply toward the door, very much as though he feared that his resolution would leave him if he did not execute his will at once. He passed into the hall, and with a grim face went toward the door of his son.

There he tapped. There was a pause which continued so long that his heart began to thunder; and finally the boy opened the door and showed his dark and solemn face.

"Come in, sir," said he, and stepped back.

"I've come with extraordinary news," said the father, as he entered. "By heaven! my lad, do you know what the people of the town have in mind now?"

"I've no idea, sir," said the boy.

"Murder, Danny! Yes, Danny, they've planned to take poor Lefty Dunlin out of the town jail and hang him to the nearest tree!"

Daniel Crossett looked in amazement at his father.

"After all," said he, "the man appears to be a ruffian and a murderer. I don't know what is to be expected for him; and if the rest of his race have escaped hanging, he might as well be used to establish a good precedent, I should think!"

"Good gad, Danny," said the father, "you don't know what you're saying! But—look down from the window!"

Danny, obediently, went to the window, but only after he had cast another glance of surprise at his father.

The moment his back was turned, Mr. Crossett lifted a corner of the bedspread, and there he saw the shining form of a new Colt revolver. He threw the spread back with a hasty jerk; but a very troubled man was Jeremy Crossett as he slowly followed his boy to the window. For he could see, now, a clear picture of Daniel walking up and down his room with hurrying step, and the gun hanging in his hand. The devil that hounded the race of Crossett surely was close behind this unlucky youth!

Daniel, from the window, turned and nodded.

"They're gathering," he said. "No doubt they'll make short work of Lefty Dunlin. Of course, that's an ugly thing—a lynching, I mean. But at the same time, it looks only like justice in this case—with such a ruffian as this Dunlin, I mean."

"Daniel!" cried the father.

"Sir?" said the boy, greatly surprised.

"But you don't understand—by heaven, Danny, we must do something to get the poor fellow out of his trouble!"

"We? We?" exclaimed Daniel, moving back a little. "I don't see that the thing has to rest on our hands. And besides—it looks a dangerous thing to interfere with the mob that's coming down there."

"It must be done," said the father firmly. "We have to do our best! Danny—God forgive me if I do wrong—but I have to tell you! That man in the jail is your own kin!"

There was no sign of great shock in the boy as he heard this. Instead, he turned on his father with an air of keen and awakened attention. There was a light almost of pleasure in his eye.

"Of course," said he, "that takes a little explaining!"

"I haven't time for details. I'll tell it to you in brief," said the father, studying the face of Daniel with a sort of frantic attention. "But you remember that your mother always was delicate, lad? She lived until you were nine, but she only lived because she didn't want to leave you. You felt that?"

Daniel was silent. It was the one theme in the world on which he could not speak, for never had there been a relationship between mother and son so close as that which had bound him to his mother.

"The doctor told us that it would be a dangerous business," said Crossett, forcing himself to continue. "And when the baby was born, your mother was desperately close to death—hardly a breath remained in her body, Danny. And the doctor said—why, I knew myself without being a doctor—that if she had any sort of shock it would be the end for her when she recovered consciousness. The fact was that the child was a boy, born dead!"

He paused, here, mopping his forehead, and staring earnestly at the boy. Daniel betrayed not the slightest emotion. He merely listened with a slightly inclined face, as though he were hearing the words of his father, but seeing at least one other face beside.

"I didn't know what to do," said Crossett, his rapid voice falling lower and lower. "There was only one great desire in my life, and that was to keep your mother with me. The doctor himself made the suggestion. That same evening, before he came to us, he'd delivered a woman in a poorer section of the town—a woman whose husband was dead, whose child was unwanted—at least a burden—and——"

He found it impossible to continue and paused again, panting, at which Daniel said firmly: "I suppose that I can guess. It was that old story of substituting children. The dead child was taken away and the false child was brought in——"

"Not false, Danny—only, you see——"

"There was a funeral from the home of the Dunlin family—I suppose it was the Dunlin family?"

The father was silent.

"And in our house—in your house, I mean to say—there was a good deal of happiness—and my poor mother—I mean," said the boy, with a sudden and terrible

change in his voice, "I mean—your wife—was saved—
and made happy—ah?"

"You're hard on me," muttered Crossett. "I wish to
God that I hadn't told you."

"You could have waited till I was older," said the boy
bitterly. "You might have waited till I was settled in business, say, or married, and with children of mine wearing
a false name—and a wife who would have shunned me
like a leper if she'd known my real origin! Yes, you might
have waited that long, sir!"

Mr. Crossett could not speak. He endured, his hands
clenched and his head bowed.

"However," said Daniel coldly, "blood always tells, and
before the end, no doubt, I'd have betrayed my bad
strain!"

"Don't say that, lad. Don't say that, Danny!" cried the
father. "Whatever name you take, there's no doubt about
your clean heart, boy! You have always been highminded
and manly!"

"Heredity is a small thing!" answered the youth savagely. "It doesn't matter, of course—it hardly counts, in
this country! But it counts with me! You can't make a
wooden ship out of steel bars. Heredity?" And then he
burst out with the theme which they both had pondered
over so long and never had mentioned to one another:
"If there's nothing in heredity, why have the black Crossetts taken their own lives for a dozen generations of
'em? Can you answer that, sir?"

The older man swayed in the storm, and he merely
answered feebly: "I should have told you when you were
younger and then the idea could have been adjusted in
your mind—you would have been able to grow into a new
idea of it—as the son of my affection, so to speak, Danny.
You understand me? I should have told you when you
were years younger—but I couldn't do it! Not while your
mother lived—I mean, while—my wife, Danny—ah, God!
Well, after she was gone, you meant doubly as much to
me. You may think this very odd, but because she'd loved
you so much, because she'd lavished herself on you, and

lived for you, I really began to feel that she had made you
her actual child!"

"A romantic emotion, sir," said Daniel, and bowed
slightly.

At that, Mr. Crossett flinched from the window, and
in the shadow into which he stepped he fumbled for the
wall, and rested one hand heavily against it.

"Romantic, perhaps," he managed to continue. "I
thought it was not particularly wrong, at the time. I
thought that you could wear a good and clean name, and
that you never would lack from me anything—"

"In the way of a fortune, sir, you could supply me. Ah,
I don't mean to bear down so hard! Only—you seem to
think that it's nothing. But it is! God knows that it is! It's
everything! It means that my life has been a complete lie.
I think of the people who have entertained me. I think—
why, all through school and college I walked in a cloud!
I was a Crossett. People used to point me out. Oh, a boy
hears everything. 'That's young Crossett. Look at him;
blood tells, you know!' They said those things behind my
back. They said them to my face sometimes! Well, I was
the aristocrat. If there was a dispute between a couple of
fellows they would come to me. A Crossett had to be
square. He'd be disgracing half a dozen centuries if he
weren't.

"You remember that there was trouble before the last
big football game and the Blue accused us of stealing their
signals and such stuff. I wrote personally to their captain
and declared there was nothing to it. Do you remember
the letter that he sent back?"

"I remember," said Crossett slowly, and his voice was
feeble in the dark.

" 'Dear Crossett,' " quoted the boy sadly. " 'I've taken
your letter to the coach and of course we agreed that
whatever you'd put your name to must be above reproach.
We're sending on formal word dropping all our accusa-
tions and offering an apology. Thank you for clearing
things up!' "

Crossett broke in: "It's wrong to look at it like that.
It wasn't a tribute to your family name but to your own

fine integrity, Danny. Dear lad, you'd stood as straight as a plumb line all your life, and the whole world knew that you were honor itself!"

"Honor?" echoed Daniel. "The honor of a Dunlin! The integrity of a Dunlin! The clean blood of a line of thieves, gamblers, murderers!"

He added with sudden violence: "I can see it all as clear as though I were looking through crystal! Ten thousand times I've had the horrible promptings to do perfectly rotten things. Dishonorable, sneaking, treacherous things; and I've had murder in me, too! I can remember a dozen times. Actual murder. But I put all those thoughts behind me. It wasn't possible. I couldn't be or do any of 'em. I was a Crossett! A Crossett!"

He began to laugh, and the jar of the sound made Jeremy Crossett tremble. He wanted to say many things, but words, for some reason, failed him. He parted his lips, but no sound came forth.

Then the boy added: "I shouldn't carry on like this. No doubt, if I were a Crossett such talk wouldn't be possible for me. If I were a Crossett in such a situation, I'd remember your kindness, and the way I've loved you, as if you really—"

He had to stop, and then went on, a trifle choked: "Some day I'll be able to thank you for the good you've done for me. Only—"

"Danny!" broke in the older man.

"Can you tell me," asked the boy, "what my real name is?"

"Good God, what should it be but—no, no! I don't know what you would have been called!"

"No name whatever, except Dunlin. Well, it's enough, I suppose. I'll be young Dunlin, or the new Dunlin, or some such thing, eh? I'll soon have my spots to wear, and the world can tell me by the pattern of 'em!"

He caught up his hat and jammed it on his head. Passing the bed, his hand made a sudden motion and caught something glittering from beneath the spread—a movement so fast that it almost escaped the eye of Crossett, except that he knew.

"Danny!" he called. "What are you going to do? Where are you going? Danny! I want you to—"

But Danny answered: "I've got to get outside—that's where the Dunlins belong!"

He slammed the door; his rapid steps went down the hall, and Jeremy Crossett sank into the chair by the window, trembling, unable to rise; and clutching the sill of the window. He was very sick; his heart was acting strangely; and a cloud of black was floating back and forth across his eyes.

4. His Own People

NOW, ON THE STREET, the youth looked calmly and sternly about him.

For all his experience on athletic fields, in the boxing ring, on the wrestling mat; at another earlier time he would have been touched with awe and fear at the sight of these rough fellows who strode through the street, with weapons in their hands. For they had a light of deadly purpose in their eyes. Whatever their plan, it had been made, at last, and now their voices were low murmurs. Most of them were wearing black masks. And they mustered under the shadow of the trees which faced the hotel in a dense and quiet mob.

But now Daniel regarded them calmly, with an eye of understanding. More than once, in the past, such crowds must have gathered to destroy his forbears, but they never had succeeded. Crafty wits, like the wits of a fox, and steady, sure hands had baffled greater numbers than these, no doubt, and of even more determined fighting men.

He was a Dunlin, and he felt something in him rising to welcome the new name, the real name. It was a sense of liberation and of strength that possessed him now, as though fetters had fallen away from his body and left him free for the first time. The Crossett name, the Crossett scruples must be gone. Sooner or later, the Dunlin nature must assert itself, and that nature was to prey upon the world as the fox or the leopard preys on the animal kingdom.

In the first place, if blood mattered in this world, he must do something for Lefty Dunlin in the jail. He wished that he could have worn his new nature for such a time as would make him familiar with more of the wiles and shifts of his kind, but as it was, all he could think of doing was to go straight to the jail.

There he found a deputy sheriff sitting on the front steps.

"Are you in control here?" asked Daniel.

"I am, young feller," replied the other.

"Do you know what's starting up the street in this direction?"

"I don't," answered the other curtly.

"A lynching mob," said Daniel.

"Is there?" asked the man on the steps.

He took the rifle which was lying across his knees and rested it against the wall.

"Did they send you on before to ask where I stand?" he suggested.

"Suppose that they have," said Danny.

"Why, then, stranger," said the deputy, "I dunno exactly where I *should* stand. I'm here for the sheriff. I got to enforce the law. But what's the law? Can you tell me?"

"Suppose we say: The law is to keep prisoners for fair trial and execution at the hands of the appointed people."

"Would you say that—joking aside? Well, youngster, I dunno. Who makes the laws? The people. Who is bigger than the laws? The people. Who are the people? The crowd down the street. What does that crowd want? To take Lefty Dunlin and hang him to the big cottonwood, yonder. Well, if they want to do it, that's the law. And the laws that are wrote down, they ain't any more important than the laws that ain't wrote down. Is that sound sense?"

Upon this train of naïve reasoning, Daniel offered no

comment, and therefore the deputy continued to answer his own questions.

"It sounds like sense, it looks like sense, and it *is* sense. Now, if those fellers think that I'm afraid to stand agin' 'em, they're mistaken. I ain't afraid. But how does the case look to me? Why, Lefty Dunlin has been seen and trailed and traced, and his crimes, some of 'em, have been saddled right on his shoulders. He's a killer and a crook. As for a trial, he's been tried already. Everybody knows that he ought to hang. I'm the same as everybody else. I know it, too. Now what good is there in putting the law to a whole lot of trouble? Besides, who can tell? If they keep him for a long time, most likely he'll slip away. The Dunlins have a knack for that sort of thing, as maybe you know."

"Certainly," said Daniel, letting nature take its course in this man.

"So what I aim to do is just to set here. When they come, I'll stand up and tell 'em that the written law forbids 'em to enter this here jail. And if they keep on, after that it's on their own heads for taking the law into their hands. Ain't that logical, right and reasonable? It is, and that's where I stand. You can go and tell 'em that!"

Daniel considered.

"Very well," said he, "but first I'd like to see the prisoner."

"What right have you got to see him?" asked the deputy.

"Why not? He's a public prisoner, I suppose?"

"Maybe he is," admitted the other unwillingly, "but if you aim to take him away with you—why, I'll see you damned first, son. Not to you, nor to any other one man, or two men, or three men would I give him up. Because why? Because they don't mean nothing, they ain't the law. But when a hundred or so comes along, why, then it's different. It's the will of the majority. It's the will of the majority," he repeated, turning the phrase over his tongue, with relish, "and I guess that I'm just a servant of the people!"

He was much pleased by his own oration, and Daniel said quietly: "I'm not a fool. I'm not trying to force your hand. But we want to know just where in the jail we can locate Lefty Dunlin. Haven't I a right to see him? I'm not fool enough to try to take him away from you!"

"Why, I dunno," said the deputy. "That sounds sort of reasonable. I got to admit that sounds like logic. Come along, then!"

He rose and opened the door of the jail and ushered his guest in.

"There's Lefty down in that corner cell. The keys," he added, "maybe I carry myself, and they would have to be taken off me by force. Yes, I'd resist. Not with a gun, mind you, but I'd resist. I got to resist force. It's my job. However, I got the keys!"

"I understand," said Daniel.

"Well, then, we'd better be going back! I think that I hear 'em coming down the street, now!"

"Go back, then," said Daniel. "I'll stay here."

"You'll what?"

"I'll stay here, I say. Go back, and tell the rest of them that if they try to rush this jail, I'll shoot them down as fast as they come through the door, and I'll shoot to kill!"

The deputy was about to speak; more than that, he was about to act, but he found a gleam of steel in the hand of the young stranger.

"By heaven," he stammered suddenly, "you're a Dunlin, too!"

"Back out the door, and hurry," said Daniel. "And remember what I told you. There'll be no lynching tonight, unless they want to pay with blood for the fun they'll have!"

The jailer backed slowly toward the door, and down the street beyond rolled a rapidly increasing body of noise.

5. In Jail

AS FOR THE DEPUTY, that continued stumbling backward became too much for his nerves, and when he was outside the door, he turned and fled at full speed. Daniel slammed the heavy door and shot home the bolts.

The rush of the crowd was coming nearer, now, and it sounded curiously like the moan of a storm wind through a forest. He began a rapid tour of inspection. Outside the cell room, there were three chambers: the sheriff's office, a small kitchen, and a sort of anteroom near the entrance. On each of these, one window opened; but he noted with relief that the means of preventing egress from the building ought to defeat ingress, also, for the windows were heavily barred with strong steel.

He found a bull's-eye lantern in the antechamber, and this he lighted, holding the match for an instant in his hand as he listened to the loud beating on the front door. Then he shut the hood of the light and stepped back into the inclosure of the cell room.

It was quite dark; there was only one dim eye of red in the distance—the lighted cigarette of Lefty Dunlin, beyond doubt, as he sat in his cell calmly smoking, and, perhaps, casting a glance or two before him into the eternity which was now so close.

The wash of the crowd had spilled quite around the building, by this time, but, from the continual shouting, the chief force was evidently centered around the front door; it was like the beating of a heavy sea along a shore of rocks and caves, the noise of one voice constantly overlapping upon another.

Then one personality seemed to dominate the rest. The jangling at the heavy door stopped; the confusion died away, and a man shouted loudly: "You within!"

"Well?" said Daniel.

"Stranger, we dunno who you are, and we don't care.

21

If you wanted some fun, you've had it. Now, open that door and we'll let you go. But if you don't, we'll beat the door down and take you out along with Lefty. We figure that you're one of his people, anyway!"

Daniel made no answer, but retreated now down the aisle to the cell of Lefty Dunlin, where he sat enscreened with steel bars.

"Lefty!" said he.

Lefty stood up. Irons jingled on his legs and on his hands.

"What's the play, partner?" he asked cheerfully.

"A stupid one," said Daniel. "I let the deputy get away without taking the keys from him. What can I do now?"

"Give me something small, and I'll pick every lock in this old-fashioned dump inside of ten minutes. We won't have time, though. They're going to beat down the door—"

The crash of an improvised battering ram sounded on the door, now, followed by the loud bang of the door as it sprang back into place after yielding a little to the impact.

Daniel loosed from the lantern a single ray that played dimly on the square face of the door; then he put a bullet through the top of it.

That shot caused a wild panic outside the jail, a departing rush of feet, a clamor of voices.

"It *is* another Dunlin!" some one shouted.

"No guts," commented Lefty mildly. "Always noticed that; you take ten of the bravest men in the world and lump 'em together—they got nothing but a nervous system and they work it overtime. Maybe we can do something with 'em, stranger. Have you got anything that I can use on these locks?" he repeated a little anxiously.

"Such as what?"

"A watch spring is the best, of course."

"I haven't one."

"You haven't got a watch?"

"I'm a fool!" said Daniel.

He snatched from his pocket a beauty cased in platinum, inclosing the finest of Swiss movements. This he dashed to the floor, and there was a sadly musical murmur as the ruined works disintegrated.

"Very well," said Lefty. "There was something slick in the way of a watch that went to hell, just then."

At the same time, he began to stir a little. Daniel, as he picked up the shattered fragments of the watch, heard the clinking chains and the murmur of the prisoner's voice, talking to himself.

Then, with a flash of the lantern, he saw that Lefty had neatly slipped the irons from his wrists. He asked for a ray of light, and when it was given to him, he took the main spring of the watch and broke off a small piece of it.

"It's a real one," said Lefty, regarding the point of breakage with a critical eye of admiration. "The finest sort of steel! If I can't work with this, I can't work with anything!"

And still he paused, holding the little broken piece of metal close to his eye, and smiling with a sort of artist's appreciation.

"Man, man!" exclaimed Daniel. "You may be throwing away your life by wasting time like this!"

Lefty put the bit of spring into a vest pocket and rolled a cigarette.

"I dunno," said Lefty. "If a gent is going to win through, he'll win through; if he ain't going to win through, he ain't."

He delivered this piece of fatalistic philosophy with a gravely nodded head, as he lighted his smoke.

"Besides," said Lefty, "if you hurry up too much, you don't get none of the fun out of nothing!"

From his very heart Daniel admired this assured young man. There were no more nerves in this fellow than in some image chipped from black Egyptian basalt.

"Do you want a light here?" he asked, preparing to drop the lantern.

"I don't," said Dunlin. "I want darkness, so's I can get a better touch with my fingers. You can't see with your fingers in the daylight, you know!"

Exactly what this meant, Daniel did not guess; but he

knew that he was the amateur, the tyro, and that he must
do what a recognized professional directed him to do.

So he merely asked: "I'll keep going the rounds of the
windows, then?"

"You?" said Lefty. "I suppose that you know what to
do as well as me! Sure—watch the windows, oldtimer.
I'll finish this little job in a few minutes."

Watch the windows? There were four in the big cell
room, but they were very high and narrow, not apt to
be forced and hardly big enough to allow a man to work
his body through. However, there were three other rooms
in the building, and on each of these opened a danger
point. The bars, to be sure, were very strong, but the
whole network of steel might be pried away from its
moorings in the masonry.

There was no sign of trouble in the sheriff's room; the
antechamber was dark and still; but in the kitchen, as he
slipped through the doorway, he heard the faintest of
sounds, rather like the ticking of a watch in a very still
place, a steady, regular creaking.

He slipped to his knees and one hand, and looking upward in this position, he could make out two heads of
men beyond the bars. They were softly, patiently working
to pry the bars away; and Daniel put a bullet squarely between their heads. No, the shot must have leaned a little to
one side of the bull's-eye, for the hat was jerked from
one fellow's head, and both of them leaped from sight
with yells.

There was a babble of voices that ran in a wave all
round the jail building, but one dominant cry was clearly
audible to Daniel.

"He's shooting to kill! By heaven, here's my hat, if
you doubt it. He clipped right along the side of my
head——"

Daniel shuddered.

And yet, stiffening himself a little, he avowed that it
made little difference; if he was a Dunlin, precondemned
to lead the Dunlin life, the sooner he painted himself in
their color, the better, perhaps, for them and for him.

He went on softly, moving like a cat, making no noise.

Never before had he known that he could step like this! A hidden talent, he thought bitterly, and useful for a thief, say, almost more than any other gift!

Yet, he was neither gloomy, frightened, nor overwhelmed by his situation. He was no fatalist like Lefty Dunlin, but he felt that in this place, hemmed in with two-foot walls of solid stone masonry and strong steel bars, watched by hundreds of armed fighting men, all that he could do was to wait for each new incident, and try to meet it as it rose.

In the meantime, perhaps the temper of the crowd would cool. They would disperse. The sheriff would arrive. And who could lay hand on Daniel for having enforced the law against the will of a murdering mob?

So Daniel thought, and he could not help smiling a little, knowing in his heart of hearts how thoroughly Lefty Dunlin deserved to hang.

Now his task of watchman was complicated by a new difficulty, for the wind leaped suddenly down the Lammer Valley and brought rain upon its flying skirts. In crashing volleys, the rain and the hail rushed against the jail; the wind grew to such violence that a heavy pounding began at one end of the building, as though another battering ram were being applied there, high up toward the roof; but when Daniel hastily ran to the back of the building, he realized by the character of the noise that it was simply a great branch of a tree being heaved by the storm, now and again, against the wall.

However, with that uproar continuing, his duty was made a hundredfold more difficult—the last glimmer of starlight was gone, and the screech and bellow of the storm drowned every lesser sound.

The crowd had neither been cooled by the violence of the rain and wind nor by their long wait. When Daniel peered out from the windows on either side, he could see the faint gleam of cigarettes under the shelter of the trees and in the high brush, and every window, along the street, was now lighted.

Still he continued his rounds until he came to the

sheriff's office, and, as he stepped into the doorway, out of the wall of darkness inside came a double report, a double flash of blinding light like a giant hornet's sting thrust itself into Daniel's side!

6.   "Never Rush a Dunlin"

WITH GREAT CROSSBARS and many hands, no doubt, they had ripped away the bars from the window, and then they had calmly waited inside the room, accustoming their eyes to the faintest light which existed there. Now they had their reward!

Daniel leaped back, stumbled and fell headlong, and that fall saved his life, for a rapid chattering of bullets poured through the air where he had been standing. Half blinded with surprise, the shock of the fall, the stinging pain in his side, he fired blindly through the doorway. A wild yell answered the shot, and then subdued cursing.

The firing stopped; men were heard scattering here and there from before the fatal gap of the doorway, and Daniel writhed a little forward, caught the edge of the door, and slammed it. There was both an outer and an inner bolt; the inner bolt he now shot home.

To be sure, they might force the door as they had forced the window; but, so doing, they were more apt to make a noise which he could hear.

He slipped into the kitchen; there, at least, the bars were still intact. He tried the antechamber, and there also the outer line had not been stormed.

Down his side, in the meantime, the hot blood was trickling, and the end, perhaps, was not far off; and yet he felt a savage satisfaction. For once in all his life he had been himself; and he who has realized himself only once is willing to die with less sense of pain.

In the meantime—Lefty!

He went hastily back to the cell barely in time to unsheath a ray from his lantern and see the gallant Lefty stepping jauntily through the opened door.

"It took a little time," said Lefty in apology. "The damned locks were a bit rusty inside, y'understand? I couldn't help it, partner!" He added: "What's been happening? I heard a little party on."

"They've got the office," answered Daniel. "They tore the bars off, I suppose; but I managed to keep them from getting in here—I closed the door on 'em. They've nicked me, Lefty, and I think I'm done. But if I can last, I'll try to help you out of this hole. What can we do?"

"Look at the nick," said Lefty instantly. "Where is it?"

"There's no time," said Daniel eagerly. "If you want to try a——"

"There's a world of time," said Lefty. "It's hurry that makes trouble in this old world, stranger! Lemme see—where was that nick you talked about?"

Daniel threw off his coat, pulled up his shirt, and Dunlin played the lantern on the spot. A red slash several inches long was bleeding freely on his left side, near the heart. Dunlin puckered the flesh with his hands and then exclaimed with satisfaction.

"Only a graze," said he. "Hold that shirt up a minute. They knew I couldn't break jail with adhesive tape, and they left a roll on me. Why, kid, we'll patch you up better than new—hold the lantern higher. That's it."

He took the adhesive bandage from his pocket, and a clean white handkerchief, and still his movements seemed maddeningly deliberate to Daniel.

"They'll spot the light—they can look in through the window and pick us off!" said Daniel anxiously. "For Heaven's sake, man, let this scratch go. It amounts to nothing!"

"Might get infected," said the calm Dunlin. "As for the light showing 'em anything—why, you always got to take a chance, with anything worth while. Here you are! Lean a little this way so I can draw the flesh together better—very neat and very easy, kid!"

He applied the strips up and down, drawing them over the handkerchief, which he had folded on the face of the wound. Then he reënforced his work with two long ribbons that passed half way around Daniel.

Even then he was in no haste, but paused a moment, and admired what he had done, opening the lantern shutter to the full.

"I got a sort of taste for this sort of thing," declared Lefty. "I ought to have been a doctor, if I hadn't found better things to do. And——"

He had snapped the lantern shutter home as he was speaking, and at the same instant a rifle clanged from the window facing them. The bullet rang on the bar of a cell like the plucked string of a harp.

"A miss," said deliberate Lefty Dunlin. "And that'll only dishearten 'em. I begin to feel that maybe it ain't my time to die. What made you horn in, though? Did Jerry send you, maybe?"

"If there's anything to do," said Daniel, almost in anger, "we have to do it now! They've broken into one room. They'll be in the others before long. They've got us cornered, Lefty Dunlin! They may break through with a rush, at any time!"

"You're green, I see," remarked the other, and yawned a little. "I haven't slept for a couple of nights," he explained. And then he went on: "You're green, kid. They never rush a Dunlin. It don't pay. Why throw away the lives of a half a dozen honest men in order to catch one thief? You see the idea? They got too much sense to be very brave! Tenderfeet would be a lot more dangerous to handle."

He deliberately unveiled the lantern and flooded Daniel with light from head to foot.

"Tenderfeet like yourself," said Lefty, and hooded the light once more as Daniel dodged instinctively to escape another rifle shot from that yawning window.

But there was no second bullet. The storm sprang on the jail and shook it with fury from head to heel almost as though some giant, infuriated by the clumsiness of the lynchers, had determined to crush the building and all who were in it.

"We'll stand here and wait, then," said Daniel, nervously enraged.

"If you rush around and get excited," observed Lefty Dunlin, "you never come to no good. Brain stops working. Ever notice a man trying to remember a name? Got it right on the tip of his tongue. He begins to frown, beats his head, damns his stupid brain. And he don't remember the name until just as he's about to fall asleep that night!

"Well, it's always the same," continued Lefty's drawl with maddening slowness. "When a fellow says: 'We got to do something!' it means that his brain is all in a knot. It don't work out that way. Just you keep loose, stranger. Wait to see what's going to happen. Don't you try to play the cards before they fall!"

He broke off and chuckled a little, highly pleased with this example he had drawn forth.

"Jerry would like to hear that," remarked Dunlin. "Jerry would sort of laugh if he heard that!"

And Dunlin laughed again, with a real merriment.

It occurred to Daniel that he had done all he could. His companion was beyond doubt a most resolved, desperate, and cunning fellow, beneath that careless exterior. And it was better not to clog the mind of Dunlin with arguments and suggestions. So Daniel kept his silence.

They made a cautious round of the rooms, once again, from the doorways, flashing one beam of light over the interiors, and this time they found that in the muffling roar of the storm the steel bars of the kitchen window had been torn loose at the bottom. No doubt they would soon give way at the top, also. And this success, perhaps, explained the slowness of the lynchers to attempt an attack through the office of the sheriff. They would wait until they had secured a double front and then make a double attack.

"Dog-gone interesting!" declared the outlaw, as he stepped back into the cell room. "I've seen mobs before. They nearly got me down in Tucson, one day. But never anything like this. It looks like they hate me pretty bad. Usually don't take more than a shower to cool off a crowd, y'understand? But these fellows, they've stuck on like badgers. I kind of admire this here town, kid. If I was to get lynche[,] I couldn't ever be strung up by none better than those boys!"

He said it with a sort of heartfelt sympathy and emotion, as though he were praising the sterling. virtues of a brother. And again Daniel listened nervously.

"There's no cellar," said Lefty, making a cigarette and lighting it.

"That shining end of the cigarette makes a perfect mark," said Daniel grimly. "If they spot that through a window——"

"We got to take chances," observed Lefty, "and I figure always that it's a lot better to take them in comfort. But there's no cellar to this place. That lets out any chance of digging away, I suppose. The windows ain't very easy come at, and I suppose that there's twenty rifles marking every window, pretty near. Suppose that we look at the roof, kid?"

"The roof? We're not birds, I suppose!" said Daniel, bad temper getting the best of him.

"Maybe we ain't; maybe we are. You can never tell till the time comes," chuckled Lefty. "Besides, I dunno that we have any other bet to place, up to this time!"

"There's the ladder to the attic, I suppose," said Daniel, taking the lantern and casting a flare to the corner of the cell room.

"It's over there, sure enough," nodded Lefty. "Come along, old-timer. We're gunna get wet. But rain water is better than blood, mostly!"

They climbed the ladder up the wall, and pushed up the trap door to which it led. They found themselves, then, in a low loft, and Lefty, opening the lantern the faintest trifle, probed delicately here and there with a single ray. He examined the floor, the walls, the roof, in this expert fashion.

"They got to get out to the roof some way," observed Lefty. "I don't see any trap. We got to go along and try the roof with our hands, I suppose. Take that side, kid, and I'll take this one——"

Here the storm lulled almost to silence, and there was

a sudden crash; then a flood of shouts filled the cell room beneath them. The heart of Daniel stood still!

"Hello!" called Lefty cheerfully. "They've got loose inside and I suppose inside of an hour or so they'll make up their minds that we've come up for the roof—and there's the trap, kid. Gimme a boost, will you?"

He had pushed out a small trap door near the center of the roof, and Daniel took him by the legs and forced him up through the opening; he was drawn up in turn, and hardly had they gained the outer surface when the unbroken force of the wind drove at them in the full might of a mountain gale. There are heavy storms at sea, and wild winds there, but at sea there is all the wide surface of the ocean to wander over, whereas in the mountains the blasts are focused, brought to a cutting point, as it were, and all their energies pooled.

So it was with this torrent of wind that streamed down Lammer Valley. And the unspeakable power of it caught Lefty on the flat of his body and floated him like a piece of dry paper in a blast.

He clutched Daniel, and the latter in turn gripped the trap edge through which they had just come. For a moment his strength was barely great enough to keep them in their place. Then the wind dropped a little, and Lefty crawled up beside him.

"A little luck, kid," he shouted, "or else we'd've been birds quicker than you thought for!"

And, in spite of that perilous position, Daniel laughed. The wind slipped into his open mouth and made one cheek a bulging pouch.

Lefty, in the meantime, giving up the attempt to speak, pointed straight ahead at the great mass of a tree which was swaying back and forth above the jail top; a branch of it had been hammering at the wall so violently. Now, as the wind abated, Lefty and Daniel crawled hastily toward this possible avenue of escape. They gained the edge of the roof and saw the billowing depth of the tree surge beneath and above them; but they saw, also, half a dozen little glowing eyes of red at the base of the trunk. That avenue was well blocked indeed!

7. Through the Trees

AS THEY TURNED from that blocked channel of escape, they saw before them the wildly waving head of another tree at the farther end of the roof; Dunlin made straight on for it, and Daniel followed him. They had to flatten themselves against the roof and wriggle like snakes to keep the storm wind from driving beneath them and prying them from their finger holds in the shingles.

But they came, at last, to the roof end, and there they could mark that the tree was a perilous distance from the roof, neither so big nor so spreading, but with a great bushy head beaten over by the gale and springing up against it, now and again, when the pressure relaxed a little.

However, beneath it there were no telltale little red eyes, though all the brush which circled around the yard was spotted with the lights of the smokers here and there. Lefty Dunlin put his mouth close to the ear of his companion and shouted: "I'm going to make the jump for the head of that tree the next time it comes back this way. If I don't break my neck and fall through, you follow me." And that instant, as the head of the tree sprang up, he rose, let the whole force of the wind-torrent strike his back, and leaped high and far. At the same time, the gale cuffed the tree back from before him, and Daniel instinctively blinked. When he looked again, Dunlin was crashing through the upper cloud of the treetop.

Down to the ground stared Daniel, to mark the fall of a limp and broken body, but Lefty Dunlin seemed to have landed safely, unless, indeed, his broken body now was caught and held in some upper fork of the tree!

At the same moment the treetop swayed suddenly upward and Daniel braced himself with tensed muscles for the leap.

His heart failed him. He sank down against the roof

fighting for his breath. Suddenly he was aware that he was cold and wet, and that the wind had blown the big raindrops straight through his clothing to the skin; and he knew that his heart was faint and fluttering, and that his brain was staggering.

He was in a funk, and the knowledge that his nerve had failed him amazed and startled Daniel. Before that moment he would have matched his pluck against that of any man living; but here he had failed to follow even after a leader had shown him the way!

Once more the tree staggered up against the wind, and Daniel, spurred by wild shame rather than by courage, stood up and leaped headlong.

He felt himself shoot forward with the power of the wind giving him literal wings; then the movement slacked, and he dropped heavily down. He closed his eyes and threw one arm across his face in order to shield it from the tearing branches. But it seemed as though a thousand little arms received him, caught at him, and, breaking the momentum of his fall, let him slide gently through.

He opened his eyes; he was dropping through the upper head of the tree, and now his feet jarred solidly on a strong branch. The impact made his knees buckle and pitched him sideways. Had he pitched upward, it would have been his last moment, but he inclined in toward the trunk, and so his hands managed to catch at and hold a stout bough.

There he dangled, found a foothold on another limb, and so braced himself against the swaying trunk, very sick at heart, indeed, but fiercely satisfied that he had been able to force himself to the attempt.

Something dropped like a shadow beside him—Dunlin.

"Nothing broken, old-timer?" said Lefty, for he could speak with comparative ease inside the envelope of the tree's foliage.

"Nothing—I'm sound. And you?"

"Like diving into water, wasn't it? I almost wish we were back there on the roof to have another header."

"Shall we go down?"

"No hurry."

"No hurry, Dunlin? Man, man, they've found that we went up to the roof, by this time!"

"And what then? Will they go exploring to see if we could have got off the roof? I don't think so. They'll probably think that we squeezed through one of the windows, in spite of their watchers."

"But why stay here, man?"

"I was only thinking," said Lefty, "who keeps the best horses in town. Or did you lay out a couple of good ones before you came in to me?"

"I didn't," said Daniel.

"Parker ought to have the best—for us. Nothing fancy in looks, but tough devils, and that's what we want for the mountains. Parker ought to be our man. Look, kid, how they've balled up this job! Instead of spreading out, and making a couple of lines, they've all huddled around in the brush. They'll do a little cursing in the morning when they find that I'm gone—and you with me! By the way, where's my gun?"

"I've only one. Here it is."

Dunlin put his hand on the weapon and then hesitated a moment.

"You've only got this one?" he asked.

"You can use it better than I can," declared Daniel. "Take it, and welcome. I don't want to be tempted into having to shoot at another man again this night."

"Ah, ah," murmured Dunlin, "I understand. Very green, and not used to the game. But you'll come on. You ain't made yet, but you'll finally learn. I'll take the gat, then!"

He accepted the revolver.

"How many shots in it?"

"Three."

"And where are the other cartridges?"

"There aren't any."

"Good gracious, man, how could Jerry have sent you on a job like this one?"

Daniel was silent.

"All right——" sighed Lefty. "Here we go! Only— don't run. Walk along slow and easy. It's hard to see slow things in the dark, but the faster you go, the more light you make, you might say!"

Daniel said nothing at all. He watched his leader climb through the branches, swing from a lower one, and then scramble down the tree trunk to the ground on the side of the tree farthest from the jail.

The alarm must have been given through the men in the jail, by this time. They had discovered that their two men were not in the building, and, rushing down, they poured out through the doors and went flooding abroad, shouting and giving their warning.

Daniel dropped hastily behind his leader, and they stepped into the heart of the thicket at once.

Just ahead of him, he saw Dunlin bump into some one who shouted: "What in hell—why are you going this way?"

"Me and my kid brother are fed up waiting here for nothing in the rain," said Dunlin calmly. "We're going home."

"You yellow quitters!" said the big man roughly. "Get out of my way quick!"

Dunlin side-stepped, and Daniel followed suit, but as he stepped on in the trail of his leader, he heard the big man shouting after him: "Hey, what's your name? Hey, you!"

Dunlin turned sharply into a hedge-like growth of firs and began to run, with Daniel following. And the latter, looking back, saw the stranger had taken after them. He was shouting words which the wind drowned; then many other shadows sprang up and headed in pursuit.

Daniel knew that they were discovered. He had no doubt about his own speed of foot, and as for Lefty Dunlin, that worthy ran like a deer.

They dodged out of the trees, hit a lane, and went down it at full speed, doubled down a footpath, and then vaulted a fence. Standing there, Lefty Dunlin leaned against the fence and gasped for breath.

"Cigarettes—no lungs left!" gasped Dunlin. "I'm near done, kid!"

A rush of men went down the footpath. That far, they

had been traced; and now, the wind fell suddenly away, and the storm which would have made their escape from this point so secure now plainly was breaking up, for the great cloud masses in the central sky were rent and torn and tumbled back from the clear faces of the stars. What so clear as mountain stars—and when was their clearness so little wanted?

Dunlin had spotted a shed behind the house in whose backyard they stood. For this he made at a stagger, with Daniel very anxious beside him. It seemed impossible that Lefty could be so spent, and that world of nerve and cool resource sapped so quickly by a little bodily exercise. What would happen if Lefty fell from exhaustion? What could be done then? How take him, helpless, out of the dangers which were swarming in this town?

The door of the shed was torn open and inside they found what they wanted—four horses in four stalls, and several saddles on pegs behind them.

In frantic haste they saddled and clapped the bridles on. They had come in from the little rear door, and as they finished their preparations, the sliding front door was shoved back with a screech along its rusty runway.

"Get the gray and I'll take the roan," said the voice of a man in the darkness.

"Where's the lantern?"

"Here by the bin. Got a match?"

"Yep. We'll have a damned long ride, if that Dunlin has busted away!"

"We'll have a damned long drink if we get him. How did he get from the jail?"

"Goodness knows! How does he do everything? Somebody come in and turned out Jeffries, the big sap! A bird like that to be a deputy sheriff! Deputy dog-catcher is his speed."

Lefty stole to the side of his companion and whispered in his ear:

"We gotta sap these on the head, kid! Are you with me?"

"No murder!" whispered Daniel, shuddering.

"No, no," answered Lefty. "Just follow me and back me up!"

And he advanced toward the farther end of the shed; at the same time a match was scratched and a spurt of blue flame flickered.

8.   For Freedom

HE WHO HELD the match cupped his hand behind it; the lantern was raised by his companion; and just as the flame touched the wick, Lefty Dunlin held his gun under their noses. "Just shove your hands up, boys," he invited them, "and turn your faces to the wall."

They raised their hands, the unshielded fire of the lantern streaming wildly to one side, and turned their faces to the wall.

"My God!" stammered one, "it's Dunlin!"

They stood like statues, transformed by that terrible name, while they held aloft the lantern which gave Dunlin light to take from them a pair of loaded revolvers and two cartridge belts with ammunition.

"I was careless at the jail," he told them in the most friendly manner. "As a matter of fact, we weren't equipped for carrying a very heavy pack out of it. I'm sorry to take your guns, boys, but I'll send you money for 'em. Surely you didn't start out without rifles—there they are leaning by the door, partner. Now, ain't it a lucky thing that you come here bringing everything that we need, to say nothing of holding a light for us, so's we could get what we needed. Into the saddle, partner, and lead the other horse outside. That's right. So long, boys. Wish us good luck, will you?"

He turned from them, leaped into the saddle, and with a twitch of the reins he turned the heads of the horses straight for a low section of the fence at the rear of the yard.

Out of the barn rose, now, a wild series of shouts for

help, and a furious proclamation of "Thief! Dunlin! Dunlin!"

Lefty Dunlin drove his pony straight forward and sailed the fence; Daniel followed on fast, his horse refused, then buck-jumped the obstacle, and he saw Lefty flying straight before him across a field, already almost out of sight beneath the stars.

He jockeyed the mustang to full gallop, and so the trees and the houses blurred on either side, the black ground flowed like water beneath them, and now on a rising hillside, he overtook Lefty at last.

They halted their horses and faced toward Lammer Falls. They could hear dim voices and sometimes one clearly raised shout.

"So," said Lefty, "they've chucked their chance at me again! Only," he added, "I wish that we'd been able to get to Parker's barn and land a pair of his horses. Now, stranger, do you stick with me, or do we split? What sort of orders did you get from Jerry?"

"I know no one by that name," said Daniel.

Lefty did not explain; neither did he ask any questions, but finally he murmured: "Well, if you've got no objection, suppose that we travel along together. How's your side?"

"No trouble at all."

"I'm glad of that. We'll push along. We'll need to drop a few miles behind us before the morning comes. There's a moon due up any time!"

They had before them, now, a steep tangle of mountains, and Lefty melted into that tangle on barely perceptible trails which he persisted in taking at a walk, even when the ground sloped down or held level. Daniel grew more and more restless behind this leader.

It was true that there was no sight or sound of pursuit behind them, but in the moving pictures the forces of the law generally won by dint of hard riding which ate up the miles. He ventured, at last, to advise: "We might hurry on a little, Lefty. Why not use the time that we've gained on them?"

The trail was narrow, at that point. On the one hand

up went the vast and sheer wall of the mountain; on the other, the ravine dropped steeply away to nothingness; but Lefty reined back his mustang and rode beside his companion, letting his pony have its head. The moon-glow was rising in the east, now, and against it Daniel saw Lefty riding, as it were, upon the naked air, but cheerfully gossiping as he went along.

"When I was new at the game," said Lefty, "I always aimed at galloping. A gallop, that's a good gait. It sort of fills up your mind, you know. But I never seen a time when it was any use, except to rock along over a bit of fine desert when the sand ain't too soft, or to burst into a town with a yell and a whoop like our daddies used to do. I always galloped, as I was saying. I had to always keep a lead horse with me; I killed off a horse about every two weeks. And yet somehow I always was getting into trouble. I picked up about twenty bullets, in those days. I still got one somewhere floating in my innards, and they had me marked as though I'd been fighting a mountain lion.

"Finally I slowed up. I learned that a trot was pretty good. A trot takes some sitting out, but it will get a horse along farther in a day than any gallop. But, after that, I learned that the walk is the best of all. Keep a horse doing three miles an hour. Work him twelve hours a day, if you have to. That makes close to forty miles in a march, and forty miles a day is faster than all the galloping and trotting horses in the world can keep up through country like this. Besides, you've got two grand advantages. You always got a fresh horse under you—or a horse fresh enough to make a sprint, and walking don't joggle your head too much. Galloping is like whisky. I like whisky pretty well, but you can't rob banks when you're full of it. I like a gallop, too, but only when I'm having a little party. After all, no horse can run as fast as an automobile, and no automobile can run as fast as the telegraph."

Lefty paused for a little, then he rambled on in his usual cheerful manner. Presently: "You're green, kid, I keep saying that, but I dont want to make you downhearted. You're green, though you got everything. Nerve, head, and everything. Only, you ain't been figuring these things out. We can't ride away from trouble. We got to dodge it. We never can run so far that we ain't in danger; we never can ride so fast that they can't catch us. All through these mountains, in the old days, the boys used to raise their little hell and then slide away into the ravines and never have to worry—like land pirates, as you might say! Now, piracy on the high seas ain't so comfortable, I take it. You get your ship and you jump a fat merchant-man. No sooner get away from him, all loaded down with millions in drygoods, or what not, than the word is sprinkled all over the doggone world by wireless, describing you, all your men, your ship, and the last course you were on. If there's a sea gull in the air over you, maybe it's no sea gull at all, but a dog-gone airplane come to spot you down. You may have a fast ship; maybe you can do twenty or even twenty-five knots, for a while. But twenty skinny destroyers, all loaded with rapid-fire guns and marines, and poison-mean things like that, come snaking after you at forty knots. The airplane tells them where to go. They eat you up before your stolen goods are a day old. And there you are. Does this tire you?"

"No, I'm interested."

"Thinking aloud is a pretty good way to think," said Lefty. "If I'm alone and get in a corner, I talk it out to the ears of a mule, even. When he cocks an ear, it says 'yes.' When he drops it, it says 'no.' Well, partner, here on land things are pretty near as bad. Once it was so easy to be a crook in the West that the boys used to die of boredom. They had to get excitement by riding into town and pulling the beard of the sheriff, or trimming his mustaches while he was asleep. But that's different, now. I could promise you three hundred and sixty-five days of fun in every year, the sort of life that I lead. All these mountains are spotted with towns big and small. They got telegraph and wireless. All those towns are connected with all the rest of 'em. And every town is full of men, horses, and guns. These here mountains look wild and terrible lonely, but they ain't. They're just a checkerboard where you got to keep hopping from square to square. Or else, this game is like chess, and you're always getting checked, with mate just around the corner.

"So you got to keep thinking, partner. There's one thing that may beat the wireless, the horses, the automobile—and that's thinking. Well, you can think better on a trotting horse than on one that gallops, and you can think better on a walking horse than on one that trots. It looks foolish, sometimes. But while your horse is walking, you can think straight, and you can shoot straight, too. Did you ever shoot a man before to-night, partner?"

The moon had risen, and now they passed out from the shadow of a peak and into a thin and misty moonshine that poured down a valley. Opposite them, they saw the silver mist of a waterfall shaking its vapors in the air and rushing ceaselessly down the face of the cliff like galloping, silent white horses, each overtaking the other with flying mane. The wind blew toward it; not a sound was heard; but now and again it seemed to Daniel that an ominous vibration hummed toward him across the empty gulf of air.

"I never shot a man before to-night," said he.

"I thought not," said the other. "Are you going to shoot a man to-morrow, or any other day?"

"I?" exclaimed Daniel.

"I mean," said Lefty, "do you like the sport?"

"Sport!" cried Daniel.

"Sure," said Lefty Dunlin.

He turned in his saddle and regarded his companion with a broad smile.

"You're like the rest. But you gotta keep thinking, kid. You gotta keep facing yourself. That's the hardest job. Every other bridge you can wait till you have to cross; but yourself is a bridge that you're on night and day and you never can get off it. Now, I'd like to know, if you never slapped the law in the face before to-night, what you expect to get out of this life you're apparently starting on."

"Freedom," said Daniel in a ringing voice.

"Freedom from what?" asked the other.

"Well," said Daniel, "suppose you tell me what *you* get out of it."

"Sure I will," said Lefty instantly. "I'll do better than that. I'll show you the whole picture, to-morrow morning!"

9.   Bulldogging Through

IT IS NECESSARY to turn back, before more time passes, to Lammer Falls and to all that happened to Jeremy Crossett.

After the departure of Daniel, he lay in his chair very sick, as has been said, and near to fainting.

When he recovered a little, he staggered to Daniel's bed and fell heavily upon it, face down, and lay there for hour after hour, barely conscious that he still lived. Finally, he passed from torpor into sleep, and in the morning he wakened with a start and a shock.

He sat up on the edge of the bed and held his head in his hands. His brain was swimming and his whole soul was shocked and troubled, he hardly knew by what. By degrees, his wits cleared and he could remember how Daniel had left him, sternly and bitterly.

He stood up, trembling as he realized that this was Daniel's room and—but perhaps the boy, finding him asleep there, had simply gone to the other chamber.

He returned, therefore, to his own room, but there he found the bed untouched and the window closed.

He pulled it open; it seemed that there hardly was strength in his arms to perform that little task, and he leaned on the sill with half-closed eyes, breathing hard.

A saying of his college returned to his mind: "When in doubt, bulldog it through!"

He prepared to bulldog it through, and for that purpose he pushed all inquiry to the back of his mind and set about making his toilet.

Then he went down to breakfast.

He was rather early. In fact, not another person was in the room, and the ubiquitous waitress was at work on the windows, her red head bobbing with the energy she put into her strokes in polishing the glass.

She gave him a cheerful good morning, with a jerk tossed on a white apron, pulled down her sleeves and fastened the cuffs as she approached him, and giving a single pat to her hair she stood before him, breathing a little hard, but perfectly neat, perfectly the waitress—not a bit of the charwoman in her.

Jeremy Crossett was not a harsh man and he was not stiffly aristocratic. But there were certain classes upon whom he simply did not waste time. He had no doubt that the blacksmith had as good a right as he to cast a vote, and he would have encouraged the son of the blacksmith to become president. However, aside from men of certain accepted position, he looked on the rest of society as "classes," and regarded them with no more personal interest than he would have regarded the strata of an exposed rock fold.

However, on this morning he looked more particularly at this girl. The eye of the sick man cannot help searching for relief. So Jeremy Crossett, out of a haze of pain, dwelt particularly on this girl, not as a woman, say, but as an object of art set in a shabby cabinet. She was as pretty as a girl can be in an apron and a gingham dress. Being an art object, so to speak he looked her up and down with care and remarked small feet and trim ankles, and exquisitely made hands.

"Shall I turn around, mister?" said she.

And with that, she extended her arms and pirouetted like a mannequin on a pedestal.

Jeremy Crossett almost smiled when she faced him again with twinkling eyes.

There was trout for breakfast, and bacon and eggs, and French fried potatoes, and oatmeal mush to begin with.

"May I have a little toast and a cup of coffee?" said Jeremy Crosset.

She brought them presently and he was glad of her return; it had become painful to be alone .

So, when she started to go away, he turned his head after her. She came back at once and wanted to know if everything was satisfactory and if there was anything more he wished.

"You're native to this place, no doubt?" said Jeremy Crossett, making conversation.

"I am which?" said she, tipping her head to one side as she regarded him. "Sure I'm not. I'm on the wing."

"Ah, yes," said he, breaking a piece of toast in two.

He began to nod, by way of holding her; but she dropped both hands on the back of a chair opposite him and tilting it back a little, leaned there and continued to chat as though she understood perfectly that he wanted diversion.

"Where am I bound? Will you guess?"

"For some pleasant place," said Jeremy Crossett out of his deep misery. "For some pleasant place, I trust!"

"Hollywood," said she, and smiled broadly. "This is almost half way; I'll soon be there! You get a lot of tips in a place like this."

"Do you? Do you, indeed?" said Jeremy Crossett.

"I always wanted to take a whirl at the movies," said she. "Finally, I decided I'd take a chance. I write a letter to the biggest producer in Hollywood. Why bother about the little fellows? I said: 'Here's a picture of me. I can dance; sing a little; and I can work. Have I got a chance?' Back comes a letter: 'Dear Miss Loren, if your picture isn't faked, of course you have a chance. Come along and tell me about yourself. Isaac Fitzbloomer.' Imagine me in a Fitzbloomer job! I can't imagine it!" said she.

After this, she laughed a little, partly out of happiness, and partly because she realized that she was a trifle absurd.

"You know about Fitzbloomer, I suppose?" she went on, when Crossett failed to continue the talk, but remained looking expectant.

"I'm afraid that I don't."

"Don't you see many movies?"

"I have seen one or two," said Crossett.

"You've seen—one or two? Jiminy!" said Miss Loren.

She rubbed her chin and regarded him doubtfully.

"You're up here to go fishing or hunting or something," she ventured.

"Yes."

"You and your son?"

"Yes, both of us."

She sighed a little, finding this conversation difficult to pursue.

"They had a great show last night, didn't they?" said she at last.

"Did they?" murmured he.

"I mean, the jail break."

"Ah!" said Crossett. "Some criminals escaped from this jail?"

"Look here—you didn't know that?"

"I slept rather heavily," admitted Crossett.

"I couldn't get as near as I wanted," said she. "How I would've liked to be on the inside of that job!"

"And what happened?"

"Why, there was a young fellow dropped down in front of the jail and bamboozled the deputy sheriff right out of the place, and locked himself in, in the face of the mob that came to lynch Lefty Dunlin."

"Ah!" said Mr. Crossett. "Ah!" he said again, and sat up. "What sort of a young man? A young desperado, no doubt!"

"I'd tell a man," said the girl with a heartfelt emotion. "Would I like to see him? I would, and to have his autographed picture. I'd frame it on my wall! He kept that crowd out, y'understand? Put a bullet through the jail door and scattered them, and then he walked the rounds of the windows and kept guard while Lefty, they say, must've picked his locks. He's a wonderful handy fellow, Lefty—don't you think?"

"No doubt! No doubt! And the other young man he was observed, of course?"

"Slimmish and darkish, sort of. Looked like a Dunlin and——"

Crossett rose stiffly from his chair and stared at her.

"What's the matter?" she asked him anxiously. "Was

it anybody you know? Was it—jiminy!" said the girl, and gaped.

He sat down again, heavily, sagging in his chair, his head fallen.

"Go on!" he commanded.

She seemed very nervous now and shrank before his piercing eyes.

"He was terrible brave," said the girl gently. "He must be just wonderful. He held them away. They broke through one of the windows———"

"The criminal?"

"The crowd. And the stranger, he held them back and shut the office door and bolted it on them."

"Held them back how?"

"With a gun."

"Did he—did he fire?"

"Only drilled Marty Lawrence through the calf of the leg. That was all. It wasn't anything to make a fuss about! But it threw a chill into the rest of 'em, you can bet! They handled that job with gloves, after that, and finally the next window was broken down. The crowd rushed in. But the two were gone. They must of climbed onto the roof where the wind was blowing great guns. How they got off the roof, nobody knows."

Jeremy Crossett mopped his forehead.

"Where have they gone?"

"Wouldn't the sheriff like to know that?" retorted the girl. "I don't know! But somewhere safe," she added very gently. "If I was you, I wouldn't worry none," she went on. "You could trust Lefty to take good care of him!"

"I could trust? What do you mean?" asked Crossett.

"All right," said the girl, and nodded wisely.

"What is it that you think?" asked Crossett, pale with anxiety.

"You can't be arrested for thinking." said she, with a sudden defiance. "I think it was your son—don't you?"

10.   A Very Good Girl

LIKE THE GIANT of some Arabian fable, escaping like smoke from a little earthen jar and finally towering between the earth and the sky, so the importance of Miss Loren had grown in the estimation of Jeremy Crossett, until now he looked up at her, stunned and helpless, unable to speak.

She appeared to understand.

"Now, don't you be worrying," said she. "I'm not going to talk about him! If nobody else knows they'll never be any wiser for me. Why, I think he's grand! If I was a man, I'd want to do the same thing. I'd want to go in, like that, and save a man from lynching, I mean. And if I was a father, I'd be proud of having such a son!"

Jeremy Crossett moistened his white lips.

"My dear," he said at last, faintly, "I fear that I've forgotten your name."

"I'm Jenny Loren," said she. "I mean, I am until I reach Hollywood. Then I'll pick up something fancy, like they all do!"

"Jenny Loren—Jenny Loren—that has an honest sound to it," said Crossett. "Come a little closer to me, Jenny Loren. Sit down here. I want to talk to you. Jenny, I am a stranger in this mountain range; this terrible thing has happened to my son; I want to reach him, I must reach him some way——"

"Oh, sir," said Jenny cheerfully, "of course he'll come back to you, after he's had his lark!"

Crossett shook his head hopelessly. How could he explain his present quandary?

Jenny was quite willing to interpret for this sick-faced and half-mute gentleman.

"Now, I know what you mean," said Jenny. "You think that maybe he'd be afraid to come back after he's had his little fling? But that kind ain't afraid, sir. Like a thoroughbred colt; when it bucks you off it takes a gallop around the field then comes back to see what happened to you. He'll come back, sure enough!"

Mr. Crossett looked doubtful. "He never will come back," said he. "He never will come back, girl. Do you hear me?"

It was not Jenny's fault, of course, and she might well have grown angry at this accusing tone; however, she possessed that deep store of woman's patience which can be poured out almost without ending. She merely lifted her head a little and folded her slender hands, all pink with the window scrubbing of that morning.

"He never will come back," insisted Crossett, "unless I get a certain message to him. God forgive me! He may not come even then! Do you hear me? He may not come even then!"

And grasping the edge of the table with both hands he looked into the future until he dared to look no more. Jenny saw that he was trembling, and tears started into her eyes. She took one of his hands from the table and found that it was cold, quivering, and nerveless; she cherished it in both her own warm ones.

"Will you look here, now," said Jenny. "You're just breakin' your heart about him. Lemme tell you something. That kind of a man don't go wrong! He ain't a colt or a two-year-old, Mr. Crossett. He's just a horse that is tired of livin' in a stall. He's busted out and jumped the fence; that's all. You'll have him back——"

"Don't talk!" said Crossett. "The point is—you know about him. God knows how you found out!"

"Through your own talking, sir, and just a mite of a guess. But I'll keep it quiet."

"No woman can keep from telling the news!" he declared.

She did not protest, and because of her silence, all at once he nodded.

"I believe that you will be quiet about it," said he. "And if you are—I'll furnish you with that ticket to Hollywood, Jenny Loren. You understand? If nothing of this leaks out, I mean?"

She stood back from him and shrugged her shoulders, saying: "Well, I understand, but we don't take money for that sort of thing. I work for my money, Mr. Crossett," she added in the gentlest of reproofs.

"You're an honest girl," said he, seeing her more clearly as his own spirits revived. For, grappling with his problem. the effort braced and stimulated him. He was able to think to some decision.

"I have to send a message to my boy," said he. "You find me the bravest man, and the one most likely to hold his tongue!"

"Doc Tolliver is the bravest, or one of the bravest," said she. "And I think nearly everybody here can be silent enough. I'll get you Doc. It will take a lot of work to find him, though, if he's with Lefty Dunlin."

Doc Tolliver was sent for and Jenny interviewed him first. Then he went up to Crossett's room, where that man of affairs had pulled himself together and was now ready to face his problem with all the courage and intelligence he could command.

He seated Tolliver by the window and observed him narrowly. Tolliver was a man worthy of observation. His nickname had been won by the professional appearance which a narrow Vandyke beard and a pair of carefully trained mustaches gave him. Tonsorially, Doc Tolliver looked like a duke; otherwise, he was merely a cowpuncher a bit on the ragged side. He was well past middle age and indeed nothing was young about him except his clean blue eyes.

"Do you know why I want you?" asked Crossett.

"I know." answered Doc Tolliver.

"And you're willing to try the job?"

"I don't know." said Doc Tolliver. "I'm fifty-three," he added, as though this were a remark strictly to the point.

Crossett waited for an explanation, which Tolliver launched into.

"Nobody would get any glory out of this job," he said.

"And there's a lot of trouble connected with it. I wouldn't tackle it for less than a thousand dollars!"

He blinked his eyes as he set this high figure upon his services; Mr. Crossett still waited, for he felt that more talk was coming.

"I might," said Tolliver frankly, "run onto somebody that could take me straight to Dunlin and—your son. Maybe I couldn't. And if I have to wander around and try to get on Dunlin's trail, what chance have I got? One in ten! Then, when I come up with him, how am I to let him know that I'm coming as a friend? If he spots a man hanging on his trail, he's pretty apt to turn around and hunt the hunter. In that case, he's a better man than I am."

This was very frank talk; yet Mr. Crossett did not doubt that Jenny Loren had chosen well when she selected this fellow as the bravest man in Lammer Falls, where brave men were a glut on the market.

"If I get the letter to your son, I want a thousand dollars," concluded Doc Tolliver gravely. "How does that sound to you?"

"I'll pay you a thousand dollars for the service," said the other instantly. "I appreciate that it's a difficult task. I'll pay you a thousand down, Mr. Tolliver; and if you manage to deliver the letter—then I'll add a bonus, according to the nature of the work that you've had to do."

So said Mr. Crossett, and Doc Tolliver stood up at once. He began to turn his sombrero in his hands and his eyes gleamed a little.

"I don't need cash down," he said. "You're offering pretty fine terms, Mr. Crossett. But maybe, after all, this try of mine won't cost you a cent. I'll be movin' along."

He moved accordingly, and Jeremy Crossett waited at the window of his room until he saw a dusty figure canter down the street on a wiry mustang and disappear around the next bend.

He felt confidence in Doc Tolliver; he felt greater confidence, therefore, in Jenny Loren, because she had picked out such a man as this.

He went down late for lunch, purposely, hoping that she might be able to serve him alone, and that was the case. For the room filled at the stroke of twelve and was empty in forty minutes regularly.

"But," said Crossett, as she placed a thin slice of over-done steak before him, "if you're not native to this place, how do you happen to know the people here so well?"

"You take a man," explained Jenny, "and he's got to make friends slow and float around gradual, like, till people get to know him and take him up. But you take a girl, it's different. In two dances she gets to see everybody. Well, that's only a couple of weeks. Then you see I'm sort of like a telephone central, here. I hear all the talk at the tables. You learn things, that way."

He regarded her with frank admiration.

"And Mr. Tolliver—did you meet him at a dance?"

"I heard about him when he shot Dickie Saunders," said she, "and afterward when 'Bud' May and 'Tiny' Sam Lawrence tried to stick him up in Thunder Canyon."

"Have those things happened in the last three months?"

"Yes."

"Then what happened in Thunder Canyon?"

"They buried Bud May in the canyon," said the girl cheerfully, "but Tiny Sam is still in bed and getting well pretty fast. He says that he'll have it out with Doc when he's up and about, but folks don't think he will. He's had enough. And when he can ride, he'll just slope! Lammer Falls will never be bothered by him again."

"And won't the sheriff call on him—a holdup man?" asked Crossett.

"It was only a joke to throw a scare into Tolliver, you see. But Tolliver didn't scare. He just started shooting and spoiled everything. Lemme get you some hot potatoes."

"Tolliver," insisted Crossett, "is a veteran fighter, then?"

"None more veteraner," she agreed. "Everybody can tell you about Doc."

Crossett fell into a study. He began to feel that a cheerful destiny might work out of this tangle, after all. For, if the letter were delivered and his boy came back to him, might it not be that the ghost which had been hounding the Crossetts would be laid forever?

Jenny Loren was pouring his coffee, and when he

looked up to her out of his thoughts, she was smiling upon him with a sort of maternal tenderness.

"God bless you!" said Crossett suddenly. "You're a very good girl!"

11.   Lefty's Country

OUT OF THE BRACKEN on the broad breast of a mountain far behind Lammer Peak, Lefty Dunlin advanced with his new companion. It was early afternoon. They had ridden until dawn, slept half a dozen hours, breakfasted on ample steaks cut from a mountain sheep that stood too venturesomely close to inspect them, and rested after their meal.

Fatigue, then sleep, then the hunt, and the drowsiness which followed the meal had reduced talk to a minimum with Daniel; but Lefty seemed at all times clear eyed, with a comment always ready to break from his lips. And in this alert and wakeful manner he could go for hours, and yet never say a word. It seemed to young Daniel that this fellow made silence into a sort of new conversational method.

Now they prepared for the next stage of their journey, and they came out, first of all, from their noon retreat to the edge of a barren and narrow plateau.

Dunlin dismounted and sat down in the shelter of a stunted tree, and his companion joined him. They were very high, verging toward timber line. The meager shadow in which they sat was cast by a pair of lodgepole pines, those hardy adventurers up the loftier slopes, and just above them the bald knob of the mountain, divested of all growth except patches of lichen and moss, and shimmering in the sun. All sound, in this rare atmosphere, was greatly subdued; the scream of the blue jay in the hollow, though not a hundred feet away, seemed vastly distant, and the white cataract below them rushed like singing in a dream. All the region above timber line lived with insects, and the fringes of that winged army passed by the two like the sounding of infinite tiny horns, imagined rather than heard.

Behind them the greater peaks of the range lifted and piled one above the other, but through three-quarters of a circle their vision could range around below them; in the remaining quarter, at their backs, was Lammer Mountain and Lammer Falls.

Now Lefty Dunlin stretched himself at ease and braced his chin upon the cup of one hand.

"I said I'd tell you why this sort of a life pleases me and what there is in it for me. I can show you pretty well from here. All that you see there is my country, partner. I been working it for fifteen years, sometimes in a big way, and sometimes in a small way; but it's always given me a good living."

Daniel looked askance, prepared to smile, but Lefty seemed perfectly serious.

"I'm proud of it," said Lefty, "and the way that it's come on. I've laid out here for hours and looked at it, years ago, and I never look at it now without seeing something changed. Ever see anything much better?"

"It's a great reach for the eyes," admitted Daniel.

For the air was pure and clear, and the vision could sweep down uninterrupted over the curving foothills, dark with great forests, and beyond these to rolling lands in a broad belt, checked and spotted with farms and farm houses, and twice broken by what seemed considerable towns. Two rivers wound gleaming through that landscape, drawing together, in the south and east, in the glistening surface of a big lake, and where each entered the waters were two more towns. Beyond the farmlands, the rolling ground turned flat and all toward the horizon the atmosphere seemed to change and to grow misty, as though storm clouds were breathing up along the edges of the sky.

"You start out there on the sky line," said Lefty. "That's the desert. A dog-gone bare one, too. You'd think it wasn't good for a thing. But don't make a mistake. You'd be surprised what I get from it! Suppose that I want a horse that's a real stayer, bound to last like leather and fast as greased lightning—I go to the desert to get it. There's nothing like the horses that they breed there. Runts, a lot of them, but one in a thousand is a wonder. Get fat on a handful of thistles once a week, and go without water for three days of hot marching. Like a cross between a camel and a thunderbolt. Mostly mean devils, but that's all right, when you get used to it. I had a pair of the best, but the sheriff gave me a tight run a while back, and one of 'em was exhausted, and just when I'd left it behind and was pulling out of range, the sheriff dropped him with a lucky long-range shot. Well, that was bad luck! But I'll take a trip down to the desert again, as soon as I have a good chance, and pick up another pair. I know where there's a six-year-old gray that was caught wild a year ago. I dropped in to see him, but he wasn't quite ripe. He ought to be fit now!"

He nodded to confirm this thought to himself, and then he continued: "You get other things out of the desert—a grand chase, for one, if they ever spot you!"

Daniel laughed aloud.

"Is that one of the good things the desert produces?"

"Of course," replied Lefty, smiling in turn. "You take the hounds and the hunters, they have a grand time after the fox, but think what a lot better time the fox has, when he can get to earth? And mostly, he does!"

"Go on," said Daniel. "What else do you get from the desert?"

"I could get a lot," said the outlaw, "but I don't want to overwork it. That's a poor section of my country. It mounts me. Well, that's about enough. I just pick out the best of their horses and let them get away with everything else. They ain't rich, you see. Hardly anybody out there in the sand mist."

He waved his hand closer in.

"This is Jackson River, running down here. You lose it in the foothills; there it comes jump onto the plains again; and that's the Lammer, winding in from the west and south. It turns around the corner of the mountains, you see. Well, that lake where they join out there is Silver

Lake. Where the Lammer goes in is the town of Silver and where the Jackson goes in is the town of Jackson.

"They hate each other, those two towns. You'd hardly believe it, how they hate each other! The logs are sent down the rivers to 'em. They each got sawmills, and each of 'em uses the force of the rivers to run their mills. Well, they've always been so jealous of each other that they can hardly see.

"Silver finally got the job as county seat, fifteen or sixteen years ago when I was a kid, and Jackson always claimed that Silver voters crammed the ballot boxes. They did, too, but so did the Jackson men, only they didn't manage it quite so well. Every year there's a few of the boys of one town killed by the boys of the other. They got a newspaper each, and the *Jackson Bugle's* editor, he spends his time cussing Silver and the Silver men, and the *Silver Clarion's* editor, he works up a heat damning everything in Jackson. I wouldn't have those two towns out of my country. They're better than a circus. I got two files of the papers cached, back in the hills in my hangout. You can get a laugh out of them every day of the year. They got some good stores in those two towns. The lumberjacks and the punchers out of the hills all come down there to spend their money, and they got the trade of the miners, too, who blow their dust in Silver or Jackson. And the miners and punchers and lumberjacks that spend in Silver, they hate worse than poison the bunch that spend in Jackson. Every now and then there's a big fight, and sometimes one side gets the best of it, and sometimes the other side does; and the only thing in the world that they unite to do together is to chase me."

He chuckled, enjoying the situation hugely.

"They make a pretty good pack, too," said he. "They got plenty of money; they always have fast horses; they know the country like a book; and they spend so much time fighting each other that they're all bang-up good shots. They've given me some fine parties," said Lefty with a growing enthusiasm. "I tell you, those boys all fight like bulldogs, and they never give up! I'm proud of 'em! I'd match them against twice their numbers of any folks in the whole world."

He continued in a more subdued but thoroughly satisfied tone: "I was saying that there's a lot of spending in those two towns, so that they got everything that your heart could wish for in their stores. What would a man want? Knives, bridles, saddles, guns of all kinds, ammunition that's first-rate and tested high, clothes good enough for a lord, and every wrinkle you could ask for. I outfit one year in Silver and the next year in Jackson, and every time I flash my dark lantern over the shelves I see that the stock is increasing. It does my heart good! The last call I paid in Silver, I had to stop and leave a note behind me, complimenting old man Bennett on how fine he ran his store and how well it was growing. I said that I would have to recommend it to the other boys in my trade!"

He laughed a little at this small joke of his and continued his survey.

"Now, you look over there to the left and you see a big splotch of rolling ground all squared with dark patches and different shades of green. Those where the sun flashes so bright, those are the wheat fields. That dark stuff, that's oats. You never seen such a rich country! All the farmers and all the farm horses get fat there, and the richer ones, they all move into the town, which is called Colin. A funny name for a town, ain't it? Maybe it was named after the race horse, or maybe the race horse was named after it. I dunno. Well, Colin gets bigger and richer every year, and the money out of that circle of farmlands all rains through the banks like wash through the rifts in a flume, and plenty of gold sticks in the quicksilver fingers of the bankers, you can bet. They got safes that are bulging with money, and when I'm short, I drop down there and pick up some capital."

He sat up, and a hungry gleam came in his eyes.

"I'm a little short now," said Lefty Dunlin, "and they'll hear from me before long!

"You can't do it too often," he explained. "It'd discourage the depositors, y'understand. But now and then

I go down and tap off some of their surplus. Never play
the pig, but take enough to keep me going easy. I need
lots of money in my business! It's a grand game, too.
You'd think that those farmers were an easy lot to fool
with, but they ain't. They're as hard as nails, and they'll
fight for their money like tigers. They're a thrifty bunch.
If they go out shooting they hate to spend more than one
bullet on a squirrel. I've heard a boy say: 'Dog-gone it,
I took out twelve cartridges, and I only got eleven squir-
rels. I'm afraid to go home and tell Dad. Jack, you gimme
a squirrel, will you? You got more'n you need!' So when
it comes to shooting at a man on a horse, it's dead easy
for 'em!"

He touched a little white seam that ran along his left
cheek as he spoke, and Daniel did not need to be told how
that scar had been made.

"Away over there beyond the river," went on the king
of this smiling countryside, "there's some more farmland,
and that's the town of Newfield. It started later than Colin,
but the ground is better and there's more of it. You never
seen a town grow so fast as Newfield has. They got three
banks, and all of 'em busy. They're getting fancy stores.
It's a real city! Candy shops where they get the best
candies from the East; and fancy toggery for the girls,
ruffles and what-not, and flimsy silks, and everything.
Jewelers, too. The last time that I went down to Newfield, I wouldn't stay just at the bank. I called in there
and drew out some funds," said the outlaw, smiling grimly,
"and then I went around and took a look at the town to
see how it had growed. Dropped in at a jeweler's, and
I got these. Kind of pretty, I think!

"They missed these at the jail when they searched me,"
said Lefty, and with that, he split up the edge of his coat
collar and took out from two separate places a number of
big, shining green stones.

Daniel regarded them with a touch of awe. He knew
something of jewels, and these were emeralds of the first
class; five true beauties cut and ready for setting, their
great square faces holding as much light as the depths of
a lake. Two of them were flawless, and three were only

slightly below first class. Daniel would have put the value of the cheapest at much over five thousand dollars.

Lefty held out this small fortune in a careless palm.

"Take a couple," said he. "It's sort of a rest for the eyes to have some around loose in your pocket and look at them, once in a while. I had seven, at first, but I lost a couple."

He dropped two into Daniel's hand.

"They're beauties," said Daniel, after he had examined them. "You've got a tidy little sum in those stones!"

"Have I?"

"Forty or fifty thousand dollars, I'd say," remarked Daniel. And he handed back the emeralds.

"Aw, keep them, keep them," said Lefty, frowning a little. "I got more than I want!"

It occurred to Daniel that a refusal of this gift would be taken most unkindly; he flushed and pocketed stolen goods for the first time.

In the meanwhile, Lefty had continued his oral survey.

"There's the railroad that feeds the towns," he said, pointing to the distinctly visible streak of the grade that swept in a grand arch from Newfield, tapped Silver and Jackson, spanned the rivers on mighty bridges, and then stretched away toward Colin, and so beyond it passed from sight in the dimness of the desert horizon.

"You got no idea how useful the railroad is!" said Lefty. "Suppose that you want a fast ride from one town to another. You can jump clear across the country while the posses are buzzing for you at Newfield, and the same evening you can raise a little hell in Colin, jump back to Jackson or Silver, and all between day-light and dawn! It's a wonderful thing," reflected Mr. Dunlin; "modern science, it's a wonderful thing. How would those small towns sell their stuff except for the railroad that snakes away their tons of wheat and hay and brings back the tons of canned stuff and some clothes and guns and saddles, and everything that a soul could want? Suppose that you get tired of the mountains and the desert, all you do is to jump the train and—*zing!*—there you are in St. Louis, say, or Chicago!"

"Do you go there?" asked Daniel.

"Once in a while, for the change," said Lefty. "But not too often, because you take a job like mine, you got to keep pretty close to it. You got to keep in touch with the politics and the way things are happening, and the new men that are coming on. Now and then I take a month's vacation, but when I come back, I got to spend a week reading newspapers and asking questions to work up the background for my next job. Well, I've told you about the outsides of my country, but here's the heart of it—I mean these mountains, and the upper foothills, where the ground is ragged, as you can see, and where everything is chopped across with washes and canyons, and where the big forests are standing, down there. The outside is where I do my work, and where I raise my income, but this is home, where I do my spending. Here's where I got my friends spotted around. I have to get food and all sorts of supplies from these ranch houses and the shacks of the miners, and such people. Well, I pay for everything I take, and I pay double, you can bet. I lend them money, when I find them straight. I help them out. I could name a dozen men, partner, that I've financed and got them on their feet, and now they're going great guns, some of them. They're my friends. They'd go to hell for me, or me for them. They have fresh horses for me; and they'd fight for me in a minute, except that I never let them go that far.

"Out there on the plains and in the lower foothills where the cows get fat on the pastures," continued Lefty, "and in the plains where the farms are, and down in the towns where the cash and luxuries are—that's my farming country that I harvest, every so often. I got my plowed fields, you might say, where I'm ready to plant some trouble, and I got my growing crops of ideas in other places, and there's Colin, for instance, like a standing crop of ripe grain, all ready to be harvested. There's Newfield, that's been worked and has to lie fallow for awhile. There's Jackson and Silver, partly a base of supplies and partly a sort of a circus for me.

"But up here is my home circle, and when I've been

hunted up out of the lowlands and hit the lower edge of
those forests that you see down there, mostly the boys
of the lowlands give up the chase, because they know
that it's no use. They know that I understand every inch
of this upper ground, and they know that I've got my
friends spotted around, here and there, very useful. I'm
home—I'm in my own back yard—I can thumb my nose
at the law. Well, kid, you asked me what I got out of this
sort of life, and I've told you. If you want to talk up for
yourself, suppose you loosen up and do it. I won't hold
you back none! I want to know how you happened to
horn in there at the jail and shut yourself in with me in
such a tight nut that you nearly were smashed at the
same time that I was!"

"Am I in your way?" asked Daniel suddenly.

"In my way? No, kid; I love to have you along!"

"Then let me wait a while. I'll tell you everything later
on."

12.   Tolliver Takes the Trail

IT SEEMED ODD to Daniel, that, if his companion had
such thoroughly proved friends as he spoke about he did
not go to take shelter with them at once, but Lefty presently explained—for he seemed to be anxious to let in
his new friend to a perfect understanding of himself and
his ways.

Of course, he would be hunted through the mountains
by the exasperated men of Lammer Falls, and perhaps
they would come upon some trace of him. If they did
so, and ran him to ground in the house of one of his
secret friends, no doubt the friends could save him, but
afterward they would be exposed to the prosecution of the
law: they might be jailed, at least they were apt to be
driven out of the country. Thereafter, the outlaw would
have one haven less, and one link to his underground railroad would be broken. Whereas, if he ran on a long trail,

probably he either would tire out his pursuers, or else he would so baffle them with many trail problems that they would be forced to abandon the hunt like men overtaken by darkness.

That very afternoon, as they started on again, the outlaw gave his companion an object lesson in the construction of a trail problem.

The great mistake, as he explained, which most men make in covering up their trails was that they erased all their signs over a considerable distance, perhaps, but then they went more or less straight ahead toward their previous goal. But the proper method was, of course, to make the trail a blank at the point at which one expected to turn at sharp angles and in an unexpected direction.

Of that he later gave a perfect example.

They had been traveling over the very top of a shoulder from which the streams started out every few hundred yards; and now they came to a place where three little ravine heads drew up toward one point, and straight before them the way split and they could pass on either side of a rocky mountain.

On their left rose the main terraces of the range in a crumbling and massive wall, rough-edged, and streaked with varying strata.

"Now," said the outlaw, "suppose that we got not more than a half hour's start. There's men coming behind us and coming fast—more men than we could stand off, say. What would you do?"

"We might dip down one of these little ravines—you down one and I down another, and agree where we would meet."

"They'd split their party and follow us, half and half," said Lefty. "Besides, we'd have to meet in the dark, which ain't so easy as you may think."

"Then we could try to make our trail disappear on those rocks ahead of us."

"And turn the mountainside?"

"Yes."

"We'd have one chance in two of beating them, then.

But here's a better idea. We'll go up that mountainside, right here."

"But where would it lead?"

"To a regular bad lands, above. But what do we want? We got no goal except safety, I suppose. Am I right?"

"Of course, you are."

"Well, then, the quickest way that we can make fools of anybody hanging on our trail, the better it is for us."

"That's a fact, of course."

"All right, now ride ahead and turn your horse in after me. Keep him at the slowest walk that you know how to manage. Just let him crawl and rest between steps. I'm going to turn onto that granite slab."

So Daniel followed, and at this creeping pace, the horses placing their feet most lightly, they gained the granite slab. Then Lefty turned his mount to the side and started for the mountain wall. He dismounted at the base and began to work his way up what seemed to Daniel the most difficult way of all, for it was the most sheer face, and, moreover, a recent landslide which left the rock raw showed that the footing must be insecure. However, Daniel asked no questions, for he must take it for granted that no piece of utter folly would be committed by this mountaineer.

Up that difficult grade they wove back and forth. Once Daniel's mustang, though sure-footed as a goat, sprawled and slid down twenty feet, sending a roaring fall of stones and gravel beneath him to the level, but after that they went on more securely to the top where the outlaw had been waiting for some time.

"Here we are," said Lefty Dunlin. "Now we'll wait for a while, and maybe we'll see a show."

They put the horses well back from the side of the ledge where there was a ragged patch of grass on which they could graze, and the two sat down to wait.

A long, silent hour they remained there, with not a single word from Lefty; then he quickly lifted one hand and dropped prostrate on the ground, snatching off his hat. Daniel imitated that example, and he, like Lefty, wriggled forward snakelike, until he could glance down from the edge of the clifflike ridge of rock. From the top it seemed even more impracticable than it had from the bottom.

Still Daniel saw nothing which could have caused the alarm of his companion; a full five or ten minutes went by before he made out the head of a horseman appearing around a rock side beneath them, and finally a whole cavalcade of a dozen riders streaming up the shoulder of the mountain.

"A whole dozen of 'em," said Lefty, with what seemed to Daniel an unnecessary loudness. "They mean business, don't they? And what a lot of work they'll have for nothing. Dog-gone me, partner, but it makes my eyes ache, just to think about it! Now watch 'em when they hit the blank spot!"

The leader rode straight on until he came to the center of the granite slab.

There he paused and called his men around him. Heads were turned toward the ravines that dropped away on the right; others glanced toward the mountain straight ahead; and one even looked up the cliff side, at which Daniel winced.

"They won't try this, I think," said Lefty calmly. "I came up where the landslide had fallen. Otherwise, we might have chipped off some edges climbing, and that would have been a blazed trail against the old rock. As it was, we tumbled down a ton or two of loose stuff; but who could tell whether it fell to-day or yesterday?"

The party, in fact, gave no further heed to the mountainside, but after a little hesitation, they rode straight ahead, divided, and passed one-half on either side of the mountain before them.

"They're simply riding blind," said Lefty. "And they'll never find this trail again. Wait awhile, though. They may come back, or else there may be some lazy riders lagging behind 'em."

For an entire half hour, then, they waited. The sun had dropped far into the west, by this time, and the thick shadows were falling heavily across the lower valleys. Then came another rider, alone, and like the posse before him, he reached the granite slab and paused in the middle of it.

"Well, well," said Lefty, "why wasn't he with the rest of 'em? Why wasn't he leading 'em? That's old Tolliver, partner, and a better head for mountaineering never was made in the world. If he did a little crooked work, now and then, to put an edge on his wits, there'd be none better than him. But he won't do it. He's too honest to be very wise!"

In the meantime, Tolliver had dismounted, and with the greatest care he went over the ground before him in circles which began at the granite slab and extended outward.

After he had worked some minutes in this manner, he turned sharply around and looked up toward the rock wall.

"He begins to think of something," said Lefty, chuckling in appreciation. "I told you that he was a rare old fellow! Look—by gad! Here he comes—and straight up our path. What sign did he find, I wonder?"

For Tolliver, in fact, had started to clamber up the wall, and behind him followed his horse, working as eagerly as a dog at the heels of its master.

Lefty, at that, went to the horses; he and Daniel mounted and rode slowly over the bad lands of that summit region, not toward the higher mountains, but doubling straight back toward the beginning of their course.

13.   What's Your Name?

THERE WAS NO ATTEMPT made by Lefty Dunlin, to the surprise of Daniel, to conceal their trail from this point, though such a keen observer was following so close behind them. Instead, he bore straight on down the tossing waves of that difficult terrain; then he turned to the left and dropped in the evening light to the floor of the mountain shoulder from which they had climbed the height.

Daniel, at last, had to ask questions, and the reply was perfectly simple.

"If you can't outwit a man, sometimes you can out-ride him. Tolliver ain't as young as he used to be, and he's stuck too long to one horse. There's a trouble with these honest fellows. They wait too long; but you take me, I can't afford to have a 'favorite' gun, or a 'favorite' horse. I simply got to have things which ain't lucky but useful—guns that shoot straight and horses that will run like hell. You, by the way, how are you with a gun, partner?"

"I've shot a good deal," said Daniel modestly. "Of course, I'm not an expert, like you fellows who live by the gun."

"I dunno," said Lefty Dunlin. "The day of the dead-shots has gone up in smoke. Lemme see you try a snap at something. There's a tree—"

Daniel drew his Colt and fired thrice, rapidly.

"Quick and neat," said Lefty in critical comment. "Neat and businesslike, I'd say; and I'd like to bet that you nicked your mark every time. Aye, accuracy is the great thing."

They rode up to the trunk and examined it carefully. They found the holes at once, and they were grouped so closely that the palm of a man's hand would have fitted over the three deep punctures.

Lefty made no further comment as they went up the mountain shoulder again until they reached that same granite slab from which they had diverged so long before.

The rose of the evening now showered over the mountain. There was no sense of shadows. Only that dim and exquisite radiance fell everywhere out of the heavens, coloring the peaks, and softly tinting the rivers that ran through even the deepest gorges. Daniel felt his very heart expanding in the midst of all this beauty.

"Accuracy," said Lefty, picking up his thread of thought where he had broken off some time before—a habit of his—"accuracy is the great thing. I've seen lightning-fast men in the draw. And usually I've seen 'em smash a ter-

rible lot of crockery and glass, and plow up the floor with
bullets, and rasp the plaster off the ceiling, and make
a room look like the insides and the middle of a junk
heap. But usually they kill more furniture then men. Those
fast fellows, they most generally just throw their bullets
in the general direction of a target and they splash at it
like water. Well, partner, if you tag a man once over the
heart, he won't complain because you weren't fast enough
to shoot him through the leg or the shoulder with the first
throw of your gun. But," added Lefty with a touch of im-
pressiveness, "now and then you meet up with somebody
that can throw a gun fast and shoot straight, too. And
that makes a good deal of difference. I ain't as good as
some fools say that I am. But I can do my share. You
take that stone, there, balancing on the top of that big
rock—"

He finished his sentence by jerking a gun and firing the
same instant that the muzzle cleared the leather of the
holster. The stone leaped out of sight from its mighty
pedestal.

"Well, that was pretty lucky," admitted Lefty frankly,
"I can't shoot as straight as all that; but if that rock had
been man-sized, I'd aim to be able to flash a shot into
him between the shoulder and the hip twenty times out
of twenty, and shooting from the hip on the first draw.
You know what that means. You get a .45 caliber bullet
between wind and water, like that, and you don't do much
more fighting, not even if you're a tiger. Well, that's the
sort of shooting you *may* run up against if you follow this
life. But a rifle is a lot better and more useful, usually,
than a revolver. And I know that your rifle work would
be up to standard. Revolver play—I could show you some
tricks about that, of course."

So, chatting cheerfully of guns and gun fighters, Lefty
led the way straight down one of those same three canyons which they had remarked earlier in the day from
the granite slab, and when the valley deepened somewhat,
Lefty rode up a side draw and there they pitched their
camp for the night.

"And suppose," said Lefty, "that old man Tolliver

should come sliding in on us here—well, we might wake up with our throats cut, kid."

"I'll sit up for the first watch," declared Daniel anxiously.

"Aw," said the leader, "you got to take a chance, now and then. What's the use of making life a burden? We ain't here like soldiers; we're here having a lark. Turn in, kid!"

They turned in, wrapping themselves in blanket and slicker while the hobbled horses grazed near by.

Then the voice of Lefty sounded sleepily through the darkness.

"You know, kid, that you ain't told me even what name you go by?"

"My name," said Daniel suddenly, "is Dunlin!"

14. A Cool Reception

IT WAS only natural that Daniel should prepare himself for a shout of astonishment and then for a burst of many questions. Half pleased and half sad, he braced himself to say what he knew. But finally he heard a quiet voice say: "Well, well! So that's it?"

Another silence.

Then he heard his companion snoring!

It angered Daniel to the heart, for if ever a man spoke a "headline" it was this little surprise statement of Daniel's; and it merely lulled Lefty Dunlin to snore!

Finally, he raged himself to sleep; he would part with this callused ruffian the very next day!

They were in a well-shadowed corner; and when Daniel awoke in the morning he saw a surprising tableau before him. The quarters of a small deer lay on his own hide upon the ground, and a cheerful little fire was sparkling through the shadows with busy Lefty crouched beside it. It was the crackling of the flame that had awakened him. He looked up and saw that the day already was well be-

gun, though a high-stretched film of clouds had shut out
the glare of the sun.

How could Lefty have done it without wakening him?
He would have sworn that, at such a time as this, he
would sleep as lightly as any wild wolf, and yet Lefty had
managed to rise, dress, do his blankets into yonder neat
bundle, stalk and kill a deer surely not very far away but
far enough to muffle the sound of a gun, and then return
with his burden of game and make this fire!

Questions would be of no use. Lefty himself probably
did not know how such silence was managed—or how
sleep could be so profound!

He nodded cheerfully to heavy-eyed Daniel.

"There's a pool down there in the hollow," he suggested.

And Daniel saw that his companion was not covered
with the grime of yesterday, nor with yesterday's beard.
In fact, he was marvelously neat and clean, and the razor
already had done its work.

He then wandered down to the pool, first merely asking: "But where did you get a razor, Lefty?"

"It was in the saddle pack," said Lefty. "They do some
riding from that place where we got these horses, and
they got a sort of emergency kit all fixed behind my saddle.
Do you want it?"

He handed the razor to Daniel, and the latter went
shivering down the slope.

He found the pool, lying black and motionless in a
deep circle of shadow. Only, in the very center, a fleck
of gray mirrored the sky overhead.

He sighed as he looked at this snow-fed water, and
moving gingerly toward it, he nudged a bush, and a
shower of dew fell and struck him through to the skin.
Ice could not have been colder!

Through the mind of Daniel flashed other pictures of
other mornings—steaming water running into a crystal-
white tub, and the soft, warm carpet underfoot——

Why were men so made as to court a fate such as this?
Freedom? He remembered what Lefty had said the day
before about his kingdom from which he drew tribute, and

a sneer of contempt and disgust appeared on the lips of Daniel.

He squatted by the edge of the water and shaved. There was only a morsel of soap; he had to make lather with his hand and ice water! But, after all, the painful process ended, though not before his fingers were totally numb. He could not turn back from the harder part of the task, however. Lefty had bathed here. The manhood of Daniel demanded that he should bathe also.

So he drew off his clothes and then stood in the slime at the edge of that gloomy pool and wrapped his body in his bare arms.

What might there be in the midst of those waters? What poisonous water snakes? What submerged branches, green with decay, what foul water insects and creepers, what skeleton of deer or goat lost here?

He collected himself, set his teeth, and dived.

The shock of the water thrust through him like the currents from ten thousand electric needles, but he was an expert swimmer, and presently he was fiercely churning the water with a powerful crawl stroke that swept him around in a brief circle. His spirits rose, half savagely. He spied a strong, overhanging bough and a rock beneath it. There he landed, and whipped the water from his body with his hands.

After that, he dressed. It was the most miserable part of the whole ceremony, for he had to work on the garments by inches over his damp skin. His socks had been splashed; the shoes stuck against them; a wind was rising and driving a chill through him to the bone; but at last he was dressed, and labored up the slope toward the fire site.

He found his companion turning chunks of venison on spits made of sharpened twigs, close to or almost in the flames. But the fire was so small that there was no warmth in it to do Daniel good. He shivered so that he could hardly say: "I thought fire-building was the same as hoisting a flag to show your hunters where you are?"

"That depends," answered Lefty with his usual philosophical air. "With old man Tolliver after us, it's risky.

But the wood's dry. Look over the heads of the bushes and you won't see any mist rising. And a full stomach is worth a scare!"

Daniel could have spoken a disagreeable word in answer, but he restrained himself; he set about doggedly helping where he could, and now, as they cooked, they ate. Roasted flesh without salt seemed a wretched fare; and roasted meat, above all, breakfast—in the place of toast, tea, and grapefruit.

But after a beginning had been made, the appetite of Daniel made by long labor, freshened by a mighty sleep, edged by the keen mountain air and by his ice bath, began to rage like a fire.

Lefty finished but continued to cook, and Daniel both cooked and devoured.

When he had finished he took one of Lefty's handmade cigarettes and sat back with a sigh.

"That was grand!" admitted Daniel.

"I wanted to talk to you last night," said Lefty, "but I didn't want to get you excited and spoil your sleep. You say that you're a Dunlin?"

"I am."

"From where?"

"The East."

"What town?"

"Winhasset."

"I come from Winhasset myself," Lefty pointed out, "and there was only one family of Dunlins there."

"What was your family?"

"My mother, the old man, Jerry, and me."

"You didn't have another brother, then?"

"No."

"Your mother never had another child after you, say?"

And Daniel sat up, his eyes keen. It did not occur to him to doubt the story which Jeremy Crossett had told him; and yet this was a direct contradiction at the very beginning.

"There was another," said Lefty thoughtfully. "It was born dead several years after me. I forget was it a boy or a girl. Why?"

"It was a boy," said Daniel grimly. "It wasn't born dead. And it was switched and brought up in the house of another man."

Lefty Dunlin made another cigarette.

"What other man?" he asked.

"Jeremy Crossett."

"You mean the rich Crossetts?"

"I mean that."

"You're him?"

"I am."

"Well," said Lefty, "go on. How did you happen to find it out?"

"When you came through Lammer Falls with the crowd around you, my father—I mean, the man I'd always called my father—couldn't help breaking out when he heard your name. He told me that we must try to do something for you. When I asked him why, he told me that you were my brother."

Then, as Lefty waited in silence, he went on to explain: "My mother was a very weak and sickly woman —I mean, Mrs. Crossett!"

"I remember her white face," said Lefty gently.

"They didn't dare to tell her that her only child had been born dead. There was another child born that same day, and the doctor arranged things with your mother— and mine! They took me away to the Crossett house; they brought the dead baby to your mother—to my mother. My God!" cried Daniel, "what a cursed piece of work it was!"

"It saved Mrs. Crossett, perhaps," said Lefty calmly. "And the old man didn't leave enough for us, let alone for another child. So there you are! Maybe it was a good thing. You were pretty well raised, I suppose? If you'd stayed with us, you'd have been snaked West with the rest of the family when you were about two years old. And there you'd have grown up like a weed, without a chance."

This was his only remark in acknowledgment of this newly discovered blood-tie. Daniel marveled at him! For himself, his voice had trembled, even as he put the story thus coldly and briefly. But Lefty Dunlin was a man of steel; there was no heart in him, it appeared.

"That was what brought you down to the jail, then?" said Lefty.

"Yes."

After this, the outlaw smoked until his cigarette was reduced to a fuming wisp. He stood up.

"I guess that we'd better be getting on," said Lefty and stretched his arms and yawned.

And this the reception to a miraculous tale! This the reception given to an heroic rescuer, now transformed into a long-lost brother! *Mirabile dictu!*

Daniel was stunned and went speechless to his horse.

15.   Here's a Friend

MIDMORNING brought them down from the highest reaches of the mountains to the broken hills beneath; they rode through a canyon choked with chaparral, from the branches of which clouds of dust washed up in waves about them, and the flying tips of the limbs whipped them, tore their clothes, and lashed their horses; those animals, however, with hides as tough as badger leather, paid little heed to the whipping they received, but plodded on, needing no directing in order to pick out the easiest way through the bushes. Out of this canyon's mouth they passed into a more open valley, where the ground was broken by jutting rocks; or rather, where the rocks were filmed over, now and again, by a thin coating of earth. It supported a scattered growth of bunch grass, however, and cattle spotted the distance in little groups.

They came upon the semblance of a house, at last. It leaned against the slope as if it barely had sufficient strength to remain there. The weight of time and winter storms had crushed its roof into a waving line; its walls sank in with the weight in the middle and bulged out at the bottom. And it was given a last futuristic touch by a stovepipe which issued from the roof in an uncertain jag like a section of a lightning flash, fixed here and corroded and blackened.

Two or three little sheds, as miserable as the house itself, cowered in the background, higher up the slope; and in a corral stood a single horse with withers and hips projecting out of its starved body; a single, weary horse, with a rear hoof pointed, eyes closed, and pendent lower lip.

"Here's a friend of mine," said Lefty. "Here's a fellow who would live or die for me. His name is Hannigan. He's Irish and a good fellow. There's only one thing to remember while you're in his house: Don't tell him your business; he couldn't stand two secrets!"

With this, he rode up to the door and knocked; it was like tapping against the side of an empty barrel, a brittle and hollow sound. And forth came a gentleman clad in overalls which were sustained by a belt not above his hips but lightly drawn around them, as one sees street laborers dressed, or Italian peasants who must have unconstrained back muscles as they bend with the hoe. He had a green-black felt hat, powdered with dust, pushed back enough to let a jag of stiff black hair hang down across one eye.

He leaned a hand against the door jamb.

"What have you come to me for, Lefty Dunlin?" he asked savagely. "Ain't you had enough plunder out of the towns, and out of the poor farmers that you've raided? Have you got to pick on a man that ain't got enough food for himself? Are you gonna come in here and take away my last flour and my last side of bacon?"

"What's your name?" asked Dunlin curtly.

"Me name is Hannigan."

"Hannigan, you got a loud tongue and a loose one. But are you out of grub?"

"I am. Or near out."

"Then I ain't going to rob you, man. Unless you'd let me pay for a scrap of something."

"Let you pay? And have the law on my head for

supportin' and maintainin' an outlaw and a refugee?" said Hannigan fiercely.

"Will you tell me one thing?" asked Lefty, his own voice rising a little.

"If I have the knowing of it maybe."

"Has there been a sight of any posse coming up this valley? Or have any scouts been out for me in this direction?"

"May I rot if I tell you!" said Hannigan. "You and your tribe, when you're scouted and spotted, and snagged again, it'll be a grand thing for the whole range!"

"If it was worth while," declared Lefty, "I'd be blowing your head off of you, Hannigan. But it ain't worth my while."

"If I'd stepped into this door with a gun," said Hannigan, "there wouldn't be so much talk; there'd be powder to talk for me!"

"Step out of the doorway and stand clear of it before I ride away. And if I see you try to dodge, I'll put a bullet through you, man!"

There was an inarticulate snarl from Hannigan. Then Lefty turned off, Daniel following his example; and keeping well about in the saddle, his rifle poised over the crook of his arm, Lefty rode until they reached a nest of young pines.

From that point they rode straight down the valley, but Lefty turned, after he had gone a little distance around the first curve, and rode back among the rocks until he had reached a point well up and opposite to Hannigan's shanty. There he dismounted and put his mustang out of sight behind a circle of rocks; there was no grass here, but the horse began to dine at once from the tender tips of twigs. In all things, Daniel followed the example set by his leader, and finally sat down beside him where they could peer out and watch steadily the face of Hannigan's shack.

Ugly thoughts came to Daniel, as that his newly found brother planned to wait here until Hannigan next issued from his shack, and then drop him with a bullet from the distance. His faith in Lefty was sadly shattered by this time. That omniscient young man certainly had mis-judged Hannigan, the trusty friend. For yonder ruffian in the shack seemed to have no keener purpose in life than to deny succor of any sort to the outlaw.

Presently, not Hannigan but another man left the shack, and, disappearing behind the house, came into view again on a pinto which he cantered slowly down the valley. Lefty, who had remained silent all this time, now rose in turn, mounted, and with Daniel returned toward the hut.

Arrived at the door, with Daniel lingering in the rear, Lefty knocked exactly as before, and once more the owner of the shack stepped forth and stood in the doorway, leaning a hand against the jamb.

This time, his mood was altered, and he grinned broadly at the outlaw.

"I handed out a pretty slick line of talk, old-timer," said he. "Could you fault me?"

"I couldn't," said Lefty, nodding. "You nearly had me convinced. Who was inside?"

"A puncher from up Jackson River. He's gone down to report in town that he's heard your voice and seen you through a crack in the door."

"He didn't shoot," said Lefty. "Wasn't he ambitious?"

"Not when he seen the fellow with you. He told me that he knew one of you would get him even if he got one of you. So he sat down and chatted about the reward on you for a while, and then he started for town. I told him when the posse came up this way to pick up the trail, I'd like to join. Get down off your hosses, friends, and rest your feet!"

In one of the sheds their horses were put up.

"Are you gunna grain these nags?" asked Hannigan.

"I am, just, if I can get the grain. What have you?"

"Crushed barley."

"Oats are better," declared Lefty, "but barley will do. This pair probably never tasted grain before, anyway. How did you get it here?"

"I borrowed the wagon of Tom Saxon, down the valley, and hauled out a few sacks along with a load of chuck and stuff. They were sort of excited in town, seeing me buy barley, but I said that I was going to try to bring on that yearling I got."

So the mustangs were richly fed, and they returned to the house.

Daniel waited a little for an introduction, but he was not presented. Hannigan, asking no questions, produced bacon, cold pone, a can of tomatoes, plum jam; then he started the fire and filled the coffeepot.

All this time he was answering the questions of the outlaw—answering them with meticulous care, puckering his brow in thought, as though he were employed over mathematical problems, where a single error made the answer useless.

A general alarm, he said, had been sent through the mountains after the escape of the prisoner, and every effort was being made to recapture him. Each town had been warned by wire, and literally hundreds of riders had gone forth, gun in hand, hunting for the reward.

"But," grinned Hannigan, "the betting is against them!"

"Has any one been here?"

"A gray-headed, skinny old chap come in and began stringing me. When he found how bad I hated you, he opened up a little. Seems as though he's more interested in your friend than he is in you, Lefty!"

Hannigan turned and fixed his beady little black eyes intently on the face of Daniel.

"It don't seem nacheral," remarked Hannigan, "but Lammer Falls is all cut up about the way that you slipped out of their hands. They blame the stranger, of course."

"What do they know about him?" asked Lefty.

"Nothing, except that he's one of the Dunlins."

"They know that?"

"They do."

"How?"

"By the general cut of his jib, and most of all by the way he performed at the jail."

Hannigan grinned broadly and shoveled some fried bacon onto Daniel's tin plate.

"That's Tolliver," said Lefty thoughtfully. "And he wants you!"

He bit his lip as he regarded Daniel; and the latter felt his heart warming a little. This slight indication of kindly interest on the part of Lefty was more than elaborate protestation from another man.

"Did he talk as if he meant to go on from here?"

"He did, if you mean the skinny old fellow."

"Aye," sighed Lefty, "he may have said that—but what did he really intend to do?"

16.   In for It Now

HANNIGAN had gone for a little ride down the valley. Daniel, rising from a siesta in the bunk at the side of the cabin, found Lefty seated in the door of the shack, drawing in the dust before him an intricate pattern into the midst of which Daniel stepped.

"Damn it!" said Lefty, "you've chucked half an hour's work for me."

"Work?"

"I been mapping the lay of the land around here."

Carefully he put in the erased lines.

"What would be in Tolliver's head?" he asked.

It was a subject upon which Daniel could offer no suggestions.

"He might head down for the lowlands," said Lefty, still thinking aloud. "Or else he might turn around and head back for the upper mountains. You can't tell. Tolliver is a fox!"

Afterward he added: "I only wish that Hannigan hadn't talked so much!"

"About what?" asked Daniel.

"To Tolliver, about hating me. He may have over-done it! And if Tolliver has a ghost of a suspicion—"

Again he advised: "If he wants you, partner, God help you to a fast draw when you meet him; because sooner or later you're pretty apt to be found. God help you, or keep me with you! Mind you, now. Never leave me for a minute, day or night."

Once more the heart of Daniel was warmed, but only a little. He simply failed to understand what might be passing in the mind of Lefty Dunlin. For his part he felt himself running over with ten thousand questions about the whole past life of this brother; not a gesture, not an act, not a thought of Lefty was unimportant in his eyes. But Lefty for his own part seemed to feel no curiosity whatever; or if he did, he concealed it well. Never a question escaped him; never a word did he ask about Daniel's past; never again did he express the slightest gratitude for that heroic effort in the jail which had given him his forfeited life. All was, apparently, as though Daniel were the merest chance-met stranger!

A bird rose with whirring wings behind the shack, and Daniel ran to take a glimpse of it, but saw nothing. When he returned: "Remember," said Lefty. "You'd better not get out of my sight!"

He said it sharply, as one accepting a responsibility whose weight he grudged; and Daniel was heartily offended.

"Very well," he said to himself. "If that's the tone, I'll be as independent as he is. I'll make a point of it!"

And yet, in his heart, he was thoroughly frightened at the thought of encountering Tolliver; there had been something in the appearance of that dusty veteran which had remained in the mind of Daniel, deeply rooted.

Hannigan did not return until the evening, when he turned up on a sadly exhausted mustang. He had been far down the valley, only pausing now and then apparently to tell his neighbors, near and far, about his encounter with the outlaw, and learn what he could of the approach of any danger.

At his farthest stop he learned something most worth knowing: At the nearest town twenty well-mounted men had set forth, in addition to all those who already had taken the main trail. They intended to try to take up the trail of the two from Hannigan's house, and they had telephoned ahead to the next ranches to have food waiting for them.

With that word, Hannigan spurred back up the valley. He delivered his tidings with a most apparent glow of satisfaction.

"I aimed to spend the night here," said Lefty with a sigh, "but we'll have to sleep out again. Feed us again, Hannigan, if you can. I'm going to have a nap."

This, when news of a hard-riding danger had just been given to him! But it was not a bluff. He stretched himself on the bunk, closed his eyes, and in another moment he was snoring loudly, though Hannigan was busy with his cookery. The latter, when he saw the long rider sleep, acted more like a mother than a man and a ruffian. On tiptoe he glided here and there. If a pan were to be moved or a stove lid lifted and replaced, he managed it with the utmost caution, making not so much as a clink of metal on metal.

And when, in his gliding, the floor creaked beneath his weight, he stopped with a sudden expression of pain frozen on his face.

Daniel was half delighted and half amused.

Then Hannigan paused beside him and whispered in his ear: "The horses, kid! No use leaving all that work for poor Lefty, when he wakes up!"

Daniel rose, accordingly, and went to the door.

He did not like this errand. For the sun had set, and only the twilight of the evening now lived in the valley. Where groves of trees stood, the shadows were black, and the pool of blackness behind every rise of ground might well contain the figure of a lurking man.

He stepped into the open and looked more carefully around him.

There was nothing suspicious that he could see or hear. A crow, bound homeward late, flapped heavily across the top of the shack and disappeared toward the nearest wood; and somewhere down the valley a cow was mourning. There was nothing to be seen or heard that indicated any danger, but Daniel had come to distrust his senses, since he started on this ride with Lefty

Dunlin. What would be a crowded page to men like Lefty or Tolliver, say, was to him a blank.

Moreover, Lefty himself had urged him not to leave his sight.

Then a voice from the doorway behind and above him, half a whisper and half a snarl: "Are you afraid of the dark, kid?"

He turned and saw Hannigan sneering, and Daniel felt more fear and shame than he did anger. His face was beginning to burn. After all, it was a just reproach, so he left the shack and marched steadily toward the barn.

As he approached it, that ugly little shed seemed fairly swelling with possibilities of danger. Of course, if any one were sheltered within it, waiting to cut off the outlaws from their mounts, they would fire without warning. Man hunters attacked as the tiger attacks, never troubled by the folly of chivalrous hesitations.

In spite of himself, his step grew slower, and his eyes strayed toward the heaps of darkness on either side of the shed.

When he had opened the door, the smell, and the dim outline of the horses oddly restored his nerve and, with a sigh of regret for his cowardice, he squared his shoulders and stepped for the saddle on the nearest peg.

Something moved before him as he did so. It was rather a suspicion than actual sight of anything, but Daniel dropped against the wall as though dodging a bullet, and snatched at his revolver.

Just as the driver can see with ease the road which seems lost in a mist of darkness to the passengers in an automobile, so Daniel, concentrating with bulging eyes, now made out clearly the form of a man rising from beside the grain bin, and the glimmer of a gun in his hand—

He fired; the flick of an answering bullet clipped the shoulder of his coat, and the boom of the answering shot roared heavily in his ears.

After that first sudden reaction from terror he was numbed and helpless; his heart hammered in his very throat as if to strangle him, and his hands were shaking and useless.

So, leaning stupidly against the wall of the shed, he watched the mustangs prance and leap from side to side while the sharp smell of burnt powder rose like a fume into his nostrils.

The figure by the grain bin had disappeared!

Or was it his terror which had blinded him once more?

Some one leaped into the doorway behind him; slowly he turned and knew that it was Lefty, coming like the wind.

An iron hand gripped his arm, the finger tips sinking to the bone.

"Are you hurt, kid?

"There was some one by the barley box—he seems to have disappeared."

Lefty sprang instantly forward; a match flared in his hands.

"Tolliver!" he cried.

The heart of Daniel raced no longer; it turned literally cold.

Then the voice of Lefty out of the dark once more: "And dead as hell! Dead as hell!"

Daniel could not speak, for a curious numbness made it impossible for him to move his lips. His brain, however, never had acted so switftly, for he was seeing before him the certain result of this action. Now he had closed behind him the door by which he might have retreated to safety. Now he had thrust way from himself his last chance to return to the ranks of the law-abiding. This ride through the mountains, that evening in the jail at Lammer Falls never could be a mere adventure, after this. Instead, they were the introduction to a long life of crime!

This was his crossing of the Rubicon!

So, sick and dizzy, he leaned against the wall of the shack and felt the loosely nailed plank trembling under the hand which he rested against it.

Lefty stood before him, raging: "You damned young fool!" cried Lefty. "I told you not to get out of my sight.

And now you've got it! You're with me forever. And you can't last it out. You ain't made for it! You——"

He seemed to choke with fury and disgust.

"And Tolliver!" he resumed shouting his rage. "You might have killed some bully, some gun-fighting swine. But a straight one like Tolliver——"

He was choked off by his emotion again, and once more Daniel was astonished. He had dreamed that this fellow was without feeling.

Then he heard the voice of Lefty going hard and cold again as the outlaw added: "You ain't cut out for this thing, I guess. They'll kill you, kid, in about three months!"

17.   The Grip of Fate

DANIEL would have gone back to examine the hurt of the fallen man, but Lefty ordered him sharply out of the barn and onto the back of his horse. He obeyed mutely; his mind was whirling.

They came on Hannigan, sprinting toward them with a double-barreled shotgun in his hands.

"There's a dead man in your barn," said Lefty shortly.

"God, God!" breathed Hannigan. "They'll hang me!"

"Load the body onto your wagon, Hannigan" continued Lefty. "Take it straight for town. If they stop you, tell them that I came here; that I held you up, and made you cook some food for us. Then—mind you, now—I left the kid in the house to watch you while I went out to the barn to look after the horses, and while I was away, you heard a shot. You understand. A pair of shots. You tore for the barn. There you found Tolliver lying——"

"Is it Tolliver?" faltered Hannigan huskily.

"It's him."

"They'll hang me!" declared Hannigan with a groan.

"Do what I tell you," said Lefty. "If you try to hide the body you *will* get yourself hanged. If you play out in the open you're going to be all right. And if anything happens, you always remember that I'm behind you with plenty of cash. Kid, let's get out of this!"

With that he turned his horse up the valley, and spurred away at a furious rate, with Daniel following half blindly in the rear.

Hannigan waited until they were out of earshot. Of all the business he had ever been connected with, he liked this the least of all. Of all the work he ever had done, he most wished himself out of this.

If he took the dead man from the barn and simply rolled the body into the next sharp crevice in the ground —into one of those narrow rifts behind his house, where, with a little labor, he could roll ten tons of stone down into the natural grave to conceal the dead——

He went into the barn, lighted a lantern, and looked at the prostrate form, lying head down, a furrow of crimson across the top and side of the head, a pool of blood beside it.

Hannigan grew a little sick. He had known this man well. Who in all the mountains could have failed to know Tolliver—so straight, so gentle, so fearless? And here was the end of him!

It seemed to Hannigan that at last a veil was snatched from before his dim eyes and he was able to look through at the truth; it was wrong to associate with fellows like Lefty. No matter what good chaps they might be, they killed and their profession demanded that they should keep on killing.

However, at least he would not take Lefty's advice and carry the body to town. That was a species of madness, it appeared to Hannigan.

He went out with the lantern, first of all, and examined the bad lands just behind the house. There, in the season of melting snows, wild waters plunged down the hillside and chiseled deeply into the virgin rock. In time the courses changed, and now there were many deep rifts which were eternally dry. They were sharp-edged little canyons, ten to forty feet deep.

Hannigan threw the light of his lantern into these little valleys, and he picked one where the water no longer ran at flood time; he picked one whose upper edges were piled with a gigantic rubble of water-hewn stones.

Then he returned to the barn and picked up the fallen body. He was not a very powerful man, but Tolliver made a light weight, and he dragged the latter easily from the barn to the ravine edge. He had a scruple about simply tumbling the body into the deep grave.

So, instead, he lowered it with care; and he turned it face down—horrible if the cascade of rocks should beat upon an upturned face, thought Hannigan.

After that he went to his forge where, at the back of his house, he did his own horseshoeing, and sometimes performed odd jobs for his neighbors, repairing a broken wagon-coupling, or fifth chains, or sharpening plow-shares, or a thousand-odd jobs of welding. He took a massive crowbar, and, returning to the appointed place, flashed down the lantern light and saw the lean form of Tolliver stretched there, face down, arms folded under his head, like one who slept.

Hannigan turned from it with a shudder and fixed the crowbar under the edge of a massive boulder. It was a sort of keystone, and once unseated it would allow a great shower of stones to descend and complete the grave at a stroke.

However, it was deeply rooted and a ponderous mass. He labored at it patiently for long moments before it finally slipped, then staggered on the brink with a rain of smaller pieces going down before. At last, it dropped with a crash that sent echoes booming and resounding up the hillside.

Then Hannigan regarded the grave with an air of satisfaction. Four or five tons of rock had filled the crevice halfway to the top, at this single stroke. Did not the Good Book speak of the dead rising at the Judgment? Well, poor old Tolliver, at that moment, would have something to do to rise through this overwhelming mass!

In the meantime he must make sure that all traces of the crime were removed.

He returned to the barn, and there he saw that at the spot where Tolliver had fallen one of the floor boards was deeply stained with red. There were many things that could be done. For his part, he was content to scrape off the upper surface with a shovel; then he scattered straw over the surface.

He had worked in this fashion for some minutes when something touched him on the back.

Hannigan whirled with a gasp and saw before him Deputy Sheriff Alvin Denny come up from the good town of Anvil on the trail of the outlaw.

Hannigan turned white; a mortal sickness smote him and made his senses reel. And he remembered, in this terrible moment, that at least he had a faithful gun belted on his hip.

Alas! behind Alvin Denny there were other shadows— half a dozen men had stolen upon him. Had he lost his wits and his hearing? Had he gone mad?

Denny was eyeing him curiously.

"Well, Hannigan? he said.

Hannigan tried to speak. The words he tried to utter slipped away and dissolved. He knew that he was merely gibbering. He must say something; they would grow suspicious!

"What're you up to, Hannigan?" asked Denny. "What're you covering up, there?"

"Me?" said Hannigan at last. "Why, what should I be covering up?"

"D'you generally clean your stable at this time of night?"

"If I been busy in the day doing something else, I finish up my work when I can. It's a free country, I guess!"

And he wound up with a laugh. He had been delighted by the sound of his own voice, free, easy, resonant, all nervousness certainly well obscured; and so he decided to make perfection more perfect by laughing. He laughed; and then in the middle of that laughter his voice changed like the voice of a fifteen-year-old boy, squeaked terribly, and broke with appalling harshness.

Alvin Denny, in the act of turning away, swung about

and glared at the laughter. Then he kicked away the
straw—from the boards.

All the blood from Hannigan's heart leaped into his
brain.

"What in hell are you looking for?" he asked. "What
do you——"

He reached forward, but he was drawn firmly back.
From either side he was held by resolute hands. Already
he was lost!

Then he remembered the advice of Lefty Dunlin: "If
you come out in the open you'll be all right; if you try
to hide the body, they'll hang you, Hannigan!"

Why should any one presume to know more than Lefty
Dunlin? He had presumed, and now he would have his
reward. And very clearly he saw before him the stern face
of the judge, who, rising from his place, decreed—"to be
hanged by the neck——"

Hannigan had heard men condemned for murder!

And never in all his days had he been guilty of that
crime. He was a careful man! Self-defense, with wit-
nesses—well, that was different!

Alvin Denny leaned above the boards. He fell upon
his knees. He took from his pocket a glass. He had three
lanterns brought and their light converged with a daz-
zling power——

"What sort of blood is that, Hannigan?"

"Blood?" said Hannigan. "Blood?"

"Blood!" mocked Denny. "Blood! That's what I said.
Who died here, man?"

Confession made the throat of Hannigan big. But he
checked the torrent of words.

"Go on!" said Denny persuasively. "You better talk
right out—but I got to tell you that you're under arrest,
and everything you say may be held against you!"

Sweat started on the forehead of Hannigan. He wanted
to talk, and the mighty spur of his innocence urged him
on, but he knew that murder is a terrible thing which
drags down all who so much as look upon it. There are
accessories before and after the fact, whatever that means.
One cannot tell. The law is a bog; all who venture upon

it may be drawn down helplessly to their death. Something like a hand closed around the throat of Hannigan; well, the rope would bite deeper than that!

All that he could say, finally was: "You got nothing on me. I ain't gunna talk. I ain't gunna say a word. I ain't gunna be bullied into talking!"

Alvin Denny looked at him.

"I always wondered when you would be got, Hannigan," said he. "Well, this looks like the night. Bring him on to the house, boys."

They went to the house and Denny, entering first, a lantern in one hand and a gun in the other, said briefly: "Who's been here with you, Hannigan?"

The soiled tins were on the table where the outlaw and his young companion had eaten. And suddenly Hannigan knew that it was fate that had him by the throat, and nothing could loose the bulldog grip of it.

18.   Through the Doorway

ALVIN DENNY stretched himself on a broken box which served as a chair.

"All right, Hannigan," said he. "Lemme have the straight of it—the long or short. Who was here? Two, I take it, by the look of that table. Was it one of them that spilled the blood on the barn floor? And what become of the body, old-timer? I'd like to know. You tell us, or we'll find out."

Hannigan had his wrists bound together with a few twists of rope. He stood in a corner, his head hanging. He wanted to raise that head and glare ferociously at the others, but there was something in their bright and curious eyes that overwhelmed him with a sense of guilt and despair.

"Well, boys," said Denny, "scatter and see what you can find; take some lanterns along—and mind that you have your rifles at the ready. You never can tell. Where you find blood, you're apt to find dead men, sooner or later."

They scattered and left Alvin Denny to guard the prisoner. That work he performed in silence, but keeping his eyes constantly fixed upon Hannigan until the latter began to perspire again. He glanced continually at the door. Outside, there was a deep and blessed darkness into which he wanted to plunge. Two bounds and he would be through it and in safety for a moment at the least. But he knew that the first leap would bring the sheriff's Colt into action, and the doorway which framed the darkness would also frame the fall and the death of Hannigan.

"What was that about Dunlin?" asked Denny.

The prisoner was silent.

"Was Dunlin really here? And if he was, what did he pay you, Hannigan?"

"You'd make me out a friend of his, I suppose," snarled Hannigan. "Well, you go on chattering. You got a right to talk, I suppose. Go on and yammer, and be damned!"

He felt better when he had expressed himself thus strongly. Then he slumped down on a stool and dropped his chin upon his fists.

The shack had become a delightful place now. And all the yawning cracks in its walls, and the worn floor, and the battered cooking utensils, and the staggering table, and the ridiculous seats seemed to Hannigan now essential elements of charm and beauty. There had been coolness here on hot days, there had been warmth here, in the winter cold; and when he was hungry, here had been food. And the shades of his friends sat about him and smiled, and talked of their exploits, and wished him well. A cordon of strong and devoted friends—but now they were weak as thinnest wind, and not one knife offered to cut the rope that bound him!

What would the searchers find? The fall of rocks, and the place from which they had been uprooted on the verge of the little ravine—of course they could not fail to find that!

They came back, a body of them walking together and

talking in subdued tones. They had returned to report their success—perhaps they had had time enough to roll away the stone and so to reveal the crushed and broken body of Tolliver!

They thronged through the doorway.

"Denny, there ain't a thing; we've looked everywhere!"

Ah, a voice of an angel! What music in words!

Alvin Denny stood up and stretched.

"Sam," he said, "come along with me. There's *got* to be something!"

And off they marched.

A half hour—a half-century—footfalls approached again, and Alvin Denny stood before his prisoner.

"All right, Hannigan," said he, "I've seen it! If you want to make a confession, maybe the judge would be a lot easier on you!"

Then desperation made Hannigan shout: "I don't care what you seen! You got nothing on me! I've done nothing. Damn you, you got nothing on me!"

At that Alvin Denny sighed.

"Take the rope off of him," he said abruptly. "You can't hold a man in jail because you've found some blood on a floor. Let him go!"

He himself led the way back to his horse and mounted. The others followed the example of their leader, only the last one pausing a moment to give one quick slash of a knife—and the hands of Hannigan were free!

He would not believe it; he sat waiting for the trap and the trick to be revealed. No, the hoofbeats swept away. Some of them, of course, had remained behind to watch him——

If he could get to his rifle where it leaned in the corner—ah! it was now in his hand, and fifteen shots were in the magazine. He crouched beside the door. There was no sound outside. Or was that the whisper of the wind in the distance?

After that he thought that he heard a footfall crunch on gravel; he waited with tingling nerves.

Again—and this time he could not have made a mistake! A stealthy foot was approaching the house, trying to muffle all sound, feeling its way forward, and coming slowly toward the front door——

Hannigan drew back into the shadows of the corner and gathered the rifle to his breast.

There had been blood in the barn, and now there would be blood in his house. He was ready for the deed! He kept his nerves tense, the butt of the rifle in the hollow of his shoulder, and the barrel resting upon one knee.

For the footfall continued and advanced closer until, at the last, he could make out a shadow among the shadows—and then the thing drew closer, and he was sure of the outline of a man.

A chill wonder came over Hannigan, for it was a strange man who stalked an open doorway through which lantern light was streaming into the night! All sound ceased; and the form came drifting straight on. Now it dipped to one side; now to another; and finally it stepped straight into the center of the doorway and loomed before Hannigan in the full glare of the light.

It was Doc Tolliver!

He came like a blind man, with his hands stretched out before him, and his face seemed a smother of dried blood, and his eyes were great, dark, sightless hollows.

Hannigan leaped up and cast the useless rifle to the corner of the room. There was only one way out of that room, and that way was blocked by the terrible apparition of Tolliver; but Hannigan, with the fury of a cornered rat, plunged straight ahead.

He thought that the blind form before him wavered a little. He leaped ahead, steeling himself—but there was no encounter of flesh against flesh—and Hannigan, in sheer horror, yelled and bolted straight ahead, reaching forward, as though the darkness were a thick water through which he must pull himself.

He glanced over his shoulder, and straight behind him he saw the lighted interior of the cabin. There was no shadow of a shadow filling the doorway. The place was empty. And Hannigan ran on, blind, desperate, with all his sins behind him.

19. Fishing for Whales

NORTH OF MOUNT LEWES and on the upper verge of the tall foothills, Lefty Dunlin and his companion pulled out of a pine forest and scanned the landscape of the late afternoon. They could see the upper bend of the Jackson River, and all to the south and west of this was shut off behind the broad shoulder of Lewes Peak. Straight before them they barely could make out the glimmer of the town of Colin, for the atmosphere was comparatively thick—a golden haze spread beneath the blue of the upper sky. Nearer at their feet tumbled the lower hills, and from the top of one of these two streams of smoke rose in thin columns which joined together after floating upward for a little distance.

"How does the land lie?" asked Lefty.

"Is that a signal?" asked Daniel, and he pointed to the twin arms of smoke before them.

"You're coming on," declared Lefty. "If you can guess that much you're coming on. You've left the tenderfoot stage; you've advanced maybe to something between the kindergarten farm age and the third grade of mountain kids on a sleepy afternoon. You're getting eyes. You can see pretty near as much as an old man of ninety, or a baby of ten months. In short, kid, I begin to think that you got the making of a mountaineer in you —and that before your sunburn has turned into a tan—"

Daniel grinned patiently under this chaffing. The sunburn had, in fact, turned to tan, except at the tip of his nose, which was a persistently peeling crimson. He was clad in new garments, now—rough jeans, a flannel shirt, a silk bandanna around the throat, a leather coat, and heavy boots, something between riding and walking. He sat in a new saddle, and he was on a new horse which was far better than the clumsy-headed mustang on which he had entered the mountains. This was like a deer, in

eye and head and legs below the knees and hocks. Above
it had strong quarters, muscular arms; and it was quite
capable of going day and night uphill and down. Lefty
Dunlin was mounted in exactly the same fashion and clad
in exactly the same manner. They were equipped with field
glasses, long Winchesters thrust down into saddle holsters,
a pair of Colts hung on either side of the pommel, and
behind the saddle, rolled into a slicker, each carried a
warm blanket, a few cooking utensils and odds and ends.
Last of all, heavy cartridge belts surrounded them loosely
and wabbled up and down when their horses trotted. But
though the enumeration of all the details may make them
appear overburdened, they were in fact lightly turned out,
and never did the sun look down upon two mounts more
apparently fit for heavy mountaineering, or two riders
more lean, wiry, and tough to endure.

"It's a signal, then," said Daniel.

"It is."

"From a friend?"

"You've hit it. Joe Tyson lives over that way. It must
be from Joe."

"Or somebody who's bribed Joe to make a trap for
you—that may be the bait."

"You never will say a truer thing if you live a thousand
years," commented Lefty dryly.

"If there's any chance of danger, let's keep away,"
urged Daniel.

"You never can catch a fish without dropping a hook,"
observed Lefty. And when Daniel said nothing in response, he added: "What you want to do about it?"

"Go and find out what it's about."

"Do you think there's danger?"

"Yes."

"How come?"

"I just feel it in my bones."

"There ain't no possible better reason for turning back,"
admitted Lefty. "Hunches are the best things in the world
to follow. A hunch is thinking done so short-hand that
you forget what the marks mean—you just read the sense

of the message. Well—we'll chuck this hunch and go ahead, if you want."

"Is Joe Tyson honest?"

"He's got a large family," answered the other. "No family man is apt to be very honest. When a man has more than three children he's got the morals of a mob, and a mob is anything between a crooked thief and a dog-gone saint all ripe to be martyred."

"Lefty, you seem to have read a good deal."

"I'm full of books; I kill a lot of the winter that way, and the off seasons when I'm letting public opinion take a rest from me. You can't keep the people talking about you all the time. If you just keep your hand in now and then, you can always be a hero to the kids and the softheads; you're always worth a headline and a couple of columns about the 'gallant outlaw' and such rot. But if you pile right in and keep busy, you get to be a public nuisance. Even the newspapers get tired of you and demand a little rest."

"What good does it do you to have the softheads and the children call you a 'gallant outlaw'?"

"So long as they're doing that, you can still have a few honest men for friends. And an honest man is worth a hundred crooks when it comes to friendship."

This singular admission Lefty made with the perfect unconcern which he generally showed when he was facing the naked truth. But now he loosened his rein and started forward toward the twin column of smoke. By his direction, Daniel swung off to the right. He was to advance within a quarter of a mile of the fires and then caching his horse in some thicket, he was to go softly ahead on foot and take the fires from the rear, while Lefty undertook the same operation from the front. In this manner, if there was a trap, one of the two was fairly apt to spot it before they were both committed. Two shots in quick succession were to be the signal which would send them scampering back for their horses and then a frantic ride to get to the spot from which they had started. That was to be their rendezvous.

Daniel worked his horse steadily to the required point,

taking care, according to recent lessons, never to show himself against the sky, for Lefty frequently would say that one must act in the wilderness as if the eye of a hawk were watching, and watching from every side.

He found no convenient copse, but a growth of brush so tall that it practically covered his pony. Here, accordingly, he left the horse with thrown reins, knowing that the well-trained animal would never graze out of the brush patch. After that he went cautiously ahead toward the rear of the fire, working with snaky caution from cover to cover until he found himself squarely behind the two arms of smoke.

He could appreciate that his position was far from safe, because to his rear he had a glimpse, through scattering trees, of a ranch house and few sheds, and before him there were thickets interspersed among big timber. But just when Daniel was making ready to stalk with his utmost efficiency, the two columns of smoke, he observed, had ceased to rise. As though the person or persons who controlled the fires realized that danger was approaching and made sure that they would not furnish a light by which enemies might come nearer, the smoke was finished. Only high above the tops of the trees sailed one last puff, thick and deep, and curling upward at the fringes as it rose like a ghost ascending.

It seemed, indeed, an unearthly thing to Daniel. But as he watched it sail upward, he heard the cheerful voice of Lefty calling not far in advance:

"Hey, kid! Come along, will you? It's all right! It's all right, kid!"

With that, Daniel went ahead, but not in blind haste, for in these days with Lefty Dunlin in the wilderness, he had learned to think with care every time he lifted or put down a foot.

So he came out on a gap in the trees where the remains of two adjacent fires were still smoldering faintly; and where Lefty Dunlin and a formidable-looking, black-haired fellow were scanning the trees in different directions.

Yet Daniel made three or four steps beyond the line of the trees before the two saw him.

Lefty grinned with broad pleasure.

"Now what do you say, Joe?" he asked. "The kid has walked onto us in broad daylight. Would you pick him for a tenderfoot, or are we two the greenhorns?"

He explained to Daniel: "Joe Tyson, here, has just been telling me that there's a rumor out in Lammer Falls that you're a tenderfoot, kid—the son of a rich bird out of the East—some millionaire, eh?"

Daniel smiled and made no reply, for he had been strictly cautioned by Lefty never to speak to strangers when he could avoid it.

"He looks like one of us," said Tyson in a sour voice, and then he turned his back on Daniel. "My business is with you, Lefty."

"I got no business except what he's in on," said Lefty promptly, and the rancher turned around and scanned Daniel again with unfavoring strictness.

"All right," said he, "but I don't know him. I know that he's broke jail with you and raised some hell around, but I didn't know that he could have a big job handed to him."

"How big?" asked Lefty.

"Oh, about a million," answered the rancher, and he stared at Lefty with gleaming eyes and flaring nostrils, the beast jumping into his face with startling vividness— the beast, and the hungry beast, at that.

"About a million," said Lefty, as calmly as ever, "would be around the kid's speed. But what would be left for me to do?"

This calm manner of speech made the rancher flush.

"It looks like small change to the pair of you, I suppose?" said he.

"If it's business, it's worth tackling," said Lefty, "but I'd rather have it come at any other time. Is it something near or far?"

"The day after to-morrow, son."

"I hate that, and I don't think I'll touch it," said Lefty.

"The country's too hot just now. They're all gunning for us!"

"They've got your nerve at last, I see," sneered Tyson. "Well, it was bound to go some time, I suppose. Not everybody is a Billy the Kid!"

He dropped the insult with a pointed manner, but Lefty took no offense. Instead he changed the subject sharply.

"What talk have you been hearing about us?" he asked.

"You don't want to hear my job, then? Is that flat?" asked Tyson, growing blacker than ever.

"I asked you a question," said Lefty.

There was a pause, as though the devil in this man were fighting against some kinder or weaker nature.

At length he said: "You and the kid, here, broke through the jail at Lammer Falls——"

"The kid broke through for me, and took me away, you mean——"

"I don't give a damn what happened. The fact is that you got loose. You shook a dozen posses clean. You called at Hannigan's shack up the valley above Anvil——"

"Well?"

"Hannigan sent in word to Anvil. They sent out a posse. They come on Hannigan cleaning up a red spot in his barn and figured that was the end of some man. Who, they couldn't guess."

"They jailed Hannigan?"

"How could they? They had nothing on him. But they scared him so bad that he's disappeared."

"Well, I understand. Go on. What next did you hear?"

"You decided on getting new horses to take the place of your beat ones. You cut down on Sheriff 'Bud' Loftus and his posse where they were camped on the upper Jackson River near Mount Lewes. You sifted into his camp and you picked out his own pair of saddle horses."

An involuntary grin of envy or admiration or both appeared on the face of Joe Tyson.

"You got away on those nags, with bullets flying after you a little. Then you dropped into Bostwick later on that same night. You raided the Jameson General Merchandise

Store, took a lot of clothes, guns, saddles, ammunition, glasses, and what-not. Then you dropped out of view again. A gang of hunters out of Eastwood viewed you and gave you a chase, but you got clean of them. And then—Joe Tyson," added that worthy, "figured that you might be coming his way just in time to get some good news, so he put up a signal for you!"

He was pleased with this ending to the story, but as he was about to speak again, Lefty canted his head thoughtfully to one side and asked: "Hannigan disappeared, did he?"

"He did."

"Is that all?"

"About Hannigan?"

"Yes."

"It's all that I've heard. What about him? They say he's very hot after you."

"Never mind. Hannigan has disappeared," continued Lefty to Daniel. "Well—now break the news to me—Joe. What sort of a job is this one that you've got lined up for me?"

"A sweet one, old son!"

"For how many?"

"Three might do it. Three good, hard, and seasoned ones," returned Tyson.

"Like who?"

"You and me, to begin with." He looked at Daniel and added: "I dunno who would make a third. Not some green kid!"

"You?" repeated Lefty with a keener interest. "Would you count yourself in?"

"I would, this time."

"What would this job come to?"

"A lot more than seven hundred thousand dollars in cash! It's being shipped by——"

"Wait a minute. To hold up a train?"

"You've got it."

"Whereabouts?"

"Anywhere along the line, say, between Newfield and Colin. That would keep it on ground that you know."

"And ground where I'm known," said Lefty gloomily. "That whole countryside is still buzzing like wasps for us!"

"They are? I dunno about that," said Tyson. "They've quieted down a good deal, I'd say. They're quieted down, I tell you, and they're going back off the trail. They've tired themselves out trying to catch the two of you. Don't exaggerate how they're hunting for you, Lefty."

Lefty lightly waved these remarks aside.

"We stop the train, and we get the stuff. How would it have to split?"

"Fifty thousand to the man that squealed to me."

"Go on."

"Then I'd get two shares. One for bringing you the business and one for helping with the job. And I'd do my part of the job, by George. When I set my hand to a thing, blood won't turn me back, Dunlin."

And he said it with a savage intentness, as though he were willing to begin with a murder, merely to prove his sincerity.

"You can't," said Lefty calmly. "You can't tackle a job like this. You got your family here, and you got your ranch on your hands. You're making a living out of this, that's a sure thing. And you're a sure-thing customer, Tyson. You won't play the long odds to win."

"You know me, Lefty, don't you?" sneered the rancher. He added hoarsely: "I don't fish for trout, but I fish for whales, kid. You write me down and remember what I say. I fish for the whales, and I land 'em!"

He snapped his jaws together to give that sentence a period.

"It's all right," smiled Lefty. "I suppose that you've done your own little jobs, from time to time. But I say, you won't chuck your ranch and your house and everything that's in it, to say nothing of your cattle——"

"You fool!" exclaimed Tyson, growing red with the intensity of his emotion. "Why should I? They're sold already. Every damn penny is paid in for them—and all I'm doing is holding down the place and the cattle for him until he comes back from a trip to St. Louis."

"The money paid down, did you say?"

"It is."

"So your hands are cleared?"

"I've got everything salted away for a new start and a bigger layout than I have here," said the rancher. "I'm ready to tackle one job in between. Now, son, I've told you what the job would be."

"Seven hundred thousand," said Lefty Dunlin. "Fifty out to the inside man. That leaves six fifty. Four shares. That's over a hundred and sixty-two thousand apiece, for me and the third man. And three hundred and twenty-five to you, old-timer?"

Joe Tyson nodded.

"Well, I got to talk it over with my friend," said Lefty.

He nodded to Daniel, and they walked away among the trees together. But no sooner had they disappeared in a thicket than Lefty turned and began to retrace his steps softly to the rear!

20.   A Golden Moment

DANIEL, uninvited by word or signal to join in this stalking, remained reluctantly where he stood; but in a few moments Lefty emerged silently through the brush, went past him, and led the way to a big pine whose gigantic branches thrust smaller trees aside and left an ample clearing.

Lefty sat down cross-legged beneath this tree and rolled a cigarette.

"Now, kid," said he, "here's the thing. You get a chance at a small fortune this way. The other way you get a chance at millions. This way you'll probably pay for the job with a bullet through the brain. The other way you escape worry and danger for you don't have to take a chance."

"What way do you mean?"

"If you go back to Crossett."

Daniel flushed and said nothing.

"You mean that you wouldn't give up your right name?"

Still, Daniel was indignantly silent.

"Then ask Crossett if he'll let you take your real name. I don't think that he'd refuse that."

"The bridges are already burned," said Daniel. "You heard Tyson say that they've traced me back to Crossett in Lammer Falls?"

"Just a scare—just a rumor," said Lefty eagerly. "Don't build on that. If they were sure about it, Tyson wouldn't've taken it all so easily. It would have been headline stuff for him. The whole country would be crazy about it. Millionaire's son turns bandit—why? I'd almost like to turn into a scribbling reporter, to write up a story like that! No, kid. If they seriously thought that you were Crossett's boy, they'd be shouting the word everywhere!"

"I don't go back," said Daniel simply.

"You don't?"

"No."

"This robbery stuff—how can you swallow that? I mean, the way that you've been raised?"

Daniel lighted a cigarette in turn. And as the fumes of smoke rose, he felt his mind clearing and growing cold like the air of an autumn morning before the sun is up. He could not help wondering if this were not the very state of mind in Lefty when that worthy was settling a problem in his mind.

"Blood tells," said Daniel.

"Sometimes, sometimes," said Lefty. "You blame the Dunlins for this?"

"Why not?"

"You been put through a college. You ought to hate a crooked job!"

"I would hate some crooked jobs," said Daniel. "I hated breaking into the store in that country town and looting it. I hated that. And I intend to pay double for everything that I took from the place! You hear me, Lefty?"

"I hear you. Of course, we'll pay double. I always do for a job like that! You don't like that sort of a job, but to snake nearly a million dollars off the train—that's nothing to you? That's a sort of a joke, I suppose?"

"No, not a joke!"

Daniel blew forth smoke. He raised his head and watched the blue-brown mist drift upward.

High above him he could see the bright eyes of a squirrel fixed upon him, as though the tiny creature were spellbound with interest in his decision. He could not help smiling.

"Not a joke," he suggested, "but a game."

"I've stuck up three trains before this," said Lefty sternly. "There's been about fifteen of us, altogether, in those three jobs. Four have been killed during the hold-ups or in the chases that followed. Three have crawled away full of lead, and all three have died, too. That's seven out of fifteen. One has disappeared. Nobody knows what's become of him. That's eight, probably dead, too! Six have been caught and sent to prison, and not one of them have come out. Well, you take that score. Fifteen employed in the game—on my side. Fourteen gone forever, or as good as forever. That leaves me, all that's left. I want you to see what sort of a game it is—the odds you're up against!"

"It shows that you've had the bad luck," said Daniel. "And probably your share has been used up. The next job ought to be simple and easy. I still say that it's a game."

To this Lefty responded with soft but venomous cursing.

"Suppose that bullets fly?" he asked. "Suppose that you kill your second man—your third man—you shoot too straight not to kill."

"I hope not," said Daniel seriously. "I'd hate that frightfully."

"What right have you," said Lefty, "to endanger the lives of law-abidin' citizens?"

The sharpness with which this query was put amused Daniel, coming from the confessed outlaw.

"Blood tells," said Daniel finally. "It's simply in me, I suppose."

"In you!" declared Lefty. "I never heard such rot! It's

nothing but kindergarten—and you a growed-up man, or supposed to be. But you ain't! You're only a damn kid!"

"I tell you what," said Daniel. "I know it's wrong. I know it endangers the lives of others. But somehow I'm not ashamed. That's frank. It's a great gambling chance, as I look at it. I think of that train and the numbers of men aboard it, and most of them, if they're natives of this section, probably armed—to say nothing of the armed messengers, picked men, who are sure to be guarding the money. Then I think of the danger and difficulty of stopping that train. And all the rest of the dangers to surmount. And three men to tackle that job—why, it seems, to me, as I said before, a game. I know that I'm wrong. But tell me, Lefty, what makes you stick to the idea? How do *you* look at it? I'd like to know.

Lefty responded with a black look which gradually cleared a little.

"I can't argue you down," he admitted at last. "You'll go through with the job, then?"

"I will."

"Tyson is serious," said Lefty. "I went back and had a look at him. He means business. He already is counting the money. What a beast he is!" added Lefty. "I never saw such a swine of a man! He'd murder you, kid, and never think twice about it. Well, we'll go back and I'll talk business with him. Come along! But I wish to heaven," he added with earnest conviction, "that I could head you off from this work, lad!"

It moved Daniel. Very seldom had Lefty allowed the slightest kindness to appear in his attitude toward this new-found brother. This was one of the golden moments, and Daniel felt that he was enriched by it, and that he had penetrated another few steps into the mysterious labyrinth of Lefty Dunlin's nature.

He issued from the haze of his thoughts as he heard Lefty's quiet voice saying: "We'll do the job. But we'll just reverse the shares. You'll get the single one. I'll get the double share as the leader of this gang."

The answer from Tyson was a gasp, and then a bull roar of rage.

21. Schemes and Dreams

DANIEL, on an unforgettable day, had heard an Irish horse dealer bargaining for hunters, but the struggle on that occasion was as nothing compared with the strife between Lefty and Tyson. The rancher spoke so fast that it was like the roar of many rapid firers in action at once; there were hardly syllables to his speech.

When, at last, he could make his words intelligible, he barked: "Who got the idea? Who got the information? Who laid all the plans?"

"Some sneak," answered Lefty coldly, "who's employed by the company that trusts him, and who knew you, Tyson, from your old record, to be the sort of a gent who would like this sort of a game."

"Who told you——" gasped Tyson, appalled, as it seemed, by this quiet analysis.

Then he paused, gathered his rage about him like a mantle of fire to cover his confusion, and cried: "I lay the plan and I take a full share in the work. And then——"

"How full a share do you take?" asked the grim outlaw.

"As full as any man. There's no yellow in me, Dunlin!"

"What can you do?"

"Everything this side of hell that you dare to do yourself."

"How can you shoot?"

"As well as that kid that you hang with."

"Just roll that stone down the hill, will you, kid?" said Lefty, and he kicked a small stone before him. Daniel's gun came smoothly into his hand and barked six times in rapid succession; at every shot the stone leaped on its way and at last disappeared in a bush.

"Can you match that, Tyson?" asked Lefty.

The latter rumbled: "Trick shooting at a stone ain't shooting a man."

But manifestly he was much impressed, and stared at Daniel with new eyes.

"Can you ride?"

"I'll sit a horse with any man," said Tyson, gathering confidence again.

"Sure. You'll sit him so hard that you'll break his back inside of an hour's galloping. You weigh about two hundred and twenty-five!"

"I never hit the scales higher than two hundred and fifteen."

"You're a tub," said Lefty scornfully, "and you talk about doing your share in this job! I'd rather have some quiet kid that would obey orders without yapping about them."

"Then get your quiet kid!" shouted the rancher. "And get your job, too. You won't figure in this layout!"

"That's the kind of talk I like to hear," said Lefty. "And I don't blame you. You've probably had enough experience to pull off the job alone. You never should have invited in a high-priced man like myself, Tyson. Just round up a few punchers that are out of a job. You could get them for five dollars a day; and for a thousand bonus they'd do anything up to borrowing fire from hell. So long, Tyson!"

He turned on his heel, waving to Daniel, and they had reached the trees when Tyson called: "A fine friend you are, Dunlin! By heaven, I'll remember this!"

Lefty, who had seemed in a cold fury, winked broadly at Daniel as he half turned.

"What has friendship to do with this? I tell you the cheapest way of doing the trick."

"With cow-punchers?"

"Well," suggested Lefty, "I hear that 'Mugsy' Murphy and 'Mississippi' Charlie are out of jail again and they'll be looking for something like this."

"Mugsy has the prison shakes," answered the well-informed Tyson, "and Charlie always was a poor ham. I gotta have class for this job, Lefty, and you know it.

I gotta have your class; only I'm sort of surprised that you want to rob an old pal like me!"

"Business is business," said Lefty. "I put the thing the way that I see it. You want two shares, and so do I."

"I'll compromise with you," said the big man in a frenzy of eagerness as he approached the outlaw. "I tell you what—I'll donate the idea, and everything, and I'll——"

"What idea?"

"Why, the whole information about how to get the money——"

"You will?"

"Of course."

"Go on, then. What information?"

"I'll tell you the number of the train, the date of shipment, and the hour that the train is due in any town;"

"Will you stop the train, too?" said Lefty. "And will you do it in a place where we'll have a fair chance to get away afterward?"

"You want the world with a rope around it!" exclaimed Tyson, angered again. "What more could you ask from me than all the information?"

"I know that the Bank of London is full of money," responded Lefty Dunlin, "and so is Wall Street. I hand you that information free of charge. They got some crown jewels in the Tower of London, and in Tiffany's, right up on Fifth Avenue. There's some free information, Tyson, and I don't ask for two shares or even one for handing it out to you. You just go right ahead and help yourself."

This chaffing brought Tyson's temperature to such a high point that, for a time, he could do nothing but stamp up and down and curse heartily in a brutal rage.

At length he said sullenly: "Well, we'll make a compromise. We'll split the purse three ways: Two parts to you, two parts to me, and one part to the kid, yonder."

Lefty merely smiled.

"Four shares," he insisted. "One for you, one for the kid, and two for me. That has to go!"

"Go and be damned!" shouted Tyson.

He added instantly: "Have it your own way, then.
You're hard on an old friend, Lefty!"

"I don't think so," answered Lefty. "I know what my
work is worth. And you know that you can trust me. Tell
this stuff to another man, and can you be sure that he'd
split honestly with you? No, I don't think that you could.
But I've never double crossed a man, Tyson. You know
that and you bank on it."

Tyson nodded, hardly less gloomy than before.

"Well," said Lefty, "you may as well sit down and give
me the information. Kid, you ramble away and get the
horses and bring them both up here. Mine is down in the
first hollow by a little patch of poplars."

Daniel, thus dismissed, wandered back to the spot where
he had left his horse, and then went for Lefty's, which he
found without trouble. And as he rode, he was not re-
flecting upon the greatness of the crime toward which he
now was pointed. As a matter of fact, it troubled his conscience, as he had said, less than the looting of the store in
Bostwick. Rather, it seemed to him like a great and delightful adventure which awaited them, and his heart beat
high in anticipation.

Blood tells! He felt his heart swelling with the old
Dunlin strain now!

By the time he had brought both the animals up the
hill to Lefty, the latter was finished with the rancher, who
had disappeared. They rode straight back on the trail they
had just covered, and Lefty chatted as they went.

It was a promising deal; but he did not trust Tyson.
There were some men, declared Lefty, whose integrity
was perfect, but there were others who could be as honest as steel—until they reached steel's melting point. And
the melting point of Tyson, said Lefty, was far lower than
the huge sum which they now contemplated stealing.

The reward, however, was so great that the thing must
be chanced. Already, Lefty had formulated a plan and
designated a site at which they would attempt to stop the
train. From that moment they must be busy collecting
some accessories for the crime.

"And I see the way out for you, kid." said Lefty. "You won't have to stick to this work long. Your first big job can be your last one. I held out for two shares, not for myself, but so that we could pool the winnings. We'll have half a million, lad! And we'll drop it in a good safe investment. Well, say, six per cent. We can get that, gilt edged! Then we blow from this part of the world, and never show our faces in it again."

"The police?"

Lefty frowned and shrugged.

"They forget. Besides," he said, "where they look for me I won't be! They'll expect somebody to be spending big in Paris or London, but you and me, we'll slide over to some little Irish town, like you been telling me about, and hunt foxes, and live easy, and you'll marry some dog-gone swell heiress, kid, and I'll hook up with something classy. We'll settle down. I can see myself!"

He raised his head with a smile; Lefty was dreaming.

"I'll study grammar. I'll study you. I'll learn to spiel the way you do, and act the way you do. They'll never know me, even if they hit me face to face. This will be the last big job, kid; after that I'll have a pocket full of excitement to last me the rest of my days. Now what do you say to that?"

Daniel said nothing at all, for as he looked over the ragged country before them, shadowed by dark-headed trees, and marked with unfathomable canyons, he knew that Lefty's dream was a dream indeed, and that it never could be realized. He was a part of this country, as surely as the waters that flowed through it and the mountains that rose out of it.

Subtract these things from Lefty's environment, and one would be subtracting them from his soul.

And Daniel himself? He wondered, as he looked before him, how he could find a taste of life in any other existence, since he had come to this playground of the world. All that he had done, all that he had been, seemed most flat and unprofitable. Before him lay the land of his desire.

22. Questions and Answers

IN LAMMER FALLS, Jeremy Crossett grew pale and gaunt of face. His sleep was broken by endless pacings of his room; his days hung terribly upon his hands; and with his whole tormented soul he waited to hear the next news of the wanderer. Then something more than a vague anxiety came to him.

He had come down late for breakfast, and Jenny Loren served him by the window when a tall man walked in and banged his sombrero on his chaps to knock the dust from them.

Jenny Loren hailed him cheerfully: "Good morning, Sheriff Loftus!"

And Jeremy Crossett looked more carefully, and pushed away the mists of his own brooding in order to see a hard-faced man of great height, with shoulders narrowed and stooped by endless riding; a weary, aging, troubled man he seemed, like some farmer who pours his soul, his labor, into a task which never can free him from debt. Yet there was nothing to invite pity in Sheriff Loftus. Whatever one might think of his pendulous arms, and his hanging shoulders, and his withered neck, and his bowed back, his chin was still that of a fighter, and his eyes were as cold and as blue as ever.

He sat down at a near-by table and asked for a cup of coffee. While he waited for it, he leaned his elbow on the edge of the table, his chin in his hand, and closed his eyes. It was not the relaxation of thought; Jeremy Crossett judged that this was a slumber as profound as it was brief.

When Jenny placed the steaming cup before him: "Two lumps!" said the sheriff.

And Jenny dropped them in, and stirred them until they were dissolved.

The sheriff slouched back in his chair until his head and his shoulders dropped against the wall.

"Come here, Jenny," he said airily.

She stood beside him, smiling down.

"You better go to bed," said Jenny.

"Gimme your hand," said the sheriff.

She surrendered it to him obediently, and the sheriff covered it with his great, gnarled paws. He was silent, his eyes closed again, and he seemed to be sleeping. Every line of his face sagged.

"How long have you been riding to-day?" asked Jenny.

"About fifty mile," said the sheriff.

And Jeremy Crossett, all his own cares forgotten, felt his blood turn cold; fifty miles of riding through such country as this—by breakfast time! And this was no youth, but a man past middle age.

"Jenny——" said the sheriff, like one too feeble to speak more than a word at a time.

"Your coffee'll be getting cold."

"Jenny—what's been happening around here?"

"It's been quiet here in Lammer Falls, Sheriff."

"Jenny——"

"Yes."

"I mean about Willie."

"Oh!" said Jenny.

The sheriff partly opened his eyes.

"You don't like him?" said he in a mournful voice.

"I do, though," she answered.

"But not enough?"

Jenny hesitated.

"If I was younger——" said the sheriff, and let his voice drawl away as he closed his eyes again.

"If I was younger," said the sheriff, his eyes still closed, "I would go and marry you, Jenny, myself."

"Perhaps you would," said Jenny, and she smoothed the great tangle of hair which shadowed the forehead of the sheriff.

Jeremy Crossett began to grow a little ill at ease. It became hard to realize that this was the public room of a public hotel.

"I was a terrible set man," said the sheriff. "When I

seen the girl that I wanted, I went for her. She didn't want me. Her folks didn't want me. Even their dogs barked at me. But——"

He paused again, wearily.

"Ah, well," said Bud Loftus, "she couldn't keep from me. I drove her man out of the country. I made her folks shut up. And one night I took her away. I drove her away. 'Where are you takin' me?' says she. 'I dunno. Home, I guess,' says I. 'Home lies the other way,' says she. 'Not my home and yours,' says I. She began to scream. I whipped up the horses. She said she would jump. I just whipped up the horses. She didn't jump. She began to cry. I just whipped up the horses. She began to beg. I just whipped those horses along. And finally she sat still, and she didn't say nothing, and the horses come out of a gallop to a trot, and out of a trot to a dog-trot, and out of a dog-trot they fell to a walk, and from a walk they stopped dead still. Because they was beat, you see. And there was a moon hanging on the edge of Mount Lewes, and every pine tree, it stood up straight beside its shadow and never moved, and——"

His voice failed again. He allowed the hand of Jenny Loren to fall away from him.

"Willie——" he said.

"Yes," said Jenny.

"Willie was her son," said Bud Loftus. "But——"

And then, opening his eyes, he peered earnestly at her.

"I would hate to let you get away, Jenny, into any other family, to live with some other man, and get your back or your heart broke, or both. And calluses on your hands. And your soul just dyin'. Because," said the sheriff, "you could be perfumin' the life of a good man, and makin' a whole town sweet, Jenny. Well, well, Willie ain't the man! Now, you run along," he went on, suddenly growing more brisk as he sat up in his chair. "You run along about your work. I got something to think of!"

He seized his coffee cup and drained it.

"Gimme some coffee, Jenny. Gimme a full cup, this time. The world has gone to hell, Jenny. There was a time, if you asked for coffee, they handed you a bucket of it; now they put a drop in a thimble. The coffee cups, the women, and the men—they been shrinking and shrinking! Is that Mr. Crossett?"

His head was erect, now, and there was not the slightest shadow of weariness in his eyes as he looked across at Jeremy Crossett.

"My name is Crossett," said the latter.

"I gotta talk to you," said the sheriff. "I want to know, is it your son that's gallivantin' around and raising hell by the side of Lefty Dunlin?"

Mr. Crossett gripped the edge of his table, and it quivered until the water shuddered in the glass.

"Why, Sheriff Loftus!" cried Jenny Loren. "That's an idea, I guess not! Him? Why, he's gone hunting up in the mountains, that's all. Him a jail-breaker? Him? But you never seen him!"

"I asked Mr. Crossett," said the sheriff. "You run along, Jenny, because I guess that he don't need you to help him talk."

"I was surprised," said Crossett.

"Nacherally you would be," said the sheriff. "And you still look kind of sick, I might say."

This observation did not help the unsettled nerves of Crossett, but under the grilling he steadied himself a little. After all, back on "the Street" there were just such encounters, games of bluff, sudden challenges, and he with the best poker face won millions, and the weaker man went to the wall. The quiver of an eyelid might mean a dozen bankruptcies within an hour.

"I've heard you addressed as 'Sheriff'?" said Crossett gravely.

"That's my unlucky job," said Loftus.

"So that you have a right to ask such questions, as a matter of course."

"And to have them answered," said the sheriff sharply.

"Naturally. It was a shock to me to hear such a remark—you understand that I have heard a great deal in the past few days about the exploits of the ruffian Dunlin and his equally ruffianly companion—to be asked if my son—it was a great shock to me, sir!"

"It was," said the sheriff keenly. "I see that it was. You turned green!"

"When a father hears his son accused of murder and robbery——"

"Murder? Who have they killed, now?"

"I thought there had been killings."

"Maybe, maybe! Maybe you've heard straighter from them than I have. Who did they kill?"

"Naturally" remarked Jeremy Crossett, "I only have to remember that my son is my son; it puts me at ease again. But the sudden suggestion——"

He waved his hand. But the sheriff did not answer the sympathetic smile.

"Where's your son now?"

"Hunting in the mountains."

"There's a pile of mountains. Where in the mountains?"

"He intended to start north," said the millionaire, "and gradually circle around through the mountains, following game as he could find it——"

"Start north, travel in a circle, follow game as he found it!" growled the sheriff. "I asked you for an answer, not for a puzzle!"

"I tell you what I know," said Crossett with dignity.

At this, Sheriff Loftus stood up and leaned upon both hands, that rested on the table top. From this position, he stared fixedly at Mr. Crossett.

"Well——" said the sheriff, and then, abruptly, he turned upon his heel and left the room.

At the door, Jenny Loren met him and looked at him with great eyes.

"Dear Uncle Bud!" she said. "Is it really Mr. Crossett's boy that's doing all the terrible things?"

"Don't you think so?" asked the sheriff.

"How should I know what to think?" said Jenny.

"He's a fine-lookin' boy, ain't he?"

"Oh, no, just ordinary."

"Fine, up-standin' kid, ain't he?" asked the sheriff.

"Him? I never noticed him particular."

"Humph," said Bud Loftus, and strode swiftly away from her, his spurs jingling upon his old and wrinkled boots.

23. Into the Wilderness

JENNY LOREN appeared on the verge of following the tall man, but she changed her mind presently and, after balancing back and forth, as an undecided person will do, she returned hastily to the dining room and dropped into a chair opposite Mr. Crossett.

Mr. Crossett was not pale, he was even smiling a little. His fighting blood had been roused and, like a thoroughbred, he responded to the challenge of danger.

"Who is Willie?" he asked.

"Willie? A poor sap!" said the unsympathetic girl. "What do you think he meant?"

"Willie is his son; he hopes that you'll marry Willie, it seems. Will you, my dear?"

"I'm not for marriage," said Jenny Loren bluntly, "unless it helps me on with my business."

"What is your business, pray?"

"The movies, of course."

"I almost forgot. Jenny, that is a very keen man."

"Him? Keen?" said Jenny.

She closed her eyes and with them shut spoke in a drawling imitation of the sheriff: "They used to have men—some—around here—long time ago. They've died —finished—dried up—all except one. That's Bud Loftus —I guess——"

She opened her eyes and smiled at Jeremy Crossett. The latter was nodding.

"You talked to him at the door," he pointed out.

"I tried to turn him off the trails; I only put him further on it. I thought that I could talk him away—but I couldn't!"

"Well," murmured Crossett, "we haven't a word from Tolliver. I'm afraid he's not so keen a man as you thought, Jenny."

"Tolliver," said the girl, "will follow a trail as good as any man in the world, and shoot as straight and die as game."

"Then what do you think has happened to him?"

"I don't know. I don't know! They couldn't just brush him out of their way, if he came up with them——"

"You mean that if there was a fight, it would be such a terrible one that other people would have to hear about it?"

"I think so," said the girl. "I'd bank on that."

"I think that Tolliver is a beaten man," answered Crossett slowly. "The more I reflect, the surer I am. He couldn't stand up to them. To the two of them, I mean. I saw Dunlin ride down the street. That was enough to make me feel that he's one man in a thousand. Then there is my boy. You haven't had a chance to know him, Jenny, but let me assure you that *he's* one in ten thousand!"

Jenny's color changed ever so little; her brown face was tinged with pink.

"Is he?" said Jenny vaguely.

"He is, my dear. And now I see what utter folly it was for me to send a fighting man on their trail. I must try some one else. I don't know whom, I don't know what expedient, Jenny. Can you suggest any one?"

Jenny sighed.

"I've been trying to think. Oh, how I've been trying, night and a day."

"What a warm heart you have, my child!"

"There's something for me to get out of it," said Jenny in the most practical of voices. "I want that trip to Los Angeles and back."

"Ah?" said Crossett, but he could not be totally deceived, and his eyes retained their kindness as he watched her.

Then he continued sadly: "They've done damage enough, even now. What they may have in prospect before them, heaven knows! Sheriff Loftus has more than a suspicion about my boy. The whole countryside is up in arms. They cannot last long, no matter how clever Lefty Dunlin may be. And every moment that I remain here alone, Loftus will grow more and more suspicious because my son stayed away so long!"

Jenny started up from the table, struck with a great thought.

"Wait! Wait!" said she. "I'm thinking something out—I—I'll come and talk to you later."

Jenny disappeared, and climbing swiftly to her own little attic chamber, there she sat down in the midst of her life, so to speak, and stared at the future. From her bureau, two pictures looked over at her—a faded woman in a little hat tied beneath the chin with ribbons, and a faded gentleman with a long beard and an air of Nestorian solemnity. They were father and mother to Jenny Loren, and though they had died, she kept their pictures continually with her, so clinging to her past, so gathering about her some vestige of an environment which was her own. A threadbare carpet-bag in the corner served to contain the total of her worldly goods, except for the dancing dress which hung from the nail near the window, giving one streak of color to that little room.

So Jenny sat among her thoughts until a little wrinkle appeared in the middle of her forehead; she banished it by taking from the dark cavern of the carpet-bag an old wallet inherited from her father, and from the depths of the wallet she removed the one treasure which it contained. It was neither a bank note nor a check, but merely a snapshot of a slender, dark, and handsome youth. She held it in both trembling hands and searched the photograph hungrily, as though she wished to receive some manner of answer from those serious eyes.

It was a picture of Daniel Crossett, and had the elder Crossett seen it he would have known that prying fingers had been through his luggage and chosen this prize from all the rest. No qualms of conscience troubled Jenny Loren for this theft, and yet often she wished that she had not taken the little print because it had given her many hours of such happy sadness as she never had known before; and the knowledge that it waited for her in her room sometimes stopped her in the middle of her work, and set her dreaming breathlessly, like a witch of the olden days, who has made an image and thereby captured a soul to torture or make rejoice.

But it seemed to Jenny, now, that her duty lay clearly before her. She could understand why it might be most difficult for any man to come within hailing distance of two such as Lefty Dunlin and Daniel Crossett, but a woman could come to them unsuspected, if only she could pick up the trail. She had her own saddle and own horse— Sheriff Loftus had given her both—and a better little mustang never rocked over the level miles or twisted through chaparral, or dipped up and down among the hills and canyons of the back country. She knew the lay of the land, also, because whenever a dance was given in a neighboring town, Jenny Loren had to go; pretty girls could not be spared!

There were difficulties. She hardly could explain to people that she was leaving in order to ride in pursuit of a young man across the mountains. So she went first to Jeremy Crossett and explained to him, briefly, that she had hope that she could persuade an old and tried friend of hers—a relation, in fact—to undertake to deliver the message. To the hotel manager she gave a different story —there had been a sudden message from a sick friend— in a week she would be back. So Jenny gathered her courage for the task.

She knew exactly what to do, the sort of pack to arrange, the supplies to take along; and out of her own money she paid for everything. Jeremy Crossett had not even thought to offer funds.

For that matter, she needed to think for him, as well as for herself, and it was her suggestion that he leave the hotel and take a horse and pack mule into the hills across the left shoulder of Lammer Mountain. In that manner, he could remove himself from the embarrassing questions of the sheriff, and it might keep the attention of Loftus from being turned to curiosity about the identity of Lefty Dunlin's young companion.

Jeremy Crossett accepted that good advice. He was in a profound quandary, now, unable to fix on anything, ready to do as any other bade him; therefore, he went in the most docile fashion toward the hills, riding an old horse, leading a pack mule behind him, with the haunting conviction that once the pack was removed from the back of the mule, he never would be able to assemble it in one homogeneous whole again.

However, such a worry as this was a small thing compared with the sea of trouble in which he was lost, and when he reached the first rise of ground beyond the town of Lammer Falls, he turned and looked back upon it with a gloomy conviction that nothing in the world could save his boy from early and terrible death except the intervention of wise Jenny Loren.

She seemed to Crossett, now, the very personification of wisdom, and he felt himself oddly humbled, as if he had become a child again, and as though Jenny Loren were a commanding presence—like a schoolteacher, say.

He smiled a little at this fancy, and then he turned his back on Lammer Falls, and went slowly toiling up the slope beyond. He was disgusted with himself. He felt that he had played and still was playing a weak and foolish game, but he did not know where he could put his hand to the wheel. All was vagueness and confusion before his eyes.

Jenny Loren was as compact of assurance and confidence as Crossett was now full of indecision and weakness; she gathered the lightest of packs, she threw on the saddle with her own strong hands, and drew up the cinches until the mustang groaned. Then she swung into the saddle like any man, her divided skirts looking for all the world like the chaps of a cowpuncher.

So she drew on her gloves, she tapped the butt of her light Winchester with an assured hand, she gathered the reins, and sitting straight and easily in the saddle she sent the mustang cantering down the main street of Lammer Falls. As she rode, her confidence grew in her, as strength grows in the workman who put his hand to task. She was singing as she saw the last house of Lammer Falls drop behind her, and the trail winding snakelike before her, into the wilderness.

24.   A Ghost Trailing

BETWEEN THE TOWNS of Jackson and Silver lay a little switch station, well within view of each city, and that was the spot on which Lefty picked for the holdup of the express. When big Tyson argued savagely that it meant running their heads into the lion's mouth—or rather, into the mouths of two lions—Lefty insisted that if they performed the job at the switch station they would have a fairly well-secured line of retreat. They could head up between the two rivers, through a region screened with many trees, and if the bulk of the pursuit rolled after them on the same line of march, they could turn either right or left and ford one of the rivers, or else they could abandon their horses and drift down one of the currents in the night; in short, they would have a hundred ways of playing dodge with their followers. Whereas, if they robbed the train at any other place, they would be isolated in the midst of widely sweeping plains, and the telegraph would send hordes of pursuers to spy them out before they could reach shelter of any kind.

"You can't dodge a man twice when he sees you in the open," summed up Lefty. "But if those two towns see the train stop, they'll think nothing of it. They can see the train, but they won't be able to see what's happening to it, and by the time they get the warning, we'll be well along our way!"

Tyson still argued, but, always, he was forced to accept the decisions of the master criminal.

When that important point was settled, Tyson set out at once. He was to ride ahead of the two others for two reasons. One was that he could go freely if he were not in their company, besides, it is harder for three to journey unobserved than it is for two. In the second place, he could execute several necessary commissions by starting on ahead; and, finally, he would be on the spot of the holdup with a fresh and eager horse, and a fresh horse was what Tyson would need when once they started to ride for their lives.

A thousand other points were discussed, also. Not a detail was left untouched by the accurate minds of Lefty and Tyson. The latter, for instance, insisted beforehand that all the loot should be left in the possession of Lefty Dunlin until they were well away from all danger of capture.

"Suppose that they snag me," said the logical Tyson, "because I'm big and beefy and will give my horse more work than a splinter like you. Well, then I'd have jail and my money gone, if I had my share with me. But suppose that you have it, it'll be a hot-riding gang of deputies that ever lay their hands on Lefty Dunlin! Then you can use anything up to twenty thousand for lawyers for me. And, after that, if I have to serve out a term, well, it'll be work that I'll be being paid for."

And Tyson grinned, it was plain that for such a stake as this he would venture not prison only, but death as well. His family already was packed and ready to move south for Mexico, where an old companion of Tyson was located. Their future address he did not fail to give to Lefty, so that in case he were killed in the holdup or in the fight, the money he had earned could be forwarded to his wife.

This was a mere sample of the foresight which the pair exhibited in every detail of their planning.

So, then, Tyson went on ahead, and the other two waited for the evening, so that they might ride down through the lower foothills under the cover of the dark; then, proceeding out into the plains toward the two towns, they could camp the rest of the night—resuming their journey the following afternoon—in easy striking distance of the right place and the right time.

They had paid careful attention to their horses, and through Tyson they had secured two temporary mounts.

These would be ridden through the hills, the regular saddle animals being led. Their strength was to be reserved for the homeward dash to the upper mountains.

The evening came, and Daniel was drawing up the cinches on his mustang substitute, when Lefty whistled a soft warning, and stepped to the edge of the little thicket which sheltered them.

Then he turned back and said softly: "It's Hannigan coming, and coming as if the devil was after him. What can he want? Why's he here? And how the devil has he trailed us?"

Brush began to crackle in the distance, and then Daniel saw the wild form of Hannigan bursting toward them with all the speed that he could command; and as he reached the little clearing inside the outer fringe of the thicket, he saw Lefty Dunlin and threw up his hands with a wild cry of joy. He saw Daniel, and leaped at him with a yell of a madman. He clutched him with one hand, and with the other, he seemed calling to some one from behind.

"I've swore and swore that it wasn't me," said Hannigan. "I've swore faithful, and he wouldn't believe. But now I've brought him to the gent that done the work."

Lefty caught Hannigan by the shoulder and swung him sharply around.

"Look me in the eye," he commanded.

"I ain't dippy," said Hannigan. "I'm close to it, but I got the wits in me still, I think!"

Lefty pulled out a flask of brandy and poured a large dram down Hannigan's throat; it left him coughing with the sting of the raw liquor.

"Now tell me how you happened to come for me here? Who tipped you to this place?"

"You done it yourself. Four years ago you remember that once you made me lay up for you here and wait while you was coming in from Anvil with——"

"I remember! I remember!" said Lefty sourly. "It

slipped out of my head. That's all. Now what's the meaning of the rest of this jabbering. Will you tell me?"

"A ghost, man," said Hannigan. "I been chased through the mountains by a ghost that says that I murdered him, but I didn't. It was the kid, and I've told him so."

Lefty glanced sharply aside at Daniel, and the latter nodded his own conviction that Hannigan's excitement must be madness.

"You mean Tolliver?" asked Lefty gently.

"Don't try to baby me!" groaned Hannigan, instantly feeling the change of expression. "I tell you, that I let down five ton of rock on the spot where I stretched out Tolliver's body——"

"You damned idiot!" exclaimed Lefty Dunlin. "I told you what to do with him!"

"You told me what," said Hannigan. "But I figured that I knew more than you. And suppose that while I was drivin' down the road, he'd stood up and took me from behind——"

Hannigan, with bulging eyes, clutched at his throat, as though he felt the fingers of the ghost closing upon him there.

"Steady up!" said Lefty. And he added to Daniel: "There's something in this. Go on, Hannigan. Tell me what?"

"There's everything in it straight and sound," said Hannigan. "I swear that there is. I ain't a fool of a ghost believer. I never had no belief in spirits. I figgered that when we died we went to ground like cattle or sheep. And I've lived thinkin' that. But I'm wrong, and you're wrong, Lefty, and every fool is wrong, because I tell you that they's spirits inside of us that look like us, and wear clothes like us, and carry our marks and our skins and our scars—and when we die, we'll wander around in the wind, Lefty, the same as Tolliver is doin' now, bringing hell after him toward me. What have I done to him? I ask you, Lefty, did I ever so much as damn Tolliver in all my days?"

This semi-hysterical speech rushed from the lips of Hannigan in a frightened babble, and Dunlin said: "Pull yourself together. Give the brandy a chance to work a bit on you, and then tell me just what happened—about Tolliver, I mean."

"That swine of a deputy came from Anvil with his posse," said Hannigan, summoning his strength again. "And he held me up where he found me—cleaning from the floor of the barn the blood of Tolliver where he fell——"

A strong shuddering seized upon Hannigan. He closed his eyes and gripped Lefty's shoulder to steady himself.

"Where he fell," said Hannigan again, in a hollow voice, "with a bullet drove straight through his brain!"

"Yes," said Lefty, growing a little pale. "But go on, Hannigan."

It seemed clear to Daniel that Lefty had lost a great deal of his nerve. He was shaken, though he kept himself sternly in hand. And his eyes rolled wildly at the shadows which encircled them, deepening every moment as the last light of the day faded.

Even Daniel himself, clear-headed skeptic though he was, felt his nerves weaken a little—not that he believed, but that he was unstrung to see such a man of steel as Lefty affected by a wild tale of spirits.

"I saw Tolliver lie dead," repeated Lefty Dunlin. "Now what did you see?"

"I saw him—after the deputy had gone, mind you— when he would have me alone to pull me down to hell with him—after I'd buried him under five ton of rock! Man, you can't bury a ghost, not even if you was to lay a mountain on top of it! It would come through solid rock the same way that a bubble comes up through water——"

He was unable to continue for a moment, and then he said in the wildest of voices: "I sat in my cabin and heard a whisper, no more, of somebody comin' toward the door from the outside. 'Danger!' says I. My blood begun to turn cold. I got into a corner, with my rifle ready. I waited. I could feel my hair lift. A chill was in the air. I was afraid—of nothin' at all! And then into the doorway stepped the face and the body of Tolliver, with his dead hands stretched out to get me!"

"My God!" whispered Lefty.

"I dropped the rifle. I knew it was no use. I rushed for the door and ran right through that body of Tolliver— and it was nothing but air!

"I ran on. I been running ever since, it seems to me. I been wandering here and there not even safe in the day. And with him—with Tolliver—stalkin' through every night, waitin' for me! My God! why should he take me for the murderer of him? It was the kid! And I've brought him to the kid. God help him!"

25.   One Chance in Three

UP TO THIS TIME, it had seemed to Daniel that Lefty Dunlin was one of those four-square figures, invincible to every wind of danger and discomfort that blows, but now it appeared to him that he saw a breach in the armor of the outlaw.

In low, rapid voices, Hannigan and Lefty conferred together—low, save when hysteria brought high the tones of Hannigan. Then, in haste, the leader mounted and motioned to Daniel to do the same, while he gave a place to Hannigan on one of the extra horses.

The imp of the perverse began to stir in Daniel.

He said to his leader: "Lefty!"

"Aye, Danny," said Lefty.

Daniel lowered his voice to a hushed whisper.

"Lefty, I think something moved back there in the brush!"

Lefty gasped and turned with a jerk in the saddle, one hand holding a swiftly drawn revolver.

"Where? Where?"

"Back there—near the birch—something white———"

There was an indistinguishable whisper from Lefty.

"Let's go back," whispered Daniel. "You take the right

hand and I'll ride through on the left—somebody is trying to spy on us, Lefty!"

"Go—go—go ahead," said Lefty, shuddering in body and voice. "Don't turn back. You don't know what you're talking about, Danny——"

But Daniel was already gone. He slipped from the clutching hand of Lefty, and drove his horse straight through the brush, which crashed loudly around him, until Daniel came to a sudden halt when he was out of the sight of the other two. He waited for a long moment; then he heard a distant exclamation, and a rush of horses away from him. Panic, certainly, had seized upon the other two riders.

He took out a white handkerchief and draped it over his face, then he prepared to follow them.

It was a ghostly moment in the wood, for the sun was long down, and the moon was now giving a faint light when something passing among the trees called the attention of Daniel to his rear.

He saw a horseman passing with strange silence through the wood. There was the faintest breeze stirring through the leaves, and no sound came from the horse and rider greater than that whisper among the leaves.

He came closer—a rider dressed like any ordinary cowpuncher, a small, thin-shouldered man; and now, passing out of shadow into the dim moonshine, Daniel saw the face of the silent rider, and it was that of Tolliver!

Within half a dozen yards passed Tolliver, and when he was opposite young Daniel, he turned his head and looked fairly into the white-shrouded face of the youth.

He made no sign of alarm or surprise, but looking straight ahead again, Tolliver passed on into the wood upon his soundless horse.

Daniel remained behind, turned cold with sudden dread. This lasted for a moment only. Then, gathering his resolution, he rode straight after the vanished horseman, gun in hand.

Twigs and branches crashed and snapped around Daniel as he galloped, but though he searched among the shadows here and there, he saw nothing whatever. Tolliver, or the phantom of Tolliver, had been snatched away from beneath his eyes!

He issued from the wood and, turning down the slope across which Lefty and Hannigan had fled, it seemed to Daniel that a voice cried faintly behind him. No doubt it was only the whistling of the wind in his ears, but he turned in the saddle and, looking back, he saw the shadowy rider issue from beneath the trees and come toward him at a silent gallop, with one hand raised, beckoning to him to return.

At that, all of the hot-blooded courage in Daniel vanished. He leaned over the neck of his good mustang and flogged it into a full gallop that whisked him down the slope, and through the next fringe of trees, and then again into the open, until the figures of two horsemen twinkled before him.

Glad was Daniel to ride again with Lefty and Hannigan. They received him silently. For his part, he neither could mock at them nor speak of what he had seen or thought he had seen. Indeed, now that he looked back upon the adventure, it seemed to him that the whole had been the stuff that dreams are made of. And yet he knew that he had not been dreaming; the shadowy rider actually had passed him, actually had disappeared from before him, actually had reappeared and followed him from the wood. Very cold and thin became the blood of Daniel.

They journeyed on that night out of the upper hills, into the lower, smoother country, and finally into the rich and pleasant region between the two rivers, which extended toward the lake. And when Daniel saw the lights of the houses flashing before him, he took a renewed comfort. Yet still he could not help turning, now and again, and glancing back along the way, and never once did they enter a woodland without the dropping of a mist of terror over the soul of Daniel.

When they camped, the thicket that concealed them was within easy sight of the lights of both Silver and Jackson, and when Daniel lay in his blanket that night he could hear the whispering rush of the river nearby. It had no soothing effect upon him; it passed into his dreams as the voice of a ghost, who rode on a soundless horse and whose words were lost in the whistling of the wind.

He wakened with the dawn.

They were two again. Hannigan had disappeared, leaving the horse he had ridden behind him, and Lefty explained briefly: "He's put the curse on us, kid. Then he's gone on, the dog! Well, it'll take more than ghosts and ghostliness to stop me today. Big Tyson will be here before noon!"

They had a breakfast of stale pone, hard as flint, and then they waited through the cold hours of the early morning until the sun rose to its full strength and burned away the last of the dew and then filled the winds with heat.

In the meantime, they kept close watch from the edges of the thicket, wary lest some one should approach them. A cow strayed into the shade toward noon, to escape from the heat of the midday; but she made a quiet companion, and nothing else living came near them until, close on the appointed hour, the burly form of Tyson came in sight, riding a mighty horse fit for the burden of his sinews and bone.

He came into the covert and stared down at the pair from his saddle for a moment.

"You look like a pair of kids playing hooky," observed Tyson.

Then he dismounted, took the bridle and saddle from his horse and watched the big animal roll.

"I paid two hundred for that," said Tyson.

"He's big enough to tire himself out," answered the unsympathetic Lefty, "but not big enough to carry you. Did you get the powder?"

"I got it. When do we start?"

"In two hours."

"I'll sleep it out," said Tyson, and stretching himself on the grass he was instantly snoring.

"Look at the ants crawling over him," said Lefty presently. "And the leaves falling on his face. And him, perhaps, about two or three hours away from hell, but still he can sleep through it!"

"What nerve!" murmured Daniel.

"What a pig!" answered Lefty. "He's got a layer of fat on his brain and no decent ideas can get through it."

For his own part, Lefty employed himself in the care of his weapons, and Daniel did the same. Also, there was the matter of masks, and this Lefty handled by cutting out great sections from the linings of their coats, and making the eye holes.

"Not too big, or somebody will get a slant at your whole face."

"And what about our voices?" asked Daniel.

"People talk about recognizing voices," said Lefty, "but it never would go down in court, I guess. You recognize a voice after you've recognized a face, most likely. Never worry about that, but take care of your face and let your voice take care of itself!"

With that, Daniel contented himself.

So the time came for the start, and the three rode out of the covert and started across country toward the switch station. From the top of every small swale they could see the light glancing on the distant rails, and Lefty consulted his watch from time to time.

"We ought to get there not more than five minutes before the train's due. That's enough to paralyze anybody in the station house and open the switch," said Lefty.

"And if the train's late?" suggested Tyson.

"Then we'll wait as long as we dare, and ride for it!"

"How long can we wait?"

"It depends on how long it would take people to get from the station house to the nearest ranch where there's a telephone."

"The people that are in the station house, we'll keep there," suggested Tyson.

"Will you keep those, too?" said Lefty, and he pointed with his field glasses, which he had been using, toward a point on the distant track.

Daniel and Tyson examined it in turn. Through the

glasses it was easy to make out a section gang of a dozen hands at work on the track.

"A fine time," said Tyson bitterly, "to run into a snag like that. You might've thought of it, Lefty, before this! The dozen of 'em will come down to mob us before we can do anything!"

"Those fellows are laborers, hobos, not fighters," answered Lefty. "They won't bother us; but we can't keep them from running to give the alarm. Say it takes them ten minutes to get across to that house"—he indicated a group of trees in the distance—"and then it will depend on how many punchers are at the house. That's the Custis place. He might have a half dozen riders right there, ready to hop into the saddle. If that's the case, we won't have a chance to do much. But this is the middle of the afternoon, and it ain't likely that they'll be so close to hand. Somebody will ride to get the men in; somebody else will be busy telephoning the alarm to Silver and Jackson. And we've got one chance in three that we'll have time enough to do the job before the rescuers come!"

26.   It's Me He Wants

THEY DREW NEARER to the switch station.

It stood in the open country, with only a streak of trees here and there in the distance, none so close as the Custis house. These were farmlands, and rich ones. Wheat stood tall and dusty yellow, ready for the harvesting machines, and there were great pale patches of summer fallow, dimly marked with the green of the grass which had sprouted since the spring plowing. Farther away, on either hand was a mist of smoke and vapor through which Jackson showed on one side, and Silver was completely obliterated on the other side.

The station house itself was a little brown building of sanded wood with a neat truck garden in the rear, a pasture inclosed beside it, and a few failing orchard trees growing close by. Sun-withered climbing vines attempted to cover the sides of the little house with green but failed wretchedly. It appeared a home, but a home very much down at the heels.

As they rode closer, they saw two small children playing before the house near the track; and a woman came from the rear door and began to hang out a basket of washing on the clothesline.

Nothing could have been more domestic, more humdrum, it appeared to Daniel; and up the track, half lost behind the shimmering heat-waves, he could see the section gang at work.

If they were only laborers and hobos, all might be well, but if there were fighters among them, armed for the work, they might lead the rest to make serious trouble.

However, now all was peacefully, dreamily lost in the heat of the sun, and never could there have been a scene with less possibilities of romantic danger and adventure, had it not been for the two parallel strips of steel which widened between them, and ran away in streaks of light, joining at a point in the distance just before they swung around a curve among trees and were lost to sight. Those flowing currents of silver brightness might lead into the humdrum quiet such a storm of wealth, power, and danger as would have filled the hands and the heart of any sixteenth-century pirate to overflowing.

They were close up before the house when the front door banged open, and the woman who had been hanging out the laundry in the rear of the building rushed out before them and ran with a scream of fear and anger to her children.

She gathered them to her, like chickens under the wing of a sheltering hen.

"You—you devils!" she panted.

She stared from one masked face to the other. "What do you want? Why've you come here? What d'you think that a woman like me would have in the house worth stealing?"

"You get inside and shut your moth," Tyson ordered her.

In response, she cupped her hands at her lips and sent a long, shrill cry echoing down the tracks toward the section gang.

"They'll hear her!" exclaimed Tyson. "The she-devil!"

And he pitched himself from his horse and drove at her. Daniel, anxious for her in the face of that charging monster, drove his horse between. Its shoulder, as it reared in excitement, struck Tyson's breast and sent him reeling and gasping backward.

He had his hand on a gun-butt, but he failed to draw the weapon. Speechless with rage and lack of breath, he glowered like an unshaven goblin at Daniel.

And Daniel, sitting easily poised in the saddle, steadied his excited horse with one hand, and kept the other ready for the draw.

He felt no fear, and he felt no uncertainty, but he knew that if Tyson's hand twitched that gun out another inch, Tyson would die. And Tyson seemed to realize it also, although he cast the blame on another cause.

"The two of you are workin' against me," growled Tyson. "But when we get this job off our hands, I'll have a talk with you, kid. You tie to that, will you?"

The mother, dragging her children with her, came close to Daniel, a protector in time of need.

"What are you people gunna do?" she asked. "What do you want from me? Or what has Jim done or got? We're poor as mice!"

Daniel lifted his broad-brimmed hat.

"Madam," said he, "we're not here to do the slightest hurt to you. It's best for you to go inside and stay there——"

"The train!" she cried, as the idea burst on her. "The train," she repeated with widening eyes, "you're gunna stop it!"

"You got your marching orders," said Tyson savagely. "Get into the house and stay there, will you?"

She shrank away from them. But at the door she turned and looked once more at them, her face frozen with fear and with wonder.

Later, when Daniel peered in at a side window to make

sure that no telephone was being rung in the house, he saw the poor young mother seated in the dining room, her frightened children on the floor at her feet, and across her knees a heavy double-barreled shotgun. There she sat like some figure out of an old tragedy, and Daniel was something between awe and smiling as he watched her.

But, after all, he felt that his two companions made terrible figures in their black masks, like midday goblins!

The section gang was still at work, a glance through the field glasses revealed, except that one man was walking down the tracks toward them.

"Turn your backs on him," commanded Lefty. "Don't let him see that we're masked until he comes close up, and then we can cover him. *He's* the husband of the woman, I figger, and he's the section foreman on this job."

So they turned their backs and waited. They heard the steps come up the cinders beside the track—then pause. Lefty whirled, a gun in his hand, and the others followed his example; but the foreman, if it were he, had already leaped down the grade and now was running through a wheat field, only his head and shoulders appearing above the tall grain.

I'll nail him!" exclaimed Tyson, and tipped his rifle to his shoulder.

Lefty promptly struck it up.

"Let him go," said he. "That money in the train ain't worth as much to us as that tramp is to those two poor kids."

"Seven hundred thousand dollars, maybe, for the sake of a pair of brats!" cried Tyson. "I never heard nothin' more crazy!"

"Of course, you haven't," agreed Lefty smoothly. "But I hate murder, friend!"

"You've done enough of it to get sick of it," agreed Tyson sullenly. "But this job—my job—"

He turned with an oath and strode away down the platform.

"He would've had the woman and the husband dead, by this time," said Lefty, "and what's worse, the two kids

squalling inside of the house. Damn such a man! Kid, what
do you think?"

"About the train? I don't think. I leave the thinking to
you. Will it be too late for us?"

Lefty stared at him.

"You're cool," said he. "Tell you the truth, kid, I
never put much faith in the wild yarn you told me before now—but it seems to me that this here is the real
Dunlin blood—or better! It ain't the money that takes
you; it's the game, Danny. Am I right? But damn the
train. That's not what I was saying!"

Daniel, listening to the compliment, made no reply.
His heart had been warming gradually to this singular man,
but he knew that not words but actions had any meaning
for the outlaw.

"I meant Hannigan's story," said Lefty. "You heard
it, the same as me. What do you think? Booze?"

A false pride tempted Daniel to put the whole tale to
scorn, but the truth came out almost in spite of himself.

"I don't believe in ghosts, Lefty," said he.

"Nor I—usually," said Lefty. "But the face of Hannigan—he's seen something out of hell!"

"I didn't believe Hannigan. I rode back into the trees
last night to throw a scare into you two. And then I saw
a rider come by on a horse that made no sound at all. You
understand, Lefty? Right through that brittle thicket and
stamping on the leaves and the dead twigs—and not a
sound more than the wind whispering. He turned his head
toward me. It was Tolliver!"

Lefty dropped his hands into the pockets of his coat
and said nothing, but he had lost color.

"I spurred after him," went on Daniel, honestly, feeling the chill of that adventure come back upon him,
"and he disappeared among the trees. That took the last
of my nerve. I spurred my horse without any pity, and
got out of that wood."

"I noticed the flanks of the mustang," said Lefty.

"And as I got out of the wood I thought I heard a
voice, and I looked back, and I saw Tolliver riding with
a white face after me and beckoning to me——"

Daniel paused; perspiration was running on his forehead, and not because **of** the heat of the sun.

Lefty began to roll a cigarette with uncertain fingers.

"It's true, then," said he. "I got a touch of the death damp out of Hannigan, I thought. I got it again from you. Now, kid, did you say that Tolliver passed by you?"

"Yes."

"And looked at you?"

"Yes."

"And still he went on?"

"Yes."

"Although you were the man that shot him! But he don't want you. He passed you by. It's me that he wants, and it's me that he'll have! I have lived my life out, kid. Maybe you'll go on where I left off. I've dodged the posses and the sheriffs, but now the devil is takin' a hand against me. I'm going down. I feel it in my bones. This will be my last job!"

Daniel fumbled in his mind for reassuring words, but he could find none. His mind refused to function. His brain was a blank.

So they sat on the bench before the station house and watched the heat-waves shimmer down the track and waited for they hardly knew what; the coming of the train certainly was not all!

27.   The Holdup

TRAIN TIME PASSED.

Tyson, meanwhile, had smashed the lock and thrown the switch onto the siding, the automatic signal, of course, giving warning to any approaching engineer. But it began to seem to Daniel that there would be no chance to wait out the train.

He had been through trying moments, and more trouble lay before him, but never did he endure such a strain of nerves and spirit as was represented by that pause on the bench before the station house. Under the shadow of the eaves the flies buzzed shrill or faint, and the sundrenched landscape slept around them, but he knew that this promise of peace was an illusion. By this time, the section boss had reached the Custis house, and the alarm was being shouted over the wires to Silver and to Jackson. From those centers, again, the warning would flash out to every crossroads village that dotted the hill country and the plains so that the riders might pour out and hem in the fugitives in a great circle.

But, as Daniel's nerves began to give way, he looked more and more often at Lefty. Dunlin was like a rock. His color had not altered; his eyes roved freely here and there, taking calm note of all around them. In those minutes, he said only one thing:

"When we start, kid, keep off the plowed ground. It may mean the straight line for you, but plowed ground is always the long way round for a horse. Go through crops rather than the plowed lands!"

That was all; otherwise, silence hung heavily over them, and the monotonous humming of the flies threw Daniel into a delirious confusion. Sometimes he was about to spring up and confess that he was beaten and bolt for his life, spurring hard. Again, he was like a passenger, calmly waiting that he might take the train to an unknown destination.

Then Lefty stood up and yawned and stretched himself carefully.

"It's coming," said he.

Daniel leaped to his feet as though he had been struck by a whiplash.

"The train?"

Lefty pointed to the tracks, and now Daniel heard a faint and far-off humming, thinner than the buzzing of a single fly across his ear, but strangely piercing, and he knew it was the singing of the rails as the train drew near.

"Is it ours?" he asked.

"Maybe they've flashed the warning in and sent out a guard train loaded with men and guns," said Lefty, "but I think there's hardly been time enough for that. All is quiet over toward the Custis house," he added, quietly surveying the distant clump of trees through his glass. "I called at that house once, kid. It's a grand place. I sat in the kitchen and made them feed me!"

"And you got away?"

"They shot my horse under me, but I switched to another in a field and got off bareback. There she comes!"

The train was suddenly before them. It had pitched around the lower bend in an instant and already seemed to Daniel to be a towering front, black and formidable, with white steam and smoke slanting straight back out of the stack.

He had wanted haste, before, but now he would have been glad of a slower train approaching.

It grew upon his vision with incredible speed; a thin streak of steam jutted up, and a whistle screamed like an angry sea-bird in a storm.

"Tyson!" rang the voice of Lefty. "If that fool of an engineer runs on and don't believe the signal, throw in the switch. Come on, kid. Help me wave it to a halt."

They stood in the center of the track and waved their hands frantically, and still the train thundered on them, reeling with speed; and from a window of the cab, Daniel could see fireman or engineer leaning out and scanning them. At the last moment, sand began to fly beneath the train, wheels screamed and then thundered, and the big train, though at a dizzy speed, hit the switch.

Tyson had not closed it. The engine crashed, keeled violently over—and after one heartbreaking moment settled back again, rocking onto the track and staggering slowly forward until it stopped.

That swift check and the keeling of the whole line of cars, apparently had thrown the passengers into pandemonium, for a roar of voices poured up from the windows with the screaming of one strong-lunged woman high above all the rest.

It seemed to Daniel that the roar and confusion closed above his head, like water. He could not think; he could hardly move. And yet it was his important task—explained in detail by Lefty—to hold up the fireman and

engineer and make them climb down from the cab. Afterward, he was to force them to flood the fire box, so that
the train would be helpless for some time after the robbers
left her.

"And watch those fellows," Lefty had said. "Some of
the men on this run carry guns and know how to use
them. There's a fat reward from the railroad to employees
who are willing to fight for the trains they command!"

He remembered that now, as he ran stumbling like a
drunken man toward the cab. His rifle he kept slung on
his back. In either hand he carried a heavy Colt, but he
knew with perfect surety that he would not be able to
shoot straight. To encounter one enemy was a different
matter; it was almost a cheerful thing; but to stand against
this iron monster broke his spirit completely.

Just before him a gun spurted smoke and fire and his
big hat jerked off his head. He replied with three rapid
shots. Other shots were sounding up and down the train.
He felt that the entire mass of the people aboard her were
about to pour out, armed to the teeth, and destroy these
impertinent scoundrels who had dared stop her.

As he ran up, a revolver was thrown down from the
cab. It exploded as it struck the ground and blew a shallow channel through the surface cinders. Then two frightened men climbed down the narrow steps and leaped to
the ground. They had their hands above their heads, and
the sight of their fear suddenly steadied Daniel. That blind
fusillade of his, no doubt, had broken their spirit as they
heard the bullets crash in the metal work of the cab.

He slapped their pockets to make sure that they carried no more weapons. Then he turned to the engineer,
a gray-headed, kind-faced man.

"Flood the fire box!" he directed.

The engineer folded his arms.

"Talk to the youngster," said he. "I'll do nothing for
you, you damn land-pirate! And if I didn't have five kids
at home to work for, I'd have this out with you. D'you
hear?"

"Back up!" said Daniel, with more roughness in his
voice than he felt in his heart, for he admired this old

fellow, and his steady, brave, blue eyes. "Back up there against the car side and keep your hands over your head."

The man showed no signs of moving until Daniel rudely jammed the muzzle of his Colt into his fat stomach. Then, protesting in a growl, he backed to the required position.

The fireman was more easily handled. He was a youngster, thin-faced, nervous. Beyond a doubt he had been the man who fired the first shot. Had it been an inch lower and killed Daniel, perhaps this fellow would have fought on like a hero, gained fame, foiled the attempted robbery, saved the train, and gained for himself an undying reputation which would have forced him into a long life of heroism. But he had barely failed with his first shot, and the crash of bullets about his ears unnerved him. Now he was shaking and weak with fear. He could hardly do what Daniel commanded—but the fire box was opened at last, and a flood of steam leaped out and covered the engine and tender with a fog; this died away in the wind, and the fire box was silent and dead. The soul had been stolen from the machine.

So Daniel, with his part of the task successfully accomplished, marched his prisoners well back from the side of the train and marshaled them at the bottom of the grade.

All this time there had been a steady fusillade.

Lefty from the front of the train, on the right, and Tyson from the rear of it, on the left, had been firing with their repeating rifles at the roofs and upper windows of the cars, so that there was a constant stream of explosions, and a constant crash of broken glass and the clang of the bullets against the steel roofs.

Not a head showed from a single window—not a gun glinted in the sun anywhere—if there were armed heroes in that list of passengers, they were not showing their hands at once!

Now the door of the car slid back close to the spot where Lefty was standing. Daniel, below the grade, could see all that happened. As the door was rushed back, a shotgun boomed with a short and heavy note, and Lefty took a snapshot in return. Daniel saw the bullet strike, and tear a great splinter from the wooden lintel of the doorway just above the fighting messenger's head.

Daniel saw, and he admired! For he knew enough about Lefty Dunlin's skill to understand that the outlaw could have driven that bullet, with as great ease, straight through the heart of the messenger.

As it was, the heroism vanished from the heart of that warrior as the splinter from above was whipped into his face. He dropped his formidable shotgun with a barrel unfired; but at the same moment, from the shadows within the car, a revolver began to chatter.

Lefty dodged as though a fist were striking at him; but it was Daniel who silenced that fire. He tried a snapshot, just in the direction of the dim form within the car, and above the level of the floor—a snapshot, a chance shot, such as flies home once in twenty times, and this was one of the lucky moments. There was a loud yell from the interior of the car, and then a sound of tremendous cursing that barked and shrilled like the defiance of a bull terrier.

Lefty, in this noisy crisis, did not fail to acknowledge the help he had received by a wave of his armed hand.

Then he called to the first messenger and that hero leaped down at once—dared not lower his hands even to brace himself against a fall—and so tumbled head over heels down the grade and lay in a heap, groaning.

The train was theirs!

28. Fugitives

ONE WOUNDED, cursing man remained in the express car, and Daniel disposed of him. As he swung through the doorway, the man on the floor twisted around and tried to fire, but the movement cost him too much time, and Daniel jammed a heel upon his arm and pinned hand and gun to the floor.

With that, the fighting messenger collapsed in a faint.

He lay in a pool of blood. The bullet which dropped him had pierced the left leg through the calf and driven up above the right knee, tearing all through the hardest and thickest muscles of the thigh. Daniel dragged him to the door of the car. He would have had Lefty help him in disposing of the hurt man, but Lefty, oblivious to all else, was examing a big safe which stood in a corner of the car, fastened to the floor by heavy steel bands. So Daniel called the young fireman and the engineer and with their help carried the wounded messenger to the bottom of the grade. There he ordered the two to care for the stricken man, while he returned to his job.

Down the line of the cars, in the meanwhile, the excitement of the passengers was growing steadily. Angry voices began to sound. And Daniel clearly heard a shrill-voiced woman upbraiding the men in her car because they would not attempt a rescue.

"Here's a dozen of you, and every man with a gun, and not a one of you game enough to step out and take a chance—enough of you to eat 'em in a meal, most likely."

Yet no adventurous heroes appeared from that car, in spite of that speech, and Daniel could not help remembering what Lefty often said—that men never risked their lives freely for the property of others unless they are either heroes or fools. Certainly there were no rash fools in this list of passengers, and the old engineer and the wounded messenger seemed the only men really capable of fighting.

It amazed Daniel, as he walked briskly around the line of the cars, his two revolvers in his hands. He had not the slightest doubt that twenty armed men and good shots were watching him as he walked, and yet no one fired.

On the farther side of the train, he encountered big Tyson, who was swelling with confidence and fighting rage.

"They don't dare to stick their heads, out, kid!" said Tyson. "By heaven, I got 'em tamed! I got 'em tamed and in hand. They know me, by this time, and when I yell, they jump!"

He laughed loudly, and then struck Daniel on the shoulder.

"You've done fine, kid. Nobody could've done better. I give you my compliments. I'm your friend, kid. You tie to that!"

He was in a perfect hysteria of expectation. His eyes rolled wildly, and his fat, thick lips trembled and twitched violently as he spoke, like those of a glutton eyeing a feast. For Tyson, a feast of wealth was coming, and perhaps a feast of death before it! There was manifest murder in this fellow—murder for the love of killing. Contempt filled Daniel as he walked on.

He did not share the feeling of Tyson that these men in the passenger coaches were completely in hand. As he went by, more than one pair of stern eyes looked calmly and quietly out at him. These fellows were not willing to rush out, unled, and with no knowledge of the numbers of their enemies in hiding. But press them too far, and they would respond with a hail of bullets which, in fact, would blow Lefty's gang to bits at the first volley.

It was nothing but the sheerest bluff that was holding this train—bluff reënforced, in this first instance, by a liberal salting of bullets showered at the windows and the roofs of the cars at the beginning. After that, those inside waited. They would not fight unless they had their backs to the wall, and hitherto, that had not happened. The railroad, the express company were losing money. But they themselves and their pocketbooks were not touched.

So Daniel estimated the situation as, on the run, he swung up between the two of the cars and darted around to the express car again.

Below, on the level, he saw that the wounded messenger was being cared for not only by the engineer and the fireman, but also by his own less heroic companion. He was sitting up with his back against a pile of tiles, and cursing with steady and terrible virulence.

In the express car, Daniel found his leader on his knees beside the big safe.

"It's a two-jacket devil," said Lefty with regret, "and we'll have to try two explosions on her. Help me here a minute, kid!"

He had laid three sticks of dynamite on the top of the

big safe, and Daniel helped him to heave up the little way safe which stood near by and place it on top of the explosive, so that the force of the detonation would be turned downward.

Then, with a three-inch fuse lighted, Lefty and Daniel sprang from the car and lay flat on the ground at a little distance.

The effect of the explosion was tremendous. The roof of the long car lifted again with a ridiculous simulation of a raised hat. The near side of the car burst out like the wall of a cardboard hat box kicked by a heavy foot. The very bottom of the car, massive as it was, had been blown through, and clouds of heavy smoke and dust boiled up around it.

For some reason, the car was driven forward a little by the blast, striking the tender and buckling that up into a foolish position, like a bucking horse. The coupling which held the express car to the nearest passenger coach at the same moment burst, and the whole line of cars jerked back a few feet with a groan.

For a brief instant, Daniel and Lefty remained lying on their faces, perforce, to let their brains clear from the shock they had received.

Then they stood up and ran to see the ruin.

They entered in an atmosphere still thick and dense and foul with the fumes of the smoke, and Lefty shouted with joy as he saw the whole corner of the safe blown off and a jagged, thick sheet of steel torn away down one side. The inner core of the safe had been little damaged, but with the destruction of the outer and probably thicker shell, they should have little difficulty in disposing of the inner one, also.

"The powder——" began Lefty.

Then he broke off and struck himself violently across the forehead.

"Kid," he exclaimed, "I've chucked everything! That's what made the explosion so big. By heaven, I left the rest of the sticks of powder lying there on the floor of the car when I jumped!"

So, for one brief, agonized moment, he stared at Daniel.
Then his teeth clicked like a trap.

"There's only one thing to do—and that's to get out.
Kid, start moving! Go for your horse!"

He followed his own advice and, leaping from the car,
he hurried around the front of the engine and summoned
Tyson with an imperious whistle.

The latter came at a lumbering trot.

"You've got it?" he asked.

"I blew all the powder in the one shot and only frac-
tured the outside of a damned double safe. Tyson, we
got all our work for nothing. Let's get out of here!"

"By the——" began Tyson, and then changed to:
"You're double-crossing me, and I know it!"

"Go look!" advised Lefty Dunlin. "I'll wait here for
you, a minute. Only—take a glance around the fields,
Tyson, will you?"

He pointed, and straight across the wheat fields, head-
ing in from the Custis place, they saw a group of riders,
half muffled in the dust which they raised from the standing crops through which they were galloping wildly.

There might be half a dozen—there might be ten of
them. At any rate, there were enough to insure a desperate fight, and Lefty could not risk staying for a moment.

Tyson, however, gave only one glance at the approaching enemy; then he lurched around the engine and raced
back toward the express car. Already it seemed the
passengers were taking heart, for half a dozen of them,
perhaps having sighted the approaching rescuers, were
pouring down the steps of the coaches.

Daniel had accompanied Tyson, at a sign from his
leader, and he saw the men from the coaches hesitate. He
was sure that he detected the glimpse of at least two guns,
and he fired a hundred yards above their heads.

That had the required effect. They tumbled back up
the steps to cover, and Tyson and Daniel sprang into the
express car.

The big man stood a moment and threw a wandering
glance over the wreckage. Then he tore from the wall,

where it was fixed in case of emergency, a massive ax. Furiously he struck at the half-shattered corner of the safe—the ax splintered under that tremendous blow, and the safe had received no damage whatever.

"We're done!" said Tyson savagely. "And a thick-headed fool has chucked a million for me! Damn his black heart for him! I'll talk with Dunlin——"

Still he hesitated, but Daniel plucked him by the sleeve and pointed.

Through the waving wheat they plainly saw eight riders coming at wild speed, and that sight cleared the enraged brain of Tyson. Still cursing, he sprang down from the car, and with the lighter-footed Daniel outracing him, they turned the line of the train again and found Lefty Dunlin waiting for them, mounted, their two horses held by the reins.

So they flung into the saddle and twitched their mounts around behind the section house, racing at full speed, not only because of the approaching riders, but because there was danger that men from the train would open on the rear of these manifest fugitives.

That was what happened. As they straightened away down the lane by which they had approached the station, revolvers began to rattle behind them, but the range was great. One good rifleman might have accounted for all three of the fleeing robbers; but in another moment they were out of range of those short guns—out of their range but by no means safe. Far, far away, dim and blue above the heat of the plain, they saw the mountains which must be their goal now, and between them lay many miles, and every mile was like a yawning canyon mouth before them.

29. Three Hungry Wolves

FOR FIVE HARD MILES they rushed their horses across country to the verge of the Jackson River, where Lefty at last turned toward the mountains.

Tyson, whose horse had stood the long drive astonishingly well, in spite of the weight of his rider, urged that they should turn, instead, toward the towns; that direction would be least suspected, and the pursuit seemed so safely distanced that they had time to double on their trail.

The answer of the leader was short and to the point: "I used to do these things. Then they started working me by opposites. Now I'm back again, doing the simple things."

So he held on his way toward the mountains.

He had chosen the river side because, along it, there was a general scattering of woods, and through this region he made his companions spread out and ride at fifty or a hundred yards distance from one another, partly so that a passer-by might not see three men riding together, and partly because the drift of the fallen leaves would cover three separated trails, but hardly three which went side by side.

For a silent hour they worked their horses at a steady trot, until the dripping flanks and the lathered neck of Tyson's mount showed that he was far spent. Then Lefty called a halt and took a package from his pocket.

He opened it, and they saw that it consisted of a sheaf of bills. He counted the money and then said with a grim smile: "We hoped for seven hundred thousand. We got one per cent of that. But we won't split this in four sections. Here's your full third, Tyson."

He passed the bundle of money to Tyson, and a similar section to Daniel. The big man received his portion in silence and then counted it, casting a suspicious scowl at that which the leader was calmly stuffing into his wallet.

"If I'd thought," said Tyson, "that you were going to bungle the job the way that you have, I'd never have chanced everything on this deal, Dunlin. You've made a fool of me!"

"And of myself," answered Lefty cheerfully. "You're no harder hit than I am, or the kid."

"Which of the pair of you has a wife and kids to look to him?" snarled Tyson.

"Listen to me," said Lefty gently. "When you start to be a crook, forget that you're a family man until you land in court. There it gets you a shorter sentence. Out here, it don't mean a thing."

Tyson made no answer except a muttered oath; then he flung himself from the saddle and began to loosen the girths to breathe his horse more quickly. Lefty and Daniel did the same.

They were in the core of the woods but from that position they could look out through several narrow vistas which opened beyond the margin of the trees, and embraced wide stretches of the countryside, hill and house, and grove and field. And all was peaceful under the floods of brilliant sun; no one could have suspected that danger was riding through that region, but Daniel could guess that trouble lay ahead of them. So far, all had been too foolishly simple and easy. Surely the law could not be bearded with such impunity? For though he and Lefty had had their adventures before, even the smallest breaches of the law had brought danger swiftly on their trail; this greater venture would surely bring a greater threat.

But he said nothing and he asked no questions. Standing there beneath the trees, with the mottling shadows falling over them, and the horses steaming from their hard work, he looked back to that nervous self which had paced the chamber in the Lammer Falls hotel, gun in hand, ready for suicide. A foolish self, as it seemed to this newly confident Daniel, filled with life and the joy of existence. He smiled at what he had been and faced the future not with a smile, but with a broad grin. The burden

of the time-weary Crossetts had fallen from him and he
was glad that destiny had made him a Dunlin!

So thought Daniel at the very time when, as a proper
hero, his mind should have been filled with misgivings, and
with the reflection that robbery attempted is as bad as
robbery accomplished, in the eye of the law and of the
conscience. Indeed, there appeared to be but little conscience in Daniel, at this period in his odd career. He
became a free bird, so to speak, and like a bird, he preyed
upon his lesser neighbors.

They left that wood when the horses were breathed a
little and rode out into a pleasant vale beyond, with a
creek twisting through the center of it; and as they let their
horses put down their heads to drink, a scattering half
dozen of riders broke from the copse on the farther side
and charged them like cavalry, with a shout.

Cunning Lefty did not turn straight back for the woods.
Instead, he drove along the bank of the stream, with his
two followers instinctively behind him, little as they
could comprehend the maneuver. But it drew the attackers
slantingly toward them and, following that line, they presently found themselves opposite an unfordable section of
the creek, a steep-walled little ravine. They had opened a
scattering fire, but from this Lefty now returned to the
woods, and as he rode he could look back and see the
posse in confusion beyond the water.

Finally they swung to the side to gain the fordable bit
of the stream; before they had gained it they had lost a
mile and the race.

"Very hot," said Lefty, when he drew his horse back
to a trot, and Daniel knew that he was not speaking of
the weather. "The hornets are out in the sun too; somebody's bothered their nest!"

He asked for no advice; he merely cast a glance at
Tyson's staggering horse, and then he made for the Jackson River at the edge of the wood. When he reached it,
he rode to the verge, scanned the farther bank, and then
rode straight in. He threw himself from the saddle and with
his rifle held above the current, he was drawn down
stream and slowly toward the farther bank by his horse.

The other two maneuvered in exactly the same fashion and luckily the three gained the opposite shore. For a cross-current hit them in midstream, and forced them rapidly on. Even with that assistance, this effort so exhausted Tyson's horse that all three men had to drag it from the water. They forced it into covert, but there it stood with braced legs and with hanging head. Manifestly it could not go on.

They stripped off the saddle. Lefty and Daniel rubbed down the poor beast to give it a better chance for life; then they threw the saddle into a thicket and turned the animal adrift. Their condition that instant became tenfold more precarious. If the three hung together, they never could escape from the pursuit of horsemen when once sighted, and their only hope for safety lay either in scattering or else in trying to steal another horse, and that at once.

Tyson squarely faced his two companions; his face was white and his hands clenched.

"I suppose that I get hell, now," he suggested grimly. "I've got to go on foot, Lefty?"

"We have two horses," said Lefty coldly, "and we'll share them, turn and turn about."

There was not a word of thanks from Tyson, only a muttered: "Thank God you got that much decency in you!"

Evening was coming, and they were glad of it. They had thrown pursuit off the trail, for the time being, by the crossing of the river, but at any moment their enemies might pick up the way.

They dared not venture out of that shelter until the darkness gathered; and it was still the half light of the day when they heard an outburst of shouts and cheers near the river bank behind them. They glanced at one another, well knowing what they meant.

Some flying posse had crossed the stream and found the abandoned and spent horse there; now, keen with hope and confidence, they would push ahead to catch the three robbers, who could not be very far distant. Tyson was for bursting out of the wood at once and striving

to make a copse a mile before them, but Lefty insisted that
they remain where they were. A dense growth surrounded
them, and they could not possibly be seen from a distance.
So they stood at the heads of the horses to prevent a
whinny which would betray them, and presently they
heard the searchers crashing through the underbrush here
and there about them.

It lasted for only a moment. Then some one began to
shout indistinct words from the outer edge of the wood,
and after that a body of fully a dozen riders poured out
of the shelter and galloped at full speed across the slope
toward the very wood to which Tyson would have had
his companions flee.

Lefty chuckled as he saw them go.

"They're beat three times," said he. "Once by the
horses, and twice by wits. Now it's time for luck to help
us out. Tyson, do you think it's dark enough for us to go
out?"

They agreed that it was, and that the need was im-
perative, for in a short time searchers would raise the
neighborhood and bring men in a host to swarm over all
the ground. Tyson suggested a return across the stream
and then an attempt to beat back up-country, but Lefty
would not hear of it.

He urged them forward, and they marched slowly
ahead, creeping snail-like across the open.

"Take this horse," said Daniel suddenly to Tyson. "We
can make better time than this!"

He dropped to the ground and struck out at a swing-
ing stride which he had learned from cross-country running in his college days. Never had his wind been better
or his condition harder, and they covered five miles of
country, the horses trotting steadily behind him.

During that stretch, he watched the lights gleaming
in the houses which stood here and there on the rich
countryside, and it seemed to Daniel that they should try
to approach one of the dwellings and get a horse; yet
Lefty made no such suggestion. Only when Daniel fell
to a panting walk, going up a hill with evident effort, Dunlin pressed up beside him.

"Can you hold out for another half mile?" said he. "We're near a bunch of the finest horses that ever stepped on iron. There's Joe Pitcher's place down there on the left—you can only see one light blinking through the trees around it. Can you run on that far, kid?"

Daniel nodded. All the way sloped gently and easily before him, and he sprinted ahead with a fresh power. So they went rapidly on. Utter night was overhead, sprinkled brightly with stars, and the rolling landscape around them was dotted with tufts of darkness and gleams of light where the houses of the farmers stood, surrounded by lofty trees.

So they came down on Joe Pitcher like three hungry wolves—starved for horseflesh!

Their own horses they left in the woods, the saddles on their backs, but the packs removed, and the packs they carried on toward the huge black outline of the barn.

"Inside," cautioned Lefty in a whisper, "you'll find some box stalls toward the front of the building. That's where Pitcher keeps his blood horses. They'll carry even Tyson and never quit. Come on, Tyson. Get in there with me. Kid, that house is full of people"—a door opened, and a noise of distant voices poured out as he spoke— "you go up there as quiet as a snake and hear what the gossip is. They'll be talking about us, I guess."

Daniel made no protest, though it seemed to him that their work should have been to get the fresh mounts and ride as fast and as far toward the mountains as possible. What questions were necessary?

However, he felt his own inexperience in these matters, and prepared for the dangerous work ahead of him by making sure of his two revolvers, and then moving straight for the rear of the dwelling, as the other two turned into the barn. He had not gone a dozen steps when the silhouette of a great dog showed before him, and the beast rushed at him with a furious snarling.

30.   In the Shadows

ALL WHO EVER have encountered a savage dog know
that there is an odd difference between its snarl and the
growl of an ordinary house dog. There is a deep intake
of breath, and the angry vibration seems to come from
the very heart. Such a sound, once heard, never can be
mistaken, and Daniel did not mistake it now. He jerked
his revolver into his hand; and then he remembered that
in the barn behind him his two companions were trying
to secure the horses on which their liberty would depend,
and the sound of a shot would be certain to bring an in-
vestigation from the house.

So, as the attacker darted at him, he turned the gun
and, grasping it by the barrel, he struck vigorously at the
dog's head. He felt the steel ridge of the butt bite into
the skull, and the animal dropped heavily, struggled for
a moment, and then lay still.

That instant a door was cast open and a man called:
"Rover! Hey, Rover!"

Light poured out from the doorway and streamed upon
Daniel so that he could see the trailers of the melon vines
at his feet and the shaggy heads of berry bushes. Certainly
there was sufficient illumination to show him to the
watcher, unless the eye of the latter was dulled by the
brighter lights indoors which he had just turned from.
That hope kept Daniel stock still, remembering a caution
of Lefty's—that a moving object is seen many times more
readily than one which is stationary.

"Rover!" called the man at the door. "Where the devil
are you? Rover! Here, boy!"

The flattened hulk of the dog did not stir, and the man
of the house hurried down the steps.

"Something's happened to Rover," he called over his
shoulder as he went forward.

Daniel was in two minds—to drop flat upon the ground,

or to slip aside into the cover of the brush, if he could. But he was certain that the least movement would betray him, now that the other was in the yard.

"Come back in and listen to Charlie," called another man from the house.

"Something has happened to Rover," insisted the searcher—but he paused. "I heard him snarl. He went for something, I tell you."

"He went after poor old Shep," called the other. "Won't let that poor dog come in the yard, any more. Come back in, Jerry. Don't be a fool."

The searcher hesitated. He screened his eyes with his hand and, it seemed to Daniel, peered straight at him. However, he turned on his heel at last, and went back into the house.

The door banged behind him, and Daniel leaned and placed his hand on the side of the fallen dog. The heart beat faintly; life still was there; but there was no stir in the body.

After that, he went on with more confidence. The light which had streamed into the yard had shown him how to pick his way and, coming straight up to the rear of the house, he climbed easily until his head was level with the first window.

He looked inside, and he saw more than twenty men seated in close order around a long table. And the very first word that he heard was:

"Nobody but Lefty Dunlin *could* have done it!"

"Read what the *Colin Evening News* says," suggested another.

A much-rumpled paper was shaken out.

"Daring Robbery of Express at——" began the reader.

"Cut out the headlines," said another. "Let's hear again what the editor says about the identity of the crooks."

"Here it is:

"The deed has all the earmarks of a Dunlin crime. There was the same boldness, simplicity, and speed with which he has accomplished all of his former exploits. With him was the same young fellow who

helped Dunlin to escape from the jail at Lammer
Falls in such spectacular fashion. The identity of this
youth has not been ascertained, though a rumor declares that Sheriff Loftus of Lammer Falls has a
shrewd notion which will be developed later on. The
third member of the gang is unknown except for the
suspicion cast on him by Mr. William Q. Bird, of the
town of Anvil, Bostwick County. Mr. Bird states that
he often has met and done business with a respectable and well-to-do rancher of that vicinity who re-
cently sold out his business and moved his family to
Mexico. Mr. Bird knows the man well, and he be-
lieves that in bulk, appearance, and voice he is sure
that the third man among the robbers is identical
with the rancher, Tyson. Inquiry has been dispached
to Mexico, to discover whether or not Tyson has
arrived there with his family, or whether the family
actually has crossed the border.

"This daring and desperate action of Lefty Dunlin
—if indeed he was the perpetrator—stamps him
finally as the most dangerous and——"

"Leave off," broke in a loud and sudden voice. "That
makes it dead sure that it ain't Dunlin. What would he
be doing with a clumsy fool like Tyson? I know Tyson.
None better. There never was the makings of a crook in
Tyson. He's a thug, I tell you.

"But he's not the kind of fine metal that Dunlin works
with. Cross Lefty off the list. After all, he ain't the only
man in the world who'd try a job like this!"

"I tell you," said he who had been reading the paper,
"that nobody in the world except Lefty Dunlin would
have tried to hold up the express with only two men to
help him. Name another that would have had the same
nerve?"

"All right, all right!" said another. "What's the use of
arguing about names? The point is, we got three thugs
here near us, somewhere. Maybe your dog was tackling
one of 'em in the back yard, for all that we know!"

This brought forth a laugh, in which Jerry, a tall and

keen-faced man, joined with the rest. And Daniel could not help smiling a little at their complacency. So great was their confidence in the strength of numbers that they seemed to feel that the very heat of their courage would keep all ill-doers at a distance.

"They're cut off from the mountains—we know that," said Jerry in a dry and practical tone.

"I dunno," answered he who read from the paper. "It's a wide swing to the mountains; I could bet that they'll break through."

"D'you think so?" said Jerry calmly. "I tell you, they won't. This ain't a fairy story. And they can't make themselves invisible. And there's a string of men watching all the way from Colin to Newfield!"

"Come on!" scoffed the doubter. "How could they watch that much ground?"

"Every man in the countryside," said Jerry, "has turned out. It's like war. Nobody dares to stay at home. They caught Sam Priest the same way, on his last raid into Silver. They'll catch Dunlin and his pals, too. You mark my word! People are tired of having Dunlin make a fool of them. They want his scalp, and this time they'll get it!"

"While we sit here and chew the rag?" suggested somebody.

"Take it easy," said Jerry grimly. "When the moon rises we'll start, and you'll have enough riding by the time the morning comes. Lew!"

"Aye!"

"You'd better go out and start the saddling. Take Bill and Tex along with you. We want a bag of barley behind every saddle, too. A grain-fed horse will outlast two soft mustangs off the grass."

Daniel slipped quietly to the ground, for it was high time to move, and as he reached the yard level again, he heard a careless query floating through the window:

"Where will they get fresh horses, the three of them? Because fresh horses they'll have to have or else they're goners. We'll have them in the bag by to-morrow, otherwise!"

Daniel had heard enough. He turned and slipped rapidly toward the barn in the distance, and as he went, he heard the screen door at the rear of the house slam with a loud rattle three times in succession; the hired men were coming out to do the saddling.

Under the shadow of the barn, he found Tyson waiting, and the big fellow snarled: "What you been doing? Eating apple pie? Shake it up, now. You've wasted three miles for us already, and damned little you've heard for it, I'll lay my bet!"

He hurried Daniel through the gap between two adjacent sheds, and there he found Lefty waiting with three tall horses in the shadows, and even by the starlight Daniel could see that they were steeds of blood and price.

31. Another Omen

ON THE BACK of his new mount, Daniel recognized the feel of the animal beneath him. Contrasted with the stiff, short-coupled little mustangs, this rangy fellow seemed to be made of springs, and Daniel knew the blood horse. Lefty had another like it, and Tyson a third, bigger of bone and broader in the quarters to sustain his crushing weight.

They drifted the horses at a dog trot through the trees and on to the moonlit hills beyond, and as they entered the open they heard loud voices shouting from the direction of the house behind them.

Daniel had pressed close to Lefty and told him what he had heard—that there was a line of watchers stretched all the way across country from Colin to Newfield. Probably there were boats at each of the big rivers to connect the line where it had to break at the water's edge, and no doubt the number of watchers would increase as new recruits poured up from the cities and the adjoining towns.

"They say that they're simply tired of having Lefty Dunlin raise the devil," said Daniel.

"That's it," said Lefty calmly. "There's enough trouble

when a couple of posses go fanning the country for you, but when the whole bunch gets fed up, then there's hell to pay. It's gonna be my last trail, kid. I've known it ever since the ghost come for us. And he ain't through. We'll see him yet, before my finish!"

But though Lefty despaired, he showed no sign of submitting. Tyson was for striking straight toward the mountains and striving to break through the line of guards. But Lefty refused to take that chance. Instead he elected to follow the bold course of attempting to outflank the line, turning Colin, and then trying to break through over the unguarded country. It was a daring and difficult tack. For the men of the law, holding the mountain way, could work on the inside lines, and by telegraph and telephone and perhaps by fire signals the whole little army of searchers could be shifted here and there to meet every feint of the three fugitives. However, they were to ride masked at all times. In any event, they were sure to be recognized as the trio of robbers; but they could prevent any personal identification by keeping on their masks. These were reduced to black strips across the eyes, with eye holes.

So they kept on veering to the right, but every step of the way was dangerous. The moon was up; the land was flooded with bright silver that rivaled the sun for strength, and perforce their speed was cut down by the necessity of keeping to cover as much as possible, and riding from one group of trees to the next. Lefty held the point; Daniel and Tyson rode in his rear.

So they kept on, never forcing the horses, though Tyson begged for more speed. However, as Lefty constantly declared, a horse has only one sprint-edge in a day, and once that edge has been blunted, any common pony is apt to overtake a thoroughbred runner.

A little after midnight, the sky suddenly clouded; a strong wind was sweeping out of the northwest, and the temperature dropped at a giddy rate until the three were shuddering with the cold.

Yet they were glad of the darkness; they were sheltered, even if they were in torment.

Rain began. It was no steady downpour, but volleys of heavy drops swept them, and every volley found their skin and drenched them. The horses, too, constantly veered from these blasts, and had to be swung back to the right point continually. Altogether it was a fatiguing and miserable night. The rain showed no sign of ceasing.

They had gone long without food; they had been riding constantly, and their brains and nerves had been on the alert for many hours. In one day they had endured enough to give them a week's famine pains, and when the gray of the morning showed them the clouds that poured and tumbled across the sky, they took stock of one another and of the horses.

Tyson's mount again was used up. He was a clumsy fellow in the saddle, and that, together with his great weight, killed horses quickly beneath him. Tyson himself showed the effects of the hunt. His red and weather-tanned face had turned to purple and yellow, and his cheeks sagged. Lefty looked gaunt and weary, and only Daniel was fresh. He was amazed at himself, but in him there was the inextinguishable fire of youth which refreshes itself with a cat nap and draws again upon the deep reserve wells of nerve energy. His mount and that of Lefty still had plenty of power remaining but their speed would be limited to that of big Tyson. The latter was, of course, aware of it. And again and again he bit his lip and scowled at the pair with a concentrated bitterness of envy and fear.

There was no soft touch about that man. He was grim, gloomy, and hard from one day to the next, and he had come to hate Lefty, apparently. All the failure of the robbery he laid upon the outlaw.

As the dawn brightened and the day was fairly launched, they came in sight of a little shack squatted in a hollow, without a sign of even a shed beside it, and only one or two little fields enclosed, in which a few horses and cows stood bunched, shivering in the rain.

"I'm gunna go down and feed," said Tyson violently. "I'm gunna go down there and get whoever is in that shack to cook me a meal, and then I'm gunna feed."

"You're a fool," said Lefty. "You eat to-day and it may make you hang to-morrow."

"Hang?" said Tyson, in a loud voice, catching at the last word. "What you mean? Since when did they begin to hang people for train robbery?"

"When they get you for anything," said Lefty, "they look up your whole record. What will they find when they look up yours, Tyson?"

With that, he stared calmly into the face of the big fellow, and Tyson turned absolutely gray.

He answered sullenly: "Me and the horse need rest and chuck. I'm gunna have it. The rest of you can do what you want—and be damned!"

He turned his head toward the house and spurred his tired horse to a canter, while Lefty and Daniel drew together behind him.

"Let him go; he wants to travel by himself," said Daniel, "and he has the right to. Let's pull our belts tighter and go on. We'll give the horses a rest in the next wood, and wait there for a few hours. Maybe it would be better to stay there till night?"

"No good," answered Lefty. "Tyson has showed himself. That will prove that we've all gone this way. Besides, it's too dangerous for us to leave the fool to hang himself, even if he wants to!"

And he added that since Tyson had given them away, they might as well take advantage of the chance to rest and eat. So the two rode on to the shack after their companion. They found his horse standing at the door, and Tyson seated at a rickety table inside with a loaf of bread in one hand and a huge piece of cheese in the other. With the dull eyes of a feeding glutton, he regarded them and saw them not.

The woman of the house, a wretched drudge, regarded them without fear but with a challenging scowl.

"If the three of you eat me out of house and home," said she, "what am I gunna do about it?"

"We'll pay double," said Lefty. "What have you got to eat?"

"Ham, bacon, eggs, coffee, pone, cheese."

"Cook it all. Where do you get the eggs?"

"My fool of a man killed my last hen yesterday."

At this point, there was a loud and ecstatic crowing from behind the house.

"We'll have that rooster!" said Daniel.

"That rooster I wouldn't sell for two dollars."

"Here's three."

"Well, you kill him, then. I would't be after murderin' him."

They started for the rooster. He was a long-legged racer, and while those two expert shots rushed after him and kept their guns roaring, he dodged here and their with uncanny speed.

A little boy and girl came out of the shack to look on, and the frightened and exhausted rooster rushed between them. The little boy picked the bird up in his arms and the rooster drove its head under the child's arm. Its wings drooped. It was spent.

"How come you wear masks?" said the boy curiously and without fear as Lefty and Daniel came up to him. "If you're bad men, why don't you shoot straighter? You better get out of here before my uncle comes back and licks the two of you and that big man indoors, too."

"Give me the rooster," said Daniel "and we'll chance the uncle afterward."

"You couldn't catch him," observed the little girl. "I dunno that you got a right to him!"

"Wring that fool rooster's neck," called the woman from the doorway.

But Daniel hesitated.

"We'll go without chicken to-day," he said to Lefty. "The rooster beat us, and so does the boy."

Lefty, with a shrug of his shoulders agreed, and they went back into the house, the little boy still with the bird under his arm.

"Gimme!" said Tyson suddenly, and his great hand shot out and snatched the bird. In another instant, he had it by the head, prepared to wring its neck; but Daniel found himself standing over Tyson with the muzzle of a Colt thrust into the hollow of the giant's throat. He was saying: "I'll take your head off, Tyson, if you hurt that rooster. Give it back to the boy!"

He was astonished at himself. The action and the words had been purely automatic.

Tyson hurled the rooster through the door; it struck the ground with a stagger, righted itself with a flurry of wings, and so reeled off around the corner of the shack.

Inside, Tyson had raised a grimy forefinger: "That's another mark!" said he to Daniel, and a chill leaped through the blood of the boy.

32.　A Message Delivered

THE WOMAN SPOKE from the stove, from the midst of a cloud of steam and smoke.

"You're Dunlin, I guess," said she. "And you're Tyson," she added, pointing to the big fellow, "and you're the kid. I wonder will they have me in court to testify when you're caught?"

Tyson stood up from the table. He looked as though he were about to strike her.

She regarded him calmly. She seemed too tired and worn to have fear.

"No," she said. "You don't need to worry. They'll kill you, Tyson. You're too big for them to miss. You'll never fit inside a courtroom!"

She chuckled dryly as she turned back to the stove, and Daniel turned to Lefty. The latter had not seemed to hear; he was standing at the door peering earnestly across the hills.

Then he said over his shoulder: "You expecting a girl to come here, ma'am?"

"A girl? Nobody ever comes here."

"There's one coming now," said Lefty. "I wish we were out of this! She's a flier, too!"

Daniel went to the doorway to observe and saw a woman riding at full speed toward them, pitching down the slope with masterly horsemanship, jumping a high rock, and then sweeping on until she came just before the house.

The men had withdrawn at once and slammed the door.

"You keep her out," they said to the woman.

There was a sharp knocking.

"Hello, hello!" shouted the woman of the house.

"Let me in, will you?" said the voice of a girl, a pleasant musical voice.

"I got nothing for you in here, honey," said the woman.

"You got three men," said the girl, "and I want one of them."

"You're talkin'!" said the woman of the house sternly. "Run along with you, you bold thing. What would you be wantin' with a man?"

"Daniel!" called the voice of the girl.

Daniel started violently, but Lefty put a hand of iron on his shoulder.

"Daniel, I got a message for you. Are you afraid to open the door?"

"I've got to see her," said Daniel. "How could she know?"

"Daniel!" called the insistent voice.

Daniel jerked the door open and stepped outside; saw before him a dimly remembered face, a little drawn as if from weariness and lack of food, but still wonderfully pretty, and rosy with the wind of riding.

"Well?" said Daniel in wonder.

"Will you come back ten steps from the house?"

He hesitated.

"I won't arrest you," she smiled.

At that, he followed her, rather shamefaced.

"I've seen you before," he said.

"I slung hash in the Lammer Falls hotel," said the girl. "I'm Jenny Loren."

"I remember."

"Thanks," said she, rather dryly, as he thought. Then she added: "I got a letter here for you."

She held out a stained and crumpled envelope.

"It's been kind of roughed in the mail," said Jenny Loren.

Daniel saw the handwritting of Jeremy Crossett; he tore the letter open, and read:

DEAR DANNY: I've tried to reach you before with a messenger who failed. Now I'm sending this brave girl, Jenny Loren, who offers to try to reach you.

I want to explain as briefly as I can and beg you to forgive me. I saw you in a terrible condition in Lammer Falls. You were going down, I thought, not because of any real mental or nervous disorder, but because you had convinced yourself that you were one of the black Crossetts, and that therefore you were doomed to an early death—a death by your own hand, most likely.

You remember that in the afternoon, from the window, we saw Lefty Dunlin brought in with the posse? You yourself remarked that he looked enough like you to be your own twin brother. And out of that, afterward, came the inspiration—a clumsy and terrible inspiration as it appears now!

Only try to place yourself in my position, dear boy. I was utterly desperate. When I went into your room that night, I saw the revolver which you had just thrown under the spread of your bed. And I knew that something had to be done quickly. I remembered Dunlin. I only wanted to do one thing, and that was to dissociate you from the Crossetts and their ugly tradition.

Besides, half of the thing was made to my hand.

I remembered that there had been a Dunlin family in Winhasset. From that starting point, I worked up the story, almost impromptu. As a matter of fact, Danny, I saw you born. I never left your bedside during the first weeks of your life, which was a very faint time with you. There was no substitution of babies. But I could remember that the doctor who attended your mother told me of another child stillborn to poor Mrs. Dunlin.

Now, my dear Danny, I ask you to forgive me, and to come back as swiftly as possible.

I hardly regret what I have done. If it has accomplished no other thing, it has, at least, been sufficient to show you that you were the prey, not of a nervous disease and a predisposition to death by your own hand, but merely of your own imagination. You have stepped into another life. You have found, I suppose, a certain wild pleasure in the terrible days through which you have been passing.

Let God favor me by bringing you through safely. Now, shake off the self which is not yours. You are Daniel Crossett, my son. There is no drop of Dunlin blood in you.

Leave that man at once. Do not attempt to meet me again here in Lammer Falls. I wait near this town only to receive word that you have started East. There I shall go to meet you. You had better proceed straight to New York and take a boat for France or Italy. Italy preferred, no doubt! The farther the better. Leave word for me in New York. We shall appoint a rendezvous abroad and go around the world without the horrible shadow of the black Crossetts falling upon us.

A new and beautiful life is now before us both, if only Jenny Loren can bring this letter to you. Talk to her freely. God never placed a stronger, more honest, more courageous soul upon the earth. She may try to tell you that she has done this for money. But I know that she has done it out of kindness and pity.

> Your loving father,
> JEREMY CROSSETT

There was an old stump near the house upon which wood was chopped; Daniel slumped down upon it and stared at the ground.

"It's all true." said the gentle voice of Jenny Loren.

He looked slowly up at her, and it seemed to Daniel that there was a misty brightness of tears in her eyes.

"He's talked to you?" he asked.

"There was no one else to talk to," said the girl, "and he couldn't keep it to himself. He didn't know the country. He had no idea what to do!"

Daniel looked wildly past her.

The whole universe had dissolved; nothing was solid. The very mountains were images taken out of a dream. He was not a Dunlin, after all, and yet he had made himself, he felt, a Dunlin forever.

"You tell me," said the girl, "where you're going to ride, and where you'll take the train. They're pretty hot after you three. But I can do some things for you. I've got another suit of your clothes wrapped up behind my saddle, here. Everything from cap to shoes. You climb into that. Then you take my horse. Burn that mask. Nobody ever will know you. They don't dare to guess. You can say you were up in the mountains, hunting. You shifted down into the hills, trying to bag a deer. You can say a lot of things. I've thought some out for you. We'll work up an alibi for every day since you left Lammer Falls. You'll see how easy it'll be to do it!"

He looked wonderingly at her. There was so much hope, freshness, and life in this girl that she made all difficult problems seem simple and easy. He felt old—stale, and unprofitable, in all the poet's profound sense of the words.

"You see——" began Daniel, and then he saw that he could not explain.

"Yes," said Jenny Loren.

She had grown a little pale, he thought.

"Yes?" she said again, in query.

"You'll see my father, in Lammer Falls again?"

"Yes, of course."

"Then I want you to tell him that I forgive him. Of course I understand. I was a nervous fool. He had to do something. I understand perfectly and I forgive him, but——"

Jenny Loren gripped a stirrup leather and waited.

"But it's too late," explained Daniel.

"What's too late?" asked the girl in a trembling voice.

"I can't go back, you see."

"But I don't see! Why can't you go back?"

"I don't want to tell you anything," said Daniel, "that you can't repeat to my father. So you can tell him that I'm in a tangle here, for the time being. As soon as I can, I'll break away. Tell him to go back East. Go home and wait there. I'll get word to him from time to time. Finally, perhaps, I can break away and go to him. Will you tell him that?"

Jenny Loren's eyes were very large.

"Such things have happened," went on the gentle voice of Daniel, "that I know that I can't return—at present, say. I'm involved—deeply. I have a duty to perform, you understand."

"A duty to whom?" asked Jenny sharply.

"I can't tell you, only—you take back the word to my father, Jenny Loren!"

She answered with a sudden flare of anger: "No! I'll never go back to him with an answer like that!"

"You won't?" cried Daniel, amazed. "Then what will you do?"

"Stay with you," said the girl fiercely, "until you come back to your senses!"

33. A Pleasant Messenger

THAT strange announcement was not a thing to be believed, and Daniel smiled at it a little. His smile went out when he noticed the set lips of the girl.

He said gravely: "You're a brick, Jenny Loren; but you can't help me. I'm sorry I can't tell you why I have to stay with Lefty Dunlin for a while. You go back to my father, if you will, and give him that message for me. Will you do that?"

Jenny Loren turned her back on him and busied herself about her horse until Daniel, much at sea, went back into the cabin and drew Lefty to one side.

"It's Jenny Loren, from a hotel in Lammer Falls," he

told Dunlin. "She's been sent off to get me by Jeremy Crossett. And she declares that she won't leave until I start back with her. How can we give her the slip, Lefty? She seems as set as iron about this!"

Lefty chuckled, and his eyes twinkled as he looked at Daniel.

"Sooner or later," said he, "sooner or later!"

"Sooner or later what?"

"Sooner or later there's a woman mixed into the business. God be good to you, kid!"

And he chuckled again.

"That's idiotic talk," said Daniel. "What time have I for a woman, a waitress in a wayside hotel———"

He stopped and colored a little. Such thoughts might be natural for the son of the millionaire and aristocrat, Jeremy Crossett; they were hardly in tune in the mouth of a Dunlin. Lefty, watching him shrewdly, nodded a little, as though in agreement with the unspoken thought. Then he went to the door and peered long and earnestly through the crack.

The woman of the house was saying: "I'll send the hussy along. Lemme have a word with her and I'll———"

Lefty turned from the door and restrained his hostess with a raised hand.

"Open the door and ask her in," said he.

Tyson clapped his hand to his mask.

"What in hell?" he shouted.

"Watch yourself, Tyson," said Lefty dryly. "There's a little lady coming in here. My mask is off; you might as well take off yours, too!"

Tyson subsided with a sound which was half groan and half curse, while Lefty nodded again to Daniel.

"You ain't interested—not you!" chuckled Lefty. He added with more seriousness: "I don't blame you, kid, I've seen 'em by the hundreds. I've been a fool about 'em. I'd be rich and settled, except that I never could pitch on a girl that filled my eye. I always kept changing my luck. But in all my days, I never seen one like this!"

While this little oration proceeded, the woman had opened the door and beckoned to the girl.

"Come along in," said she. "They say you're to come in, so in you come!"

Jenny Loren stood in the doorway, more than a little frightened, more than a little determined.

It was characteristic of Lefty that he went to welcome her and make her at ease.

"Jenny Loren," said he, "I'm Lefty Dunlin; I hope that you've never heard of me before. You seem to know the kid. Here's another friend of ours who wants to keep his mask on. Being respectable is a part of his game, so maybe you'll understand it and excuse the cloth over his eyes. He ain't improved so much when he takes it off, as a matter of fact. Sit down here and take the end box at the table. Ma'am, steam up some more coffee and throw some more bacon and eggs in the frying pan. Miss Loren is pretty near starved."

Jenny Loren sat down in the corner. And when she was seated, all at once she seemed to Daniel amazingly young and almost childish.

He could not help looking at her with more attention, after that odd eulogy from the lips of the wise Lefty; and it seemed to Daniel that he was seeing the girl for the first time. She had been a lay figure in the background, at the hotel. Now she was something more. As an artist draws on canvas the lines which he sees, so Daniel looked at Jenny Loren now and traced the lovely profile, though he neither had paper nor canvas. Yet he printed the impression so deeply that somehow he knew he never would have a need of a photograph to call up the picture again and at will.

He began to feel an odd flutter about the heart, too, and a strange sense of possession simply because she had come this great distance to find him.

Lefty was making conversation to put the girl at ease.

"How did you find us?" he asked. "With all the posses out and all the wise heads trying to work out our trail, how did you hit on it?"

"When I came to the line they've stretched between this and the mountains," said Jenny, "I guessed that you wouldn't try to break through."

"Is it strong?"

"They have hundreds of men out," said Jenny. "It's sort of like an army, you'd say."

"Go on."

"I thought that you'd have to get back to the mountains—you'd try to slip around one of the ends of the line. Which end? I didn't know. I just chanced this way and rode on hard, as if I knew. Then I spotted this little house. If you wanted to rest and eat, you'd be more apt to take a little place than a big one. That's all there is to it."

"Simple, simple, simple," said Lefty, with a sigh. "Clever people always make the clever things look simple. You're a wonder, Jenny Loren! You are! Have a couple slices of this bacon? And here's some cold pone. It's a bit stale, but it's pretty good. Where's that fresh coffee, ma'am?"

Jenny ate heartily.

"When did you have breakfast?" asked Lefty curiously.

"Yesterday morning," said Jenny, with a faint smile.

Lefty exclaimed and rose to get her more food, and all the while Daniel could not speak!

Indeed, he wanted very much to talk to this charming girl, but when he fumbled in his mind he could find nothing to say—nothing whatever. Oddly enough, the mere thought of addressing her sent a tingle up his spine.

She paid no attention to him. Only once her eyes flashed up at him; but then her glance dropped hastily, and pink ran into her face.

Daniel knew that he had been staring, and he was so confused, so unhappy at his boorishness, that he started up and hastily left the shack—to keep watch on the outside and look after the horses, as he said!

Behind the little house, he made the merest pretense of being busy. Tyson had scraped together a feed for the stock, and they were still eating. Daniel eyed them without interest. Then he thought of the girl's horse, and hastily he went to it.

She was a beautiful filly, well-bred, with an eye as soft as milk and a mist of blue in it. Now, steaming from

her work, she had not let her head fall, but kept it high,
looking curiously about her.

Daniel led her around the shack, and he felt an odd
pleasure in robbing the other horses to feed this one. An
odd pleasure, too, in watching her eat. He touched the
soft silk of her neck, and the heart of Daniel leaped
when she pricked her ears.

Then a step came about the corner and he started
guiltily as Jenny Loren appeared. He was so much unnerved that he failed to notice that Jenny had started,
too.

She pointed to the feed which her mare was enjoying;
she started to speak; her words stumbled.

"I—you're very—it's not so hot to-day," said Jenny
Loren.

"No," said Daniel.

He fumbled wretchedly in the back of his numbed
brain.

"It was pretty windy this morning, though."

"Yes," said Jenny Loren. "It——"

She rubbed the mane and the neck of the mare; the
eye of Jenny was blank with confusion. To Daniel it
seemed filled with the profoundest mystery.

"She looks a good mare," said Daniel, drawing a little
closer, and clearing his throat, and speaking with a sort
of bass.

"She really is."

"Faithful, eh?" said Daniel.

"Oh, yes—faithful!" said Jenny, and raised her eyes
and looked at Daniel, and grew suddenly much pinker
than before.

The heart of Daniel leaped, as the wild colt leaps when
after the winter mountains it sees the green fields of
spring below it.

"She has a good eye," said Daniel.

"Yes," said Jenny. "I'm glad that you——"

Her voice, for no obvious reason, trailed away.

"She's deep, too," said Daniel, cursing the empty head
which limited him to this sort of talk.

"Yes," said Jenny faintly.

"And she has a good heart, I suppose," said Daniel.

"Yes," said the girl, and she looked up to him again. It seemed a great effort, and when her glance met his, her eyes widened suddenly and wonderfully, and it seemed to Daniel that the misty blue of tenderness in the eyes of the mare appeared in the eyes of the girl.

As a keen fragrance strikes into the brain and a dizzy sense of pleasure comes, so Daniel drew a long breath.

She had looked hastily down once more. He wanted to beg her to raise her head again, so that he could make sure about the blue mist.

But he had run out of words. He heard the rapid, cheerful voice of Lefty coming toward them, and suddenly Daniel turned on his heel and bolted without further speech.

Lefty halted.

"Great Scott!" said Lefty, "you look as if you'd seen a ghost, kid! What's up?"

"I don't know," said Daniel faintly.

And he had told the truth.

34. A Decision

NOW LEFTY, having marked that expression in the face of Daniel, went on around the corner of the house and there he found Jenny Loren, who was holding hard to the stirrup leather at the side of her horse and looking rather white and staring in just the same manner that he had marked in Daniel.

The amiable Lefty put two and two together with wonderful speed.

"You ain't agreed, yet," suggested Lefty, "but you're on the way, all right!"

She did not seem to understand until she looked up to him, and saw the breadth of his grin. Then Jenny Loren flushed.

"I dunno what you mean," said she.

"Aw, but you do," said Lefty.

He waited for her to answer, but answer there was none.

"I see how it is, and it's all right," said he with tolerance. "You're a good girl, Jenny Loren. I wish you luck. Because he's the grandest lad that ever rode a horse crooked. Only, you ain't going to bother him now when he needs to think about nothing but getting loose from the hounds that are following us?"

"I have to take him away," said Jenny Loren.

"Sure you do, if you can," answered Lefty cheerfully. "But you can't. Neither can I—just yet."

"You've tried," said Jenny Loren with infinite sarcasm.

"I've tried," answered Lefty. "Tried hard and worked like a nailer on him to get him away from this life. But I can't. You think that I've been pulling him down, of course! Well, Jenny, I haven't. I've been square by him."

She nodded, looking curiously at the outlaw. They were drawn to one another by a common interest; a great feeling of intimacy had sprung up between them on the moment.

"Well," went on Lefty, "if we can get him clean out of this trouble, he can come looking for you."

"I think," said Jenny Loren slowly, "that I understand what you're driving at. But you're all wrong. We—I—I mean that we're just strangers to each other."

"Are you?" smiled Lefty. "I passed the kid, a minute ago, and there was the same look on him that you got on you. Well, what does that mean, I ask you? You're both a little dizzy about each other. Well, trust it to me, Jenny, I'll work the thing out for you!"

Jenny had turned the brightest crimson. And as she cast about for a means of terminating this profitless conversation, she could think of nothing better than to say: "He's the son of Jeremy Crossett. D'you know what that means?"

"Don't I?" grinned Lefty. "I come from the town where the Crossetts was high and mighty. I was one of the poor kids from across the river, and the Crossetts lived on the hill on the far side. They lived on the whole hill. And every time that I dreamed about heaven the entrance to it was the wrought-iron gate of the Crossett place. Sure I know about them. And the grandfather, and the great-grandfather of the kid. I've seen 'em all. But there's one thing where you're wrong."

"Am I?" said Jenny.

"You don't believe me?"

She waited very cautiously.

"Look here, Jenny," said he, "I want to play this game with the cards on the table, all of 'em. I like you. Now you listen. You think that the kid's a mile above you. He ain't. If anything, you're above him. Only that's a fool way to look at the thing. He's a grand kid. You're a fine girl, I'm all for you. Well, then, he ain't a Crossett at all. I'll tell you the bitter truth and maybe it'll spike the guns of the fool ideas that you've picked up. Maybe it'll finish the kid, in your eyes. He ain't a Crossett at all! He's a Dunlin!"

It made her step back a little. She had felt, from the first, that Lefty was far too hard-headed to swallow the strange story with which Jeremy Crossett had sent away his son to the outlaw. But there was no doubt about the conviction of Lefty. His eyes and his face shone with it.

"He can't be!" she exclaimed.

At that, a faint flush appeared in the cheek of Lefty.

"We got a pretty black name," he admitted, "and we've deserved it, of course. But you get a white blackbird, once in a while. It ain't what a man is that counts. It's what he's raised up to be. It ain't what he's got inside his head that counts. It's what's put there. That's the way with the kid. They called him a Crossett. Well, he toes the mark and everything was straight as could be with him. He found out he was a Dunlin and what happened? He busted a jail open as wide as the sky. Then he started out to raise hell!"

"And you helped him!" said the girl bitterly.

"It ain't true," replied Lefty with heat. "I played fair with him. I begged him to give up the game and go back to his own way of living, but he simply told me that there was no way except mine. He loved the ways of the wilderness, Jenny. He took to it nacheral like. He was a fish in water, for the first time. And so he's stayed with me. I got him into this train robbery deal—you see I'm putting all the cards on the table for you, Jenny, and——"

"That was brotherly, all right," said Jenny with anger. "That was helping him along."

"It was to be the last job for him and for me," replied the outlaw. "I was goin' to go straight, if we'd won."

"You go straight!" she replied with disgust.

"Couldn't be done? But you're wrong, and I'm the very man that could. I could live on a farm or in a village for the rest of my days, and there never would be a touch of restlessness about me. I could do that, only I never seen any fun in the idea, until lately."

"Until they had your back to the wall?" asked Jenny, with the same cold, incredulous curiosity.

"You'd think that way," replied the outlaw, "but lemme tell you straight that the reason was something different."

"I'd like to hear," said Jenny.

"It was him—it was the kid."

She listened in amazement, for there was a most real and undeniable emotion in the voice of Lefty Dunlin.

"He changed you?" she asked.

"He did. Because, Jenny, I seen that if he was a Dunlin and could be as white as he is—which he ain't nothing but—then why couldn't I be the same thing? I always would've laid money, from the time that I was a kid, that no Dunlin could be anything but a crook. The kid has showed me different."

"By robbing stores and trains with you?" she asked grimly.

"You'd see it that way," replied the outlaw calmly. "But it ain't what a man does that always writes him down; it's what's in his head when he does it that counts the most. But now you want to get him away from me, and I tell you plainly, honey, that it can't be done!"

"You'll persuade him, of course," said the girl bitterly.

"Persuading never would make him do what he thinks is wrong."

"Train robbery, and what not. That's not wrong in his eyes?"

"Why does a colt kick?" asked Lefty. "Because he wants to knock your head off, or because he's full of life?"

She could not help smiling a little at this rather apt comparison.

"But," concluded Lefty, "the kid won't leave me; nothing could drag him away from me until we're through this trouble that has us snagged now. You write it down in red. He'd never welch; he'd never show yellow!"

He added gently: "I know that you want to get him safe away. Well, suppose that you leave it to me to help you. I'm through with the old life, Jenny. I'm gunna break loose from it and cut away for something better, and I'll take the kid with me. Does that satisfy you?"

As though she felt a sudden impotence, she threw out both hands in a gesture of surrender.

"What can I say?" said she. "But I know what will happen. There will be no change. You'll make some good resolutions and then—the resolutions will go up in smoke. Oh! I've done what I could, but I'm only a woman—and—"

Here Jenny turned and buried her face in the mane of her horse. Lefty, not a little moved, stepped up behind her and even extended a hand to touch her shoulder. But he seemed to think better of this, and slowly turned away.

He entered the shack again and growled at Tyson: "The horses are rested and fed. Are you ready?"

"I'm ready. Is the kid leaving us?" asked Tyson, his voice sharp partly with fear and partly with dislike.

"I dunno. Where did he go?"

"Yonder by the woodpile."

Lefty found Daniel seated on the chopping block, idly weighing the ax in his hand.

"It's time to go," said Lefty Dunlin.

Daniel looked up. Then, as though by mighty effort of the will, he raised himself and sighed.

"I'm ready," said he.

But he was filled with a great temptation. It would be simple enough to let Lefty and Tyson ride on, while he himself turned back with the girl and tried to find his father. It was one thing to feel that he was riding into peril at the side of a blood-brother; it was another to know that a Crossett was living like a ruffian in the wilderness, turning his back upon a higher destiny; and there was Jenny, also turning the scales in favor of a peaceful life.

Yet a sense of duty to this man held him strictly to his work as it had held him before. He could not abandon Lefty before the adventure was ended. So he went to get his horse, and mounted slowly, so slowly that Lefty and Tyson already were a hundred yards away and waiting for him impatiently.

He rode to Jenny, where she stood leaning against her mare.

"You've been a great trump to come after me like this," said Daniel. "I have to go on, Jenny. But I'll get through with this. Once Lefty is safely back in the mountains I can break away from him honorably. I can't leave the ship when it's in the storm, you know. Good-by!"

"Good-by," said Jenny faintly.

"I——" began Daniel.

There he stuck, and at last she looked up. Like two children they stared at one another with great wide eyes. Then Daniel twitched his horse around and galloped hard after his two companions.

35. What Next?

NOW IT SEEMED to Jenny Loren as she stared after Daniel that some sort of madness must have possessed her, and she could not understand what was passing in her own mind. For there was Daniel, whom she had come to draw back to civilization and safety, and there was Lefty Dunlin, both speeding away together, and she could have stopped them both, she was reasonably confident, if she had told Lefty the plain truth of the matter.

And, indeed, had not Lefty opened the door for such an explanation when he had spoken about the effect of blood and position in this world?

And yet, somehow, he had managed to disarm her as he spoke. She had found it impossible for her to let the outlaw know that there was, indeed, as great a gulf between him and his pseudo-brother as there possibly could be between two men in this world.

But he clove to the sameness of their blood and the difference in their deeds and in their manner of thinking. He saw salvation for himself in this difference. He saw the gates of the future opened to him and an honest life in prospect, and the pathos of that hope appalled and amazed Jenny Loren.

So she condemned herself grimly saying to her heart of hearts: "I'm a fool! I'm a great fool! I should have talked. I should have opened Lefty's eyes."

And yet she could not really regret it, for something told her that there was one faint hope of escape for Lefty now—escape from himself and his old life!

None of those doubts occurred to Lefty. He was, primarily, an optimist, and he saw in the future for himself and the kid one great coup and then rest and retirement thereafter, while he schooled himself in all the ways of a gentleman, and Daniel carried on with the life which had been interrupted by this excursion into the wilderness.

Keen as he was to get back to the mountain from which he could strike again for fortune, like a hawk climbing to a point of vantage before descending upon its prey, yet Lefty dared not hurry in his ride too much on this day. Already they had been tracked to the ground by one person, and that person an inexperienced girl. It seemed very probable indeed that some one of the party of head-hunters would also be able to track them down. Therefore the three had their field glasses constantly at their eyes.

Before they left one wood, they searched every hill and copse before them; then they rode in a straight line, driving their horses hard.

The day had turned unseasonably bad. The wind leaped at them again from the cold mountain heights, burdened with rain and sleet and chill from the snows above. On man and beast that weather was hard, yet Lefty welcomed it, for, as he said to Daniel, men are more apt to spend their time looking at a warm fire than searching against the wind for dangerous fugitives in weather such as this, and if the skies had been blue and the wind soft, the pursuit would have been tenfold keener.

At any rate they journeyed on until the darkness came upon them. Their horses long since had been too spent for even a footing pace, except downhill, and in the gray of the evening when they saw a shadow of trees below them in a hollow and the glimmer of a few lights, they were all happy when Lefty said: "That's the Gillian place. If Tom Gillian's there, I think that we can sleep safe and give the horses a rest and a feed."

"Five more miles," said Tyson sternly, "and we could take a chance at turning for the mountains."

"Look at the horses," answered Lefty. "Have they got it in them, I ask you?"

The bobbing heads and the staggering shoulders of the three animals made an eloquent answer.

So they turned down from the hill into the hollow with the wind screaming in their ears and freezing one side of their faces. At the door of the house, Lefty leaned from his saddle and knocked. The door reopened at once and a gray-haired women stepped out into the storm, regardless of the wind that dragged down her hair and blew it wildly.

She threw up her hands, crying: "Lefty Dunlin—God bless me! Are you here? And they ain't got you yet?"

"They ain't," Lefty assured her, "and they're not going to. Can we have something to eat?"

"All there is in the house, and that ought to be plenty," said Mrs. Gillian. "Wouldn't Tom be glad to see you, now, if he was home! Fetch your horses back there to the barn and feed 'em, will you? Then come in here. I'll have supper started before you have a chance to get back. What a howlin' night, ain't it?"

They hurried for the barn. Tyson's horse was too tired to drink; the other pair were too hot to be trusted with more than a mouthful. So they put the horses in the stalls in the barn, and bedded them down deep. Even crushed barley, however, would not tempt Tyson's horse; he stood with hanging head, and Lefty said with decision: "That horse'll either be dead or sick in the morning. You can't ride him again, Tyson. We'll have to borrow one of the Gillian mustangs!"

Tyson went to look at them on the other side of the barn; they were small, ugly-headed, perfectly typical mustangs, but Tyson swore that they were good enough to get him back into the mountains and, once there, he knew how to make himself safe and head toward Mexico.

When they left the barn, it was like striking against a wall, so heavy was the wind. They had to lean far forward; and when Daniel tried to speak, it was impossible to hear him.

Sleet, too, whipped and stung them, but they managed to march on to the little farmhouse, where Mrs. Gillian welcomed them in the warm kitchen, and where the savor of cooking meat and steaming coffee was more than a welcome in words to them.

They slumped into chairs and Lefty proceeded to pump his hostess for information. She had plenty, and of the most dangerous nature.

No less than four times that day she had seen parties of horsemen near the place. That very afternoon the most feared of all man hunters had come in person to her house and left his men in the distance while he interviewed her.

It was Sheriff Bud Loftus with a dozen hand-picked men at his back.

"He says to me," quoted Mrs. Gillian, " 'Mrs. Tom Gillian, I know that you been friendly with Lefty Dunlin. Well, I don't blame you. Lefty's a good kid, in lots of ways, and I'd like him if the law'd let me. But it don't. He pays his way as he goes, I know. He's done nothing but good for you. But the person that turns him over

to the law, Mrs. Tom Gillian, will get something around
five thousand dollars, right now, and maybe more. And
if you was to flash a lamp three times across one of your
windows one of these nights, you'd have a party down
here in no time!' "

Tyson started to his feet, evidently much alarmed.

"I just laughed at him," said Mrs. Gillian. "I told him
that I'd sell my own soul, let alone a rascal of an outlaw, for five thousand dollars. And he went away and
seemed satisfied with what I'd said. I tried to find out what
they knew about your trail, but he kept a tight mouth. He
don't talk none except to please himself, I'd say!"

Tyson said hoarsely: "He's got a watch put on this
here house!"

Lefty imitated the croak in scorn: "And what of it?"
he asked.

"My heavens! what of it? If he's watching the house,
he's seen us come in—we've walked right into a trap!
Damn a woman that couldn't talk out and say what was
worth knowing before we got settled down here and the
horses turned cold!"

Lefty raised one finger: "Watch your tongue, Tyson,"
he said with a gentleness which did not deceive Tyson.

The latter complained in a half whine: "They've got
their eyes on us, I tell you. Let's start now—a swallow
of coffee, and I'm for the trail!"

"Aw, stay where you are," replied Lefty. "Stay where
you are, will you? They're in eye-shot of a light signal.
They couldn't've been close enough to see us when we
came down here. Through that rain and sleet we could
hardly see each other! Sit back and take it easy, Tyson.
It'll spoil your shooting, if you get heated up like this!"

Tyson slumped heavily into his chair.

"There's gunna be trouble and right here in this house,"
he announced prophetically. "I smell it the same as a dog
smells a wolf. I dunno why I don't get up and go on!"

Lefty explained seriously and simply: "Of course, there's
a chance that we'll have trouble. There's a chance that
we'll have trouble anywhere along this here range. But
there's this to look into: Bud Loftus is too wise an old

fox to waste time coming back to search the same spot twice in a day. He's been here; now he's rode on. I'm glad of it, because I dunno any man in the world that I'd less like to have dealings with than Bud at a time like this here. But he's been and gone. We need our strength for the run to the mountains, and that run comes tomorrow—if the storm will keep up to make a screen for us to ride behind. Mrs. Gillian has some horses that we can borrow. Well, what could be beter all around? Kid, what do you say?"

"I say," said Daniel soberly, "that it's better to keep moving, no matter how fagged we may be. Now we're here, let's have some food and coffee. Then let's start marching. If we can get horses——"

"Sure," said Mrs. Gillian with a grin, "I can't keep you from takin' them by force, can I? But man, man! would you be going out into the night in weather like this? Would you be havin' the darlin' face of you ate off by the cold like a wolf? Ah, don't you be thinkin' about it, but mind what Lefty says. There never was a wiser man than him; not even my old grandfather when he robbed the Phoenix bank—God rest him!"

This singular advice caused Tyson to yawn and stretch himself.

"I leave the decision with you, Lefty," said he. "Its on your head."

"We'll stay, then," Lefty replied. "There's dinner ready for us. Sit down and feed, Tyson, and try to be cheerful. You're worse than the storm."

Their chairs had barely stopped scraping as they settled down to the table, when there was a loud knocking at the front door. The three outlaws sat transfixed, listening intently. The knock was repeated, and louder than before.

36.   Out of the Night

MRS. GILLIAN fell into the wildest panic at once. She almost dropped the platter of fried bacon which she was carrying to the table, and then she clasped her hands and with a white face began to whisper: "What's gunna happen? What's gunna happen? Oh, they'll be murderin' us all!"

"Go open the door," said Lefty.

He slipped from his chair and took her by both shoulders.

"You're a brave woman, Mrs. Gillian," said he, "and you won't be trembling and showing whoever it is a white face will you? If it's a marshal or a sheriff—well, we'll know by the way you speak. If it's only a friend or a neighbor, then open the door and let him come in. Go ahead!"

Mrs. Gillian set her teeth and nodded. She appeared, after all, to be what Lefty called her—a brave woman. For she left the kitchen rubbing color vigorously into her face, and presently they could hear the bolt of the front door scratch in its rusty frame as it was drawn back.

"Whoever it is," said Lefty, "you'd better slip out the back door if you don't want to have that black mask seen, Tyson."

Tyson glared at his leader. Nothing that could be said to the big man could be made to please him.

He stood half crouched at the rear door, listening, and they heard the voice of Mrs. Gillian call out cheerfully: "Hello, Martie Orval! What in the world you doin' out on this sort of a night?"

"Well," answered the man, "you wouldn't believe it! If I didn't get blinded comin' up against the storm so's I dropped far wide of my course goin' home. Then I seen the lights of your house. Made me see that I'd missed my way, and I was so cold that I made up my mind that

I'd come in here and warm myself a mite, if I could, thank you?"

"Come on in," said Mrs. Gillian, not very brightly. "Of course, you're welcome to warm yourself. Step right on into the kitchen. I got a couple of cousins of mine from up Anvil way in there."

Martie Orval stepped into the kitchen.

He was a big, red-faced man, with an old-fashioned circle of whiskers around his chin and a great expanse of stomach and chest now covered with a wet canvas coat. He kicked each foot against the jamb of the door to knock some of the water from his boots, the while he nodded at the two men who sat at the kitchen table.

Mrs. Gillian, smiling, produced a pair of names for her "cousins" when she introduced them, describing Martie Orval as one of her near neighbors, with a house not more than three miles away.

Martie Orval sat down beside the stove; and as its powerful blast of heat struck him he began to steam at once.

"Don't you be minding me," said Orval. "Go right on and feed!"

"Wouldn't you sit down yourself, Martie?" said Mrs. Gillian. "It'll take me only a minute to set another place, and I'm sure that there's plenty of bacon left on the side!"

"Thanks," said Martie. "My old woman will be wanting me, though. I gotta go on, pretty quick. I'll just thaw the surface. How is things in Anvil, boys?"

"All heated up," declared Lefty. "Dunlin has been raisin' so much hell through the mountains that the folks are mad. They're wild this time and want his head!"

"Do they, now?" asked Martie Orval, pausing as he stuffed a pipe. "Do they want his head? I been hearin' that they was all plumb friendly to him, up that way."

"You can stand bein' robbed," said Lefty with decision, "but you can't stand bein' made a fool of!"

"That's true," said Martie Orval with sympathy in his voice. "That's a true thing. But I thought—fill your pipes while I got this pouch out, will you?"

Neither Lefty nor Daniel smoked a pipe, and said so, which caused Martie Orval to ramble on: "It's sort of fallin' out of fashion, ain't it? I mean pipe smokin'? Now, your man don't smoke neither, does he?"

"Not a whiff of a pipe, thank God," said Mrs. Gillian, who was finding something to employ her hands every moment. "I don't mean you not to smoke, Martie Orval. I got the window open, and I can stand it fine."

Martie Orval did not hesitate long, but lighted his pipe, and instantly half of the kitchen was engulfed in smoke.

"Set down, set down, Mrs. Gillian," said Orval. "I see you laid out a place for yourself. Don't you let me keep you from eating!"

"I laid out a place, but I got no special appetite," declared she. "The heat of the stove, it sort of takes away the taste for eating, sometimes, if you know what I mean!"

"My woman is the same," volunteered Orval. "You take her in August, she don't hardly touch nothin'. We got an iron roof over the kitchen and it's like an oven.

"Going back to the way you folks think in Anvil," continued the talkative Orval, "I was surprised a good deal to hear that you was so tired of Dunlin up that way. I thought that in the mountains he mostly paid for what he took, and paid high!"

"Some say that he does," answered Lefty at once. "But suppose I got a fine young three-year-old in my yard and Dunlin comes by. He's got a beat horse under him. He leaves his beat horse and he takes mine. Maybe he gives me some boot; but he kills that three-year-old. I got a damn leather-lipped mustang in its place. That's the sort of thing that made me mad. And a lot more like me!"

Martie Orval nodded.

"It's mean," he observed. "It's a mean thing. Still, I got a sort of sympathy for Lefty Dunlin."

"Have you?" drawled Mrs. Gillian. "Well, I dunno that I can agree with you. The murderin', train-robbin'——"

"He's got his faults," said Martie Orval, "but I dunno that he ever done nothing that a lot of other folks wouldn't do, if only they had the nerve to try it. But they ain't got the nerve."

Martie Orval seemed to have steamed himself enough, and he stood up and took his pipe in his hand.

He made this farewell speech: "I tell you, I've always said that there was never a man of us that wouldn't be apt to be doin' wrong if he could do wrong safely. It's them that are scared that make the laws. It's them that bolt their doors at night, that vote for the laws and shake in their beds. We don't live, we that stay at home. Them that have the nerve to go and do what they want to do— they're the folks that live. They got blood in them!"

"Why, you talk like a regular outlaw!" observed Mrs. Gillian, smiling.

"Maybe I'll be one in the finish!" said Martie Orval with a grin. He waved his hand carelessly at the others, and then disappeared through the front door.

"Is he straight or crooked?" asked Daniel curiously of Mrs. Gillian.

"Bless your heart," sighed she, sinking into a chair now that the strain of Orval's presence was removed, "I dunno. He—well, he's just a man."

This vague description did not satisfy Lefty, who observed at once: "He comes in here to warm himself, and he leaves his horse outside to freeze!"

"He's a carelesslike sort of man," agreed Mrs. Gillian.

A great shadow loomed in the doorway. It was Tyson, and as he entered the wind screamed at the house from a new corner of the sky, and gray moth-wings of sleet began to blanket the side window of the kitchen.

"There's a change of wind," remarked Daniel. "Perhaps that will bring us better weather."

"Out of the northwest and into the north! That sounds better, don't it?" asked Tyson with his usual sneer. "It's like all your ideas—not worth a damn, kid. Not worth a damn!"

Then something very strange happened to Daniel. He had endured a thousand insults from Tyson and a thousand slights. Now something snapped in him. He felt something like a hot iron run across his forehead—no, it was inside his forehead, darting burningly through his brain.

So he came out of his chair with a leap and his left hand caught the beard of Tyson; his fingers tangled in it; and it seemed to him that fellow turned into a weight of loose feathers before him. He jammed Tyson's head back against the door with a crash.

Strange words, also, burst from the lips of Daniel.

"You fat-faced sneak," he was saying. "You four-flusher! You damned, sneering blockhead! Get out your gun. You've got your hand on it! Make your draw, and I'll take that gun away from you and make you eat it. I'll feed you a yard of steel, you cur."

There was not so much as a quiver from Tyson. A baleful fire glistened in his eyes and continued to glisten when Daniel suddenly loosed his beard and sprang back, on guard. Still Tyson did not speak.

It did not seem that he was overwhelmed with fear. His face was not white but a purple red, and he seemed restrained not in the least by terror but simply by caution. Never in Daniel's life had a glance of such terrible malice fallen upon him.

Tyson stepped back to the chair from which he had risen as Daniel leaped at him. He sat down, and he began to finish his meal, but with the greatest rapidity. He ate enormous mouthfuls, swallowed his coffee at a single draft, and then kicked back his chair with a violence that made it slide drunkenly across the room and crash up against the wall.

He rose again, wiped his beard on the back of his hand, and turned slowly toward the door, eyeing Daniel. At the door, he turned again, and hesitated as though he were about to speak. But all that he did was to stare at Daniel again.

Then he was gone.

As for Daniel, after the brief ectasy of his rage, he was filled with remorse and with shame. He could not understand that passion. It had been born full grown, like the goddess, and now he sat numb and dizzy, gripping the edge of the table with numb hands.

Lefty was studiously avoiding his eyes. Mrs. Gillian's

voice trembled as she asked if he would have another plateful.

"Good Heavens!" said Daniel, "don't act as though I were a murderer. I'm ashamed. I'll go and apologize to Tyson——"

"You go to bed," said Lefty. He pointed his finger like a gun at Daniel. "You go to bed and go to sleep!"

37.   Fifty on Their Heels

DANIEL LEFT the room obediently. Silence remained in his wake.

"Is he often like that?" asked Mrs. Gillian, still white, her voice trembling with anxiety.

"Never before," said Lefty.

"Him so soft and gentle; almost like a girl! Almost like a girl! And then all at once——"

She covered her face with her hands.

"I thought that the big man was dead. I could almost see him falling! It was a terrible thing!"

"Don't I know it was terrible?" exclaimed Lefty. "Don't it mean more to me to see him act that way than it possibly could mean to you?"

"Ah, he's a real friend to you, Lefty?"

"He is. One of the best lads that ever stepped."

"Now, mind you," said Mrs. Gillian grimly. "I ain't a fool about men. I've seen 'em young and I've seen 'em old, and mostly those I've seen have been bad! My two uncles, and my own father, and my brother, Harry, and Cousin Lew Smithfield, and more than those—they none of them died in bed. But of all that I've ever seen and of all that I've ever dreamed of, there never was none such a tiger-cat as him!"

And she stabbed a worn, bent finger in the direction of the door.

Lefty raised a hand in sudden protest.

"I heard enough of that," he said. "Knock off, will you? Knock off! I don't want to hear no more!"

"He's a friend of yours?" asked the woman, growing uncontrollably excited.

"The best in the whole world to me!"

"Some day," said Mrs. Gillian, standing over her guest in a manner, "some day he'll leap at you like that, and then Heaven help one of you! Because you won't stand like that great bear of a man to be mauled around!" Lefty had grown very yellow. He began to fumble at his chin as though, indeed, a beard were there, and the hand of Daniel were fixed in it. At length he sighed and shook his head.

"Let the kid alone," said he. "I'll try to handle him, only—I never thought he had that sort of an explosive in him. And——"

He fell into a long silence. Then he said: "Now tell me some more about this Martie Orval."

"Do you think that he suspected anything?" asked Mrs. Gillian.

"I don't know. There's only one suspicious thing, it seems to me."

"That he lost his way, you mean?"

"No, there was enough storm to blind a man. But does he know you pretty well?"

"Yes. He comes by pretty near every day."

"Well," remarked Lefty, "for a friend and a neighbor he didn't seem particularly excited about the two cousins that had come down from Anvil."

"No," agreed she. "He didn't."

"As I recall it, he didn't even ask what business had brought us down here."

"He didn't," answered Mrs. Gillian. "What business was it?" she added with a smile.

"Hunting Lefty Dunlin, of course," answered Lefty, chuckling. "But this Martie Orval——"

"You stop worrying about him," said Mrs. Gillian. "He's a pretty honest fellow, I take it. I've known him a good many years. I never heard of him doing anybody wrong, except Jeff Calkins, who says that he was bad beat in a horse trade."

"There's a price on my head," said Lefty. "There's a steep price on my head, and I'd hardly trust you, Mrs. Gillian. Well—it's only one more chance to take. We need sleep—the horses need rest—in the gray of the morning we'll ride on. Good night!"

Daniel in the meantime had fallen soundly asleep as soon as he had coiled his blanket around him.

He slept in the fashion that Lefty had taught him, with one revolver at his right side, one under his head, and his rifle on his left, the muzzle pointed toward his feet. In this fashion he could waken at any moment, no matter from how sound a sleep, and find himself armed.

So, being satisfied with this arrangement of his weapons, bewildered by his strange exhibition of passion, and thoroughly weary from the day's riding, he felt his brain reel as he lay down, and then sleep clouded his wits like an opiate.

When Daniel wakened, he saw that the beams of the attic room were visible. There was no moon, the storm still howled wickedly; and he knew that it was dawn. He sat up.

Long, knifelike rays of cold draft pierced his body and he was tempted to crawl back into warmth and sleep again. For there was an unexpended weariness in him that could have soaked up, he felt, a hundred hours of utter sleep. He was kept awake, simply by the fear of death. For now he began to remember everything with a clear brain.

He crawled to the little slitlike window at the end of the attic. Lefty was somewhere in the shadows, lost, for he always slept face down; there was Tyson on the left, a faint blur of white where the light touched his face. And Daniel, remembering, was filled with wonder. He could not understand how Tyson had allowed this night to pass without stabbing to the heart the man who had so grossly insulted and challenged him.

From the window he looked over the countryside only dimly visible in the half light of the coming day. It seemed impossible that this drowned and darkened world ever could be rescued by the kind sun again. Trees were standing ghosts. And the shed roofs were faintly aglimmer with water.

Still the storm rushed on out of the north with a force that made the old house tremble like a violin under the bow.

At least there would be no fear of pursuit on this day, decided Daniel, and he went back to pull on his boots.

He never drew on those boots in the morning without regretting the change from the old to the new life. For always there was a sore place on heel or toes, and the boots were too tight.

However, he had those boots on at last, and then he paused, chin on hand, as the events of the evening before slid through his mind like the pictures on a screen. He came to a point that made him start and then frown. He brooded over it for a moment, and then he went exploring for Lefty. He found him after some groping, and Lefty waked and thrust the muzzle of a Colt into Daniel's stomach by way of a question mark.

"I've had a thought," said Daniel, brushing the gun aside. "Sit up here and hear it."

"Not for another hour," yawned Lefty, and pretended to snore again.

Daniel took him by the nape of the neck and said in a low savage voice, "I think we're done for."

So Lefty raised himself upon his elbow and listened. The pale dawn light showed not all his features but drew his face in free-hand, impressive fashion.

"You remember that Orval asked if either of us smoked pipes?"

"I remember that," said Lefty.

"And then he asked Mrs. Gillian if her husband smoked."

"Probably he did. I don't remember."

"I do, though. I remember perfectly."

"All right, Sherlock. What do you get out of that?"

"That Orval spotted something wrong!"

"Out of the pipe stuff?"

"Don't you remember? Tyson was smoking his pipe before he sat down to eat."

Lefty suddenly sat erect.

"Go on, kid, you're on the heels of something."

"And then Tyson sat down and put his pipe on the window sill beside his chair—and that was the pipe that Orval was looking at. He must have been looking at it. I remember how his eyes wandered from our faces as he talked. You can understand the questions he must have been putting to himself. We didn't smoke. Neither did Gillian. Why was that pipe lying there, filled with fresh ashes? There was another in our party. He had sat in the third chair. Why had he left? Who were we, after all? That explains, too, why he wasn't more curious about us—why he didn't ask our business away from our home town."

"I thought of that," said Lefty grimly.

"He'd made up his mind about us before," said Daniel. "He knew exactly who we were. And once he had any suspicion, of course we'd tally with the descriptions of us that must be floating by this time around the countryside!"

"You're right," said Lefty slowly, as though unwilling to admit it. "You're right, and the hound went for the sheriff when he left here. You're right—and Tyson was right when he said that we might be seen riding to the house. We *were* seen—by Orval—posted by the sheriff to keep watch. And by this time——'

"The storm may stop them!" suggested Daniel.

"It might," said Lefty hopelessly. "I've been a fool. I've been a damned fool. Tolliver——'

Whatever strange thought had connected his mind with Tolliver, he fell silent again, and rousing Tyson, with a word they set the big man dressing in wildest haste. All three climbed down together to the lower floor, and there they saw the door dashed open and Mrs. Gillain ran in upon them. She threw up her hands with a wild cry.

"There's about fifty men—in the barn—in the sheds —and they've got you, Lefty! Oh, Heaven save you! They got you—fifty of 'em, I think! They tried to catch me——"

She began to weep loudly; the three men stood silent, unmoving, until Daniel noticed the storm which was pouring through the open doorway. He went to slam it, and as he did so a rifle clanged and a bullet scraped noisily across the ceiling above his head.

38.   Many Against Them

THAT FIRST BULLET, which so narrowly missed its mark, was the opening gun of a fusillade which began to crackle all around the house, but the only answer from within was the loud clattering and clanging of the kitchen pans and pots as the lead struck them where they hung on the wall.

Mrs. Gillian screamed. Plainly she was about to become hysterical. Lefty grabbed her by both shoulders. He shouted in her ear: "Who's leading them?"

"Nobody but Bud Loftus!" she shrilled. "And we'll all be murdered!"

The first fury of the firing ended at once. But steadily and almost with a regular rhythm, bullets still were pumped through and through the house. It was a flimsy structure of wood; now and again a slug entered on a line with the floor beams or the rafters and was stopped with a heavy, pounding sound in the mass of wood. But three bullets out of four whipped cleanly through the building. Little eyeholes of light began to open here and there in the walls. Tyson's coat was laid open at the shoulder, and a ball cut neatly through Mrs. Gillian's topknot.

"Nobody'll believe it of Bud Loftus," said Lefty "that he would hammer away at a house where there was a woman. Tyson, stick that towel on the poker and shove it through the window, will you?"

"You yellow dog!" answered the savage Tyson. "I'll be shot before I surrender—and if you try to——"

He ended on an ominous rising note of danger, but

Lefty answered shortly: "Shove out the white flag, you fool. I'm not surrendering, but I simply want to get that woman out of the house. Go on, man!"

Tyson obeyed, and the instant the flag appeared there was a yell from outside, a cry that seemed to come from many throats in derision and in triumph.

Lefty turned black.

"They'll yell another tune before we're through," he vowed. He added to Mrs. Gillian: "Take that white flag and go through the open door with it."

"They'll murder me!" sobbed she.

"They won't touch you. If Bud Loftus is there you'll find that you won't be hurt. No man will shoot at a woman. Go on. Good luck, and you've been a trump to us!"

"Heaven help you," murmured poor Mrs. Gillian, forgetting her own troubles. "Only Heaven can! And—they're going to ruin all my pans!"

She picked up a kettle, and with that in one hand and the flag vigorously waved in the other, she marched through the doorway.

"Tell them," said Lefty as she went off, "that we want no quarter and that we'll give none!"

They could hear the note of triumph in the besieging party end as they saw that the woman was coming out alone.

Lefty caught Daniel by one arm and whispered to him: "Now, kid, you've done fine. You've never welched on the job once and you've showed as much nerve as any man in the world. But there's no use in you going to hell with the rest of us. You'll do us no good here. You'll simply be one more man for them to hit as they comb the house. Get out, kid. Take that dishcloth and wave it as you go—and God bless you!"

Daniel stared, for this outlaw, this pseudo-brother, this wild man of the mountains, was trembling violently and his face was pale.

"I'll take care of one side of the house," said Daniel calmly. "Don't talk nonsense. I'd never quit. What sort of stuff do you think is in me?"

A veil seemed to be snatched from before the eyes of Lefty. Suddenly they blazed with joy and he muttered: "That's the Dunlin way! Take the south side. There's three windows there. See that they never get a chance to show a hand there! Step!"

Daniel moved, accordingly, to the side of the house which was assigned to him.

He had had a chance, now, to take note of all the surroundings of the house; indeed, he felt he could have charted every blade of grass within two hundred yards of it.

Exactly north, the nearest point of danger was a small outhouse which had been, in fact, the first dwelling that Gillian put up on the site. It was a little affair with one room, now used as a shed and storage place; it was so flimsy that even a revolver bullet at long range could puncture it like paper, but it had one formidable defense, and that was a stone chimney. This rose broad and strong at the base, and about five feet from the bottom it curved in to normal chimney width. It made a perfect breastwork, in this fashion, for all that the defenders needed to do was to cut small holes in the wall above the shoulders of the chimney and then they could fire with great security, their bodies being completely covered, and only their heads and shoulders being for an instant exposed—and even these parts were screened from view though not from possible bullets.

A little distance east of the outhouse there was a tall barn, its red-painted roof turned to a dun color by the density of the storm, and though no part of this was bulletproof, yet it had many windows, and a thousand cracks through which guns could be fired, and having poured in shot from one spot, the assailants could shift their places quickly.

Running south and east of the house was a scattering apple orchard and there were a number of possemen concealed there; some merely trusting to the meager shelter of the trunks, and some having scooped up shallow trenches in the loose, plowed ground, lay flat and only raised themselves from their muddy couches in order to take a hasty snapshot at the shack.

There was no effective cover to the west, with the possible exception of a dense thicket, but in this every movement could be traced by the waving of the shrubbery, and the assailants had not cared to risk the lives of any of their men in this partial cover.

It seemed to Daniel, at first, that toward the west they could all three retreat with safety enough, but then he saw that either the log house or the apple orchard commanded every inch of ground to the westward except a shallow cone just under the wall of the house. There would be a hundred yards to run to the thicket and no three men in the world could possibly reach that distance in safety when covered by the fire of such riflemen as Bud Loftus would be sure to have with him.

That was the situation when Daniel went to take charge of the southern front.

How did he feel then, when he went into actual battle against the upholders of the law?

To his own amazement he had no more scruples about opening fire upon them than if they had been red Indians! A few hours before, he would have attributed that cold-blooded indifference to the Dunlin blood in him. But now he knew that he was a true Crossett, with generations of upholders of the law behind him—and yet here he stood in the shack, rifle in hand, standing well back from the windows as he walked across and peered carefully out at the enemy.

He was not long in spotting one.

It was a tall man who stood side on behind the thickest trunk in the apple grove; now and again he suddenly slipped his rifle to his shoulder and fired.

He was sending his bullets accurately at the height of the floor or a few inches above, and making such good play that the moment that Daniel spotted him, he marked the report and then heard something splinter on the floor. He looked, and observed a clean furrow plowed across the boards.

So Daniel waited for the next appearance of this marksman, and the instant that the rifle barrel gleamed again, he fired, not at the edge of the trunk, but two inches inside it, for he was sure that the steel-jacketed bullet would cut through the wood and do execution on the farther side.

There was a frightened shout; the tall man leaped away from the tree and appeared spread-eagled in the air. Then he fell to the ground and began to crawl away as fast as he could go. Every inch of him was in sight and Daniel tried to draw a bead; laughter prevented him; it shook him helplessly.

That one experience was enough for all who were keeping behind the narrow trees for shelter; they dropped, and from their shallow rifle pits they sent a spite storm of bullets to repay Daniel for his good shot.

He replied to that storm as well as he could, following the example of Tyson and Lefty on their sides of the house, for they jumped to a window, fired, and then leaped back to escape the return. If those return shots passed through the window, they would be safe enough, but many a shell was pumped through the walls, and Daniel, as he leaped back and forth, suddenly saw that blood was streaming from his right knee.

He had barely paused to glance at that wound when there was a sound of cursing from the door, and Tyson limped in, wounded twice, for there was blood on his right thigh, and on the right sleeve of his coat.

He held his arm at that point with his other hand.

"I ain't going to stick it," said Tyson. "It's plain murder, and we can't murder back. I'm gunna run for it, and if you got sense, you'll come with me."

"What does Lefty say"

"I dunno. Let him stay there and keep them going. We'll slip out and he'll never know!"

Daniel strode past him in scornful silence.

As he entered the front room where Lefty was fighting he thought that his pseudo-brother had lost his wits, for Lefty was singing as he fought, springing lightly into one window, and then moving swiftly to another.

Even as Daniel entered, a gun appeared over one shoulder of the chimney in the outhouse, and Lefty fired at it instantly. There was a small puff of plaster and then an ear-splitting yell.

"You've killed that fellow," said Daniel coldly.

"I've done better," answered Lefty. "I've filled his eyes full of dust. What's up at your end of the house?"

"Tyson wants to quit."

"I knew he'd get tired first. How are you?"

"Ready to stick. But is it worth while?"

"No," said Lefty, pumping another shot into his gun, and holding it poised, "but I think that Bud Loftus is yonder in that shack, and I'd like to put my mark on the old boy before we slip out. And how can we slip?"

"I think I know a way," said Daniel. "Go back to my side of the fight and wait there for a minute at the kitchen door."

39.   A Painful Passage

LEFTY LOOKED TWICE at Daniel—once at his powder-streaked face, and again at his wounded leg. He said not a word but obeyed the suggestion and left the front room.

Daniel climbed straight up to the attic and took his place at the side of it, where two boards had warped apart and left, under the eaves, a gap large enough for a rifle muzzle.

Through that same gap he looked down upon the apple orchard and, as he had expected, he found that he could see every one of the men who lay in their improvised rifle pits. He smiled grimly to himself. They were in the hollow of his hand, and yet as his grip tightened on his rifle, he could not help remembering what Lefty had said —it was better to fill the eyes of an enemy with dust than to put a bullet through his brain!

Besides, his own wound in the knee was beginning to ache; up to that moment though he had seen the blood there he had not had the slightest sensation of pain or weakness.

He took careful aim low down on the leg of the man in the farthest pit. There were five fellows in that orchard, and all of them were in the plainest view. He could see them from their shoulders down to their heels. When one lifted himself to put in a shot at the house, Daniel had a perfect target for the whole body. And he could not help smiling a little, and then shaking his head in wonder. For no doubt these were old hands and fighting men of the very first water. They were clever campaigners, unquestionably, and yet they most childishly had forgotten to consider that from the house they could be under two lines of fire—a low line and a high line. Now, if he chose, he could break their backs for them.

Five men in the hollow of his hand.

And yet he thought less about that moment of sinister power than he did about the folly of these warriors. It seemed that every man who took up a life of violence or shared in violent deeds lost some of his intelligence. There was Lefty, who made a philosophy of taking chances, and overlooked a dozen of the most simple and necessary precautions. All his cunning and boldness in holding up an express train in the sight of two large and formidable towns had been thrown away because he forgot to take care of his powder for the second blast. Now he ventured into a trap which even Tyson, with far slighter wit, had foreseen and warned him of.

He, Daniel, would manage matters better if he were to continue this life in the wilderness. No more following. He would lead, and he would plan every step he took before he took it.

He shook his head at his own presuppositions, for after all, he was human; and he could not pretend to understand this mountain warfare better than Lefty. If Lefty erred, all men must err. What was outlawry, then? It was the daily taking of one's life in one's hand—it was a terrible and knife-edged peril.

So Daniel looked down upon the five exposed figures and in one moment he knew that, if he possibly could, he would abandon all thought of the outlaw's independence and carefree existence. Not all the peril in the shack had been able to convince him, but the sight of that five-fold folly persuaded him.

He had thrown his bead. He fired calmly, and knew that his accurate bullet had gone through the calf of the man's leg—knew that it had passed through arteries and quivering flesh and perhaps had even drilled cleanly through the bone.

He saw his victim double up, and heard the cry of pain. Then he turned his attention to another. Suddenly he could not fire at helpless human flesh, and instead, he plumped down a bullet beside the head of a puncher in a yellow canvas coat.

The cow-puncher sprang up with a shout and fled headlong. The wounded fellow already was creeping for succor, and the two examples were enough for the rest. They rose in a mass and fled at full speed out of that unlucky apple orchard.

Daniel climbed down to the kitchen.

"They're out of the orchard," he announced. "Let's run that way."

"Not till we've had one go at that shack to the north," answered Lefty. "Come on, the two of you! Let's blast three holes through that dump. Each of you take a window. Aim close to the chimney edges—and we'll each put in five shots for luck. It may make them think that we plan on rushing them in that direction. Then we'll double around and make for the rear!"

"Run?" growled Tyson. "How can I run?"

However, he hobbled back with the others. They made their rifles ready. And Daniel could remember that at that moment the bullets of the besiegers were clanging on the kitchen stove as some pair of marksmen centered on one spot and drove slug after slug through the little place.

Then, with Lefty, they opened fire. Five shots apiece in rapid succession they poured on the outhouse in a storm and they heard a yell of fear and pain answer them.

"That's not the voice of Bud Loftus," grumbled Lefty. "Come on, now, boys, and we'll get out of this."

They left as fast as they could.

The rapid roar of their rifles as they poured in the fifteen shots from the northern face of the house apparently convinced the besiegers that this was the covering fire, after which the besieged would attempt a frontal attack. They stopped firing. A short half hour before, the wind had fallen to nothing. Only a thin mist was falling out of a dead gray sky when the three left the Gillian shack, and after the constant clang and rattle of the guns, there was utter silence.

Through that silence they fled toward the orchard and Tyson, in spite of his earlier complaints and his two wounds, ran much faster than the other two. Daniel was delayed by deadly pain in his wounded knee. Lefty made no attempt to press forward too rapidly, but, as Daniel never could forget, hung in the rear and held his rifle ready to cut off any hasty pursuit.

Then, behind them, guns began to bark. Daniel imagined that the next instant mounted men would be sweeping down after them; but next they heard the familiar clang of slugs on the kitchen stove and knew that the besiegers simply had resumed their fire upon the shack. Their flight had not been noticed.

And now the rain dropped in a roar. Sheets of water instantly formed even on the dead level and that water was beaten to a froth by the showering pellets of the rain. Such was the din that the noise of the rifles became in the distance like the petty sound of pop guns; and presently even this was lost.

They had crossed the orchard.

Now Lefty put himself in the lead, warned them with raised hand to a walk, and then moved straight down toward a deep thicket.

He plunged into this. Tyson followed on his heels, and Daniel now made the rear guard. He hobbled and once or twice he was tempted to slink to one side and lie down in the brush. He knew that Tyson never would inform the leader that one of their number had dropped out. But

he also knew, suddenly and surely, that when Lefty discovered that Daniel was gone he would turn back into
the face of certain death and try to find him again.
Whether it was the tie of kindred or the tie of friendship,
it seemed to Daniel that in this moment of flight, weariness, pain, and terrible, piercing rain, it was revealed to
him with a perfect fullness that in Lefty there was a faith
as great as possibly could be lodged in a human heart.

So he manfully kept up the rear as best he could.

The thicket grew denser. He was glad that the great
bulk of Tyson was breaking trail for him through the
labyrinth. So they came out on the sandy and rock-strewn
bottom of an empty river bed. The downpour had filled
pools and puddles here and there, but the main bed was
without mud or water; either it was sand or rock or big
pebbles, partly rounded by the friction of the spring torrents.

Here Lefty turned to the side which pointed north and
east, the direction of their mountains, and he went on
steadily for a half hour.

At the end of that time he stopped their march and
made Tyson and Daniel lie down in the partial shelter of
a scrub oak. There he examined their wounds.

With strips torn from shirts he made bandages.

"If I could get you off your feet," said Lefty, "you
wouldn't need a doctor. Tyson, here—he's just cut a bit.
Your knee might get infected, kid, and if it does, you've
got to have a professional man look at it. Now tell me,
kid, what are the two things that man most needs when
he's traveling?"

"A gun and a horse," suggested Daniel.

"Salt and iodine," answered Lefty, chuckling, and he
produced a small orange-colored bottle from his inside
coat pocket. With that he anointed their wounds, making
sure that the strong liquid entered deeply, while Tyson
cursed furiously with pain.

"There you are," said Lefty. "The bigger the man the
more there is of him to be hurt. More nerves he's got.
Why are women heroes? Because they're smaller. There's
less of 'em to suffer. Get up boys, Now we got to travel."

Travel they did.

Straight up the bed of that river, with the wet pebbles slipping and rolling underneath their feet, they marched on for three hours, and during that time the rain did not stop. It was a shifting curtain before them and behind. It smothered the world about them. For some reason, it became impossible to speak; with mute signs the three communicated with each other.

As for Daniel, his spirit had dropped to nothing. If he had not been led, he knew that he would have surrendered the battle there and then. And, indeed, all that supported him was a sense of shame, and an unwillingness to confess himself weaker than the others or less filled with resolution.

He tried to analyze that sensation, but it would not analyze.

A worthless ruffian and an outlaw with a price on his head; and yet he shuddered at the thought that he might lose their good opinion.

The pain in his knee had spread. His whole leg was throbbing. He felt sure that blood poisoning had set in. He could feel the flesh swell in his boot. The infection mounted to his hip. His whole leg grew numb and only mechanically could he go through the movements of walking. He began to wish for death.

"Boys, can you stand it?" said Lefty suddenly. "Or do you want to turn aside? There's a house beyond that bank. You can be in doctors' hands in an hour."

"Damn the doctors," said Daniel. "We'll fight it out!"

And he was amazed at the ring in his own voice; he was amazed at the strength he had found and at the sudden soul which had leaped up in him.

40. The Following Phantom

THAT SUDDEN OUTBREAK from Daniel brought a weak but not unexpected protest from Tyson.

"One real man outvotes three half men," sneered Lefty. "We'll keep on!"

They pressed on up the creek bed until they saw above them the dim arch of a bridge, cleaving the grayness of the storm. For still the rain came down, streaking the air with long, unbroken pencilings. Tyson, in sheer exhaustion, leaned on Lefty's shoulder. Every breath he took was a groan.

"I gotta stop, boys," said he. "For Heaven's sake, don't keep on! I'd pretty near rather lie down and die in the rain than to keep on."

"Steady up," said Lefty; "don't you be turning back when you're right under the Wishing Gate. There's the road passing over us, and we'll get horses there or bust."

He helped Tyson up the slope; Daniel could manage for himself, though with pain, and as they came into the brush at the roadside, the two wounded men threw themselves down in the wet of the grass, regardless of the water that came down in their faces and soaked them. They were fairly water-logged, and their bodies and their spirits could endure but little more.

Lefty, in the meantime, kept lookout. He reported the passage of a man on foot—some wretched tramp with a small bundle at his back. Then one rider went by.

"On a ragged-lookin' horse," said Lefty. "That'll be no use to us. Besides, we got to bag more fish when we fast for 'em! Hey, God bless me!"

The fervor in this exclamation left Tyson insensible, but it made Daniel turn to his hands and knees and crawl to the edge of the brush. Looking toward the bridge he could see a covered wagon coming down from the arch and settling on the level roadway again.

"Luck sent us that," said Lefty with simple fervor as it appeared. "We got to have that, I tell you. Kid, can you stand up and pretend to be able to use a gun? When I step to the head of the horses, you shout and show a gun from the brush."

"That wagon may be filled with armed men hunting for us," said Daniel, whose tired mind had become suspicious of every shadow.

"It may be full of sheep," grinned Lefty. "No, but it might have some hard-boiled farmer on the driver's seat with a rifle stuck in his boot."

"I'll do my share," muttered Daniel. "Go ahead!"

He unslung the rifle which had been such a weight during the last miles of the march, and as Lefty stepped to the heads of the horses with a revolver in either hand, Daniel leveled the rifle in plain view from the shrubbery.

There were two long-haired men in the driver's seat; but they attempted no resistance. They simply lifted their hands at once over their heads.

"Ho'd 'em!" said Lefty to Daniel. "I'll search the wagon!"

He ran back and peered in through the rear flap of the canvas.

"By George!" exclaimed Lefty. "Here's a regular house for us! Call Tyson. Tell him here's a chance for him to sleep. That ought to rouse him."

It would not, however. Tyson lay like a dead man, with eyes filmed over and half opened. Daniel cruelly shook him back to consciousness.

"Wake up, or stay here and rot in the mud," said Daniel. "Here's where we start."

He moved as though to leave the big man, and Tyson heaved himself to his feet and crawled helplessly after, wailing for Daniel to come back to him.

"If you leave me alone in this rain, I'll kill myself!" cried he. "I swear I'll kill myself! It'll be blood on your head, kid! Danny, for Heaven's sake, don't you leave me! I always was your friend. I may not have talked that way but I feel that way. Danny! Come back and——"

Daniel returned and helped him to his feet. Tyson had

broken down completely with the pain of his wounds, his exhaustion, and his fear. He began to blubber; he reeled as he walked, with one arm resting across Daniel's shoulder. So they gained the wagon.

It was driven by two Indians who sat upon the driver's seat with blank eyes turned toward these white men and their guns. There was no fear, excitement, or anger in their manner. They watched calmly while Daniel helped big Tyson to crawl through the rear sheet of the wagon, and saw him collapse along the wagon bed. Then Lefty entered, and seating himself behind the pair of semi-civilized red men, he commanded them to drive on up the road, not briskly enough to attract attention.

He explained himself quietly and clearly. If they did their work well and helped him and his two friends through the mountains, they could count on a fat reward of a hundred dollars apiece. If they showed any intention of betraying the nature of their wagon load to any passer-by, two bullets from a Colt would be the sum total of their payment.

They heard threat and promise with equal equanimity, and sitting stolidly on the seat they jogged their patient horses over mile after mile of the road. It was a road by name only. It was a wet, muddy cut across the face of the country and it held on its way with the blind and amiable persistence of a cow. Upon the most level and easy going, it wandered lazily back and forth; but where the rocks were piled and the way was steep, it proceeded as straight as an arrow. It turned aside from a nettle, and it drove straight over a mountaintop.

The joltings inside this springless vehicle were too terrible to be borne by ordinary nerves. Daniel endured it as long as he could, and then he stood up and rose on his toes, so that in this manner, with a spring of muscles, he might be able to break the jarring a little.

Only Tyson was not affected. He lay on his back, wabbling like a great jelly, and his snoring threatened to betray them when they passed near any human habitation.

"You get 'em like this," commented Lefty, "so close to pigs that pig life and pig ways are a lot better for 'em

than human ways. When he wakes up, this here Tyson
will be fit again. He'll be able to walk a hundred miles
without stopping, and go two or three days of work without food. But when he plays out, he plays out complete.
You can make a good horse work till he dies on his feet.
But if you should attempt to drive a pig—or Tyson—
past a point, why then he just lies down—and sleeps!"

Daniel asked him, quietly, if he thought that the two
Indians had the slightest idea of what their cargo was, but
Lefty assured him that the Indians knew everything about
the party of three which had commandeered transporta-
tion. He pointed out that the hands of the pair never were
still, but maintained a constant stream of communication.
Their sign language was so full, fluent, and thoroughly
mastered, that they could express every thought in their
minds.

In the meantime, the miles were beginning to drop behind them. The weather cleared a little; the clouds lifted
and the rain fell away to a thin Scotch mist.

"So much the worse for us," said Lefty. "Another
couple of hours of that heavy rain, and we would have
been through the danger zone. Listen, kid, and tell me if
you hear horses?"

In another moment, Daniel could hear them with perfect plainness.

They swept up behind in a volley of sound and developed into the beating of many hoofs. Through the
slightly parted curtains to the rear, the fugitives had
sight, now, of a dozen or more riders, coming at the
Western canter, which eats up the miles as the easy trot
of the wolf devours the distance.

They poured around the wagon suddenly, and Daniel
heard a voice speaking to the driver:

"What's been up this way, boys? Anything on foot!"

"Bud Loftus!" whispered Lefty to Daniel, and as he
spoke, crouching low in the bed of the wagon, he put
a gun muzzle into the small of each Indian's back.

"Nothing," answered the driver. "Not seen."

"Nothing not seen!" said the sheriff, who was not in
a good humor. "Most likely this is a pair of Indians that

have had a college education, and that's what they answer up; 'Nothing not seen!' I remember a day when we used to have you talkin' the kind of language that we liked to hear," said the old fighter. "Shake up your heads, will you, and make your brains work—your collegiate like brains, maybe they are! We followed the trail of three train robbers onto this road, and there the trail went out. There's money in it, my friends. There's a thousand apiece for you if you can put us onto the right way of finding those three. D'you hear?"

The two on the driver's seat stolidly shook their heads.

"It's no use, Bud," said one of his companions.

"I think they know something," growled Loftus presently. "I'll have a look inside their wagon, anyway!"

Daniel sat up straight, his eyes very big.

And into his hands, sad to relate, came two heavy, long and powerful Colts. There was no doubt about it; he was prepared to shoot, and shoot to kill.

Lefty, watching him, said not a word. He seemed more interested in the actions of Daniel than in the nearness of their danger. His eyes narrowed, and he looked into the very soul of his companion.

"Wait a minute, Bud," said another of the riders. "Would they trust themselves to a couple of Indians? They'd murder the pair of them and start with free hands."

"I think they would. I think Tyson would, anyway," said the sheriff. "Let's get on out of this, then. Come on, boys."

Away went the horses at a steady gallop, but they were still sounding close and loud when there was a sudden waving of the curtain at the end of the wagon. It parted and a rider was revealed peering in upon them.

His face was very pale and drawn. His very hands seemed bleached to an unnatural color.

It was Doc Tolliver! As in the flesh? No, changed and grown thinner, paler.

He looked steadily in. Then the canvas curtain dropped.

"Look up the road!" said Lefty in a terrible whisper. "Look up and down the road and see if he's in sight!"

Daniel, quaking a little himself, looked boldly out.

But neither up nor down the road was there any trace of the phantom rider. Only in the far distance was the diminishing group of the sheriff's posse. The blood of Daniel turned very cold.

41.   Tyson Quits

THE COVERED WAGON shook and groaned and swayed down the road; the span of little horses grunted in lifting their burden over a hilltop. But Daniel and Lefty Dunlin sat and stared at one another.

"It's my last trail" said Lefty Dunlin at length. "I knew it before, when he followed us, and the heat left my blood when he looked in through the canvas there. Of course you couldn't see him, Dan. And why? Because a ghost can disapper."

"It means nothing," said Daniel, "to you. If there's any meaning at all to the strange appearances of—of Tolliver—it has to do with me. I fired the shot that killed him—or seemed to kill him. If he haunts any one—but there's no such possibility, Lefty, old fellow. The fact is that he didn't die. The bullet——"

He paused.

"Just went through his brain and stunned him a little," said Lefty with a dismal smile. "Is that what you mean?"

"I mean that there is no harm to come to you, Lefty, out of this. Trouble may come this way, but only to me. Man, man, you're safe and sound. We'll split. Go one way, and I'll go another with Tyson——"

"You'd eat Tyson raw before you'd been an hour with him," declared Lefty. "No, kid. I never left a pal in trouble."

"Is it likely that I'd leave you?"

A pause followed that, and it was generously filled by the heavy snoring of big Tyson. It seemed clear to Daniel that he must not allow this man to throw himself away for the sake of a relationship which did not exist.

So he began a sudden confession.

"Lefty," said he, "I want to tell you what I found out from Jenny Loren, the other day."

"That she'd wait patient and true for you?" grinned Lefty.

Daniel colored a little. Then he went on, without paying any heed to the last remark.

"She brought me a letter from my father. I mean, from Jeremy Crosset. You see, Lefty, it appears that after all I haven't the right to claim any relationship with you. The story that he told me in the hotel at Lammer Falls was merely concocted because of—well it's hard to explain. He was worried—"

Daniel felt himself falling more and more hopelessly into a tangle. To explain the nervous, hair-trigger creature which he had been in the past seemed, in his present eyes, the most shameful and ridiculous thing in the world. And that he, Daniel Crossett, could have been hounded to the verge of suicide by a fool's weakness, a womanish superstition—he who under the name of Dunlin had ridden so far and done so many wild deeds—

He stared at Lefty, unable to continue, but Lefty nodded with the utmost cheerfulness.

"You don't have to explain," said he. "Lemme ask you, kid. Did I ever claim you for a brother?"

"No," said Daniel, and suddenly he remembered that the word never had been on the lips of the outlaw.

"I thought it was some crazy gag, at first," said Lefty. "Then I saw that you meant it. There was no good in me telling you what I knew. But I was old enough to remember seeing my mother crying over the dead baby. There wasn't a chance for any substituting. Besides, I could see the difference between you and a Dunlin. Any fool could see that with his eyes half blind. Take it easy, kid. You got nothing on your conscience. But only you remember that blood ain't the only thing that holds two men together."

He rolled a cigarette, while Daniel sat silent, full of

amazement. Now that he looked on the past days in the light of these words, he could see that they were true, obviously. Lefty never had been convinced. Lefty never had pretended to be convinced. He had accepted the companionship of Daniel, but he never had accepted the relationship.

Daniel hardly knew whether he should be amused or grieved.

At length he smiled.

"I seem to have been a champion fool, Lefty," said he.

"Only young," said Lefty, lighting his smoke. "Grain fed and nothing to carry but your skin. That always makes trouble bust loose. If your old man would cut off your allowance, you'd never have the blues, kid, and, another thing, you'd never get too hot for harness."

He grinned at Daniel through a white mist of smoke, and the latter, in a way, felt himself put in one corner like a schoolboy by his teacher.

So Daniel came to the heart of his other message.

"Since we're not kin, Lefty, you see that you're a fool to put your head into a noose, man, by staying with a pair of cripples."

Lefty yawned.

"If they ever get you, Lefty," said the boy, "they'll surely hang you. It wouldn't matter so much for me. My father's money and lawyers would probably get me a small sentence—unless a mob lynched me. But I don't think that money could save you. If you will——"

"You've said your piece," said Lefty. "Now keep an eye up and down the road, will you? I'm gunna have a snooze!"

And with that, he curled up on the floor of the wagon and fell into a profound sleep in spite of the jolting which soon rolled his hat off and made his hair flop at every jar of the wagon bed. Daniel regarded him with deepest amazement. But he knew that no words could persuade this outlawed man from the performance of what he thought to be his duty.

So Daniel sat in deepest study of the sleeping Tyson, of Lefty, of the two stolid Indians, of the jogging, down-headed, patient horses which switched their tails mildly as the whip stung and cut, of the winding, jagged, muddy road, of the sky line that drew near or fell away according as the storm gathered or cleared, and finally the thought of himself and what he had been, what he was, and what he would be if he lived through this affair.

The future, it appeared to Daniel, was a difficult matter to decide upon, because in spite of his greatest effort at clear thinking, it was confined to the pretty face of Jenny Loren, which had fitted neatly into his heart and would not come out again.

But chiefly—as always during these last wild days— his thoughts clung to Lefty. If only the world could have the chance to study this man, it would have to revise its moral code and its estimates of good and evil. No doubt he had done much wrong to society. But he had done much good to man. And, vaguely, Daniel perceived that there is a double truth and a double standard of judgment. There is the way for the weak, and there is also the way for the strong who may transcend precedent, and custom and law.

And it seemed to Daniel that he saw in Lefty if not a brother in blood at least a brother in kind. For they had one nature between them. What Lefty's fate threatened to be, such was his own. He felt that he had seen the handwriting upon the wall.

Suddenly Tyson sat up with a growl.

He rubbed his eyes, peered grimly at Daniel, and then announced: "In the same leaky boat! What's the way out this time?"

There was no clear way out, and Daniel told him so.

"Him a leader! Him a wise thief?" sneered Tyson, pointing to Lefty. "He's a fool, and he's made a fool out of me! How he ever won a reputation, I dunno, but from the beginning to the end of this trip, he's bungled everything. I'm through with him. We'll split the trail!"

Daniel wondered at two things—at the malevolence and the passion of the man, and at the prodigious strength which enabled him, after a brief sleep, to rouse himself from a trembling, cringing wailing weakness, to almost his normal strength. He could have believed such a thing of a beast, but not of a human being.

He told Tyson to be quiet and not waken Lefty. Then he pointed out that it was his turn to sleep, and directed Tyson to take up the watch upon the two drivers of the wagon.

Tyson returned no answer, merely lowering his black brows; and Daniel curled himself up in what comfort he could. At first, the shuddering and the jolting of the hard wagon bed made sleep impossible. But his vast weariness would have conquered greater obstacles than this. Presently he slept.

When he wakened the vehicle still was staggering along the road; his wounded knee was in a fever, his brain dulled by a mist. Opposite him sat Lefty, cross-legged. But Tyson was gone.

And, as Daniel raised himself dizzily into a sitting posture, Lefty said with a grin: "Tyson gave us liberty. The minute that you put him on guard and got to sleep he took a look at you and me. He wanted to brain the pair of us, by the look of him. But his nerve failed him at the last minute. I watched him pretty careful. Finally he slipped out of the back of the wagon, shook his fist at us, and that was the end of him. I never was gladder to get rid of anybody!"

"The poor fool will be caught," said Daniel.

"He will," answered Lefty with a contented nod. "There never was a fellow in the world that needed a long rest in jail as badly as Tyson needs it. Forget about him, kid. We've got ourselves to think of."

"Where are we?"

"We're through the lines, I think," said Lefty. "While you were sleeping, the wagon was stopped. That was ten minutes ago. Three gents stepped up and questioned the pair of wooden faces. But they learned nothing, and they were too careless to look inside. Look out, kid!"

Daniel, accordingly, peered out through the front of the wagon.

The sky was still covered with a thin gray, but the rain had stopped, and all around them was a rolling sea of hills, and just beyond, the tall, shaggy mountains thrust upward against the heavens.

That was their promised land.

The road they followed now was unbelievably rough. In fact, as Daniel soon saw, it was no road at all, but a mere bridle path, and presently this in turn ended in a twisting way at so steep a grade that no wagon possibly could be drawn up its face.

There they climbed to the ground, Daniel with a very stiff and fevered leg. Lefty bargained with the pair of Indians for the two horses. They wanted three hundred for the span, but they readily accepted two hundred. The little ponies were as tough as leather, but their heads were hardly up to a man's shoulder when they stood at attention.

"Now," said Lefty, "here's two hundred for your ponies. Here's two hundred for your time. You can buy a couple of mustangs for another hundred and come here and salvage your wagon. And there's one thing more. You forget about seeing us. Forget where you took us. Forget where you left us. Forget what we look like. But if any man asks you where Lefty Dunlin and his pal are and you tell 'em, Lefty Dunlin will come and break you in two. You understand?"

They nodded. Even now, with the money in their hands, and Daniel busily stripping the harness from the little animals, there was not the slightest shade of expression in their eyes; but climbing down from the driver's seat, they turned down the trail with no word of farewell and went off at a soft dog trot, one behind the other, Indian fashion.

"They'll never stop," grinned Lefty, "until they come to the first town——"

"And there they'll tell everything they know!" suggested Daniel.

"They may," said Lefty, throwing his leg over the back of one of the ponies, "but I know something about Indians. They have sense, kid. And they want peace more than they want money. The main question is: Can you ride?"

Ride? There was nothing simpler. No matter for the pain in the leg. Above them stretched the welcome darkness of the mountain forests. Behind them lay the terrible dangers of the open plain. And it seemed to Daniel that, for the first time in his life, he had come home!

42.   A Meeting

THAT NIGHT, Daniel luxuriated on a bed of softest pine boughs—of all beds in this world the most luxurious, the most fragrant—and ate a dinner of roasted venison.

For Lefty shot a deer before the ponies had climbed three miles toward the heights. After that, he slept a dreamless sleep, and awakened in the morning refreshed, clear-headed, and quite able to stand. The wound in his leg was a perfectly clean one, and his blood was in such prime condition that the healing began at once. However, Lefty would not risk moving from their camp.

Above them were the safer heights. But here in this forest glade they were fairly secure and, for that matter, once the hunt turned toward the mountains, it would be the upper and more distant fastnesses which would be explored, rather than such an easily accessible spot as this. It was like hiding the letter on the letter rack!

Seven long days and seven peaceful nights slipped away and left Daniel limping easily here and there, making the camp more comfortable, cooking the game which Lefty brought in, sitting in the firelight—for they risked a small blaze, well-housed with shadowy rocks—and listening to the long tales of Lefty which sent his imagination ranging from Guatemala to Alaska, all through that wild Western land where he had ridden and robbed, and sinned.

But he heard these tales, now, with a new attitude. For in the beginning he had listened to Lefty as to another voice from his own lips; all that a Dunlin had done he must be able to do; all that Lefty had experienced was a book in which he himself would read. But now it was, otherwise, and he heard the tales as one reads a book interpreted from a strange tongue, of deeds done long ago, never to be repeated.

No human being came near them, during that week. Within easy marching distance were the houses of several of Lefty's hired friends, but he would not trust them, he said, even for information, until Daniel's leg was strong enough to carry him easily and comfortably wherever they had to walk or ride. Their chief problem was how they should secure horses, and good ones. The little ponies which they had taken from the Indians would bring them comfortably wherever they wished to go, but they would not suffice to elude pursuit if resolute horsemen once came on their trail. It was planned, therefore, that on the morning of the eighth day they would ride for the nearest of Lefty's retainers, and there they would get capable horses and comfortable saddles. Then they would be free to consider their next step, which, Lefty declared, must be to get Daniel in touch with his father.

So they sat on the seventh night and listened to a rising wind which sighed or moaned through the upper branches, though never a breath of it came to them or so much as shook the narrow tongue of flame that rose from their fire.

Lefty was deep in a narrative of happenings in Chihua-hua when he stopped in the middle of a sentence and slowly rose to his feet.

Daniel turned, and just behind him he was horrified to see the white and drawn face of Doc Tolliver—a face without a body—merely a visage drawn in white on the blackness of the mountain night!

Then the lips parted: "Don't shoot, Lefty," said the voice of Tolliver. "I'm here as your friend, and what a time I've had to get to you!"

He stepped forward. The firelight showed all of him, now, to his chaps and spurs. He pushed back his sombrero to ease the pressure on a bandage that encircled the upper part of his head.

"A grand time I had of it," said Tolliver, "since I first got in touch with you, and that young hell-cat dropped me with his bullet!"

He turned and scowled in most unfriendly fashion on Daniel.

"By Heaven!" breathed Lefty. "You ain't dead, Doc? You ain't a ghost—you—you——"

"Is that the gag?" grinned Tolliver.

"Hannigan swore that he buried you under five ton of rock!"

"He done his best," said Tolliver. "I come to, lying in a sort of a nacheral grave, except that there was an open end to it. A rock or two dropped down close to me, and I managed to get onto my knees and start crawling. I hadn't gone ten feet before there was a roar and a crash behind me, and the little gully filled up at my heels with broken rock.

"I fainted again. Then I managed to crawl out of that gully. I seen a light and started toward it. When I come into the open doorway, Hannigan bolted past me.

"I never seen a scareder face. Well, I was glad to have the use of his cabin. I washed the cut in my head. It had been luck that made the slug slip from my forehead and run back along the skull. Lord knows why the bullet didn't go straight through me! But after I'd borrowed a drink of Hannigan's whisky, and put on a bandage, and thrown a feed under my belt, I felt well enough to sleep, and when I woke up, I was well enough to ride. So I started on to try to find this fool kid, here!"

"The forest——" gasped Daniel, who had listened, entranced with interest.

"Where you rode past me like mad? I couldn't catch up with you. You had a better horse under you than the one that I rode. And there I was carrying a letter that would've kept you from train robbery, young man!"

Lefty staggered back and mopped his forehead.

"And when you looked into the covered wagon?"

"What could I do? The sheriff wasn't a hundred yards away. I spotted you, and then I faded."

"It don't seem possible!" said Lefty. "How'd you disappear from the roads?"

"The trees weren't six yards off."

How easily the impossible could be explained away!

"And then," said Tolliver, "I met up with the girl. She was riding the same trail. I found out that she'd located you before me. But since she wanted to find you again —I dunno why—we went on. There's the letter, kid. I suppose that she gave you the brother of it!"

A travel-soiled and crumpled envelope was given to Daniel. It repeated, word for word, almost, what had been told in that which Jenny Loren had given him. But he placed it carefully in a breast pocket, for it was a memento too priceless to be thrown away.

"But now that you're found," said Tolliver, "what are you gunna do?"

"We'll get horses and ride," said Lefty.

"Where do you get the horses?"

"I have friends."

"There ain't a friend in the mountains that wouldn't sell you, Lefty. They've piled fifteen thousand on your head."

It was enough to turn even Lefty white.

"Fifteen—thousand—dead or alive!" murmured Lefty.

"Every penny of that, and a couple of bonuses throwed in."

"It's the finish," said Lefty gravely.

"But," went on Tolliver slowly, "something might be done about it."

He whistled sharply.

In the distance there was a crackling of brush.

"Tolliver," said Lefty in sharp warning, "you're a square fellow. But if you try a double cross now——"

"Son," answered Tolliver dryly, "you don't need to warn me. No danger in me forgetting. I've got the warning already printed in my scalp!"

And he touched the bandage.

Out of the circle of darkness where the trees stood broke the approaching noise, and now they saw a number of horses, with pricked ears and glistening eyes, being led forward by one person, no larger than a boy.

"Here," said Tolliver, "we got five good horses. We figured that the party might be three. That was before we heard that Tyson had been caught and tried to turn State's evidence."

"The hound!" said Lefty.

"But the State didn't need his evidence," said Tolliver. "All that they wanted of him was his time to spend in prison, and that's where he's bound. Step up, honey. These gents have met you before!"

So Daniel saw her again, and gasped, and went forward as Lefty had gone toward his ghost, and found Jenny Loren with the five reins fallen from her nerveless hand.

Postscript

THE SEA BREAKS on the great rocks of Winhasset, and above the rocks stands the little town, and behind the town is the Mansion. It has that name all through the neighborhood, and those who dwell in it rarely are referred to except as "the people on the hill." The small boys of the village pause and look through the iron gates, and they see a winding driveway, and then a stretch of lawn, and beyond the lawn the glimmer of white columns, tall and thin.

Winter had stripped the trees of the Crosset place of their leaves; the graveled paths were black with wet; and the three pools were sheeted with heavy ice where white dust flew from the skates every day. The ocean under the rocks was cold and gray, the rocks themselves dripped ice, where the spray had frozen before it could fall; all the roofs in the village glistened with frost, and the outer twigs of the trees in the Crosset estate were cased in ice; but in the library of the big Mansion the logs which fumed and spat and roared on the hearth made a second summer.

So it seemed to Jenny.

She could close her eyes and that warmth reminded her of the wide Western landscape, and the torrents of white sun, and the pools of black shadow, and the burned hills, and the shadowy forests on the upper mountains; but when she opened her eyes and looked over the window again, all she saw was the white of ice and snow and the black gauntness of the trees.

And her heart swelled and ached in her breasts.

Some one stood in the doorway. She had a feeling, suddenly, that he had been there for a long time, waiting and watching, and she started out of her chair in fear.

"Steady, steady!" said a familiar voice.

"Lefty!" cried the girl. "Lefty! How—why—good heavens, Lefty, how terribly glad I am to see you! But how did you come? How did you dare? How did you escape and——"

"Sit down," said Lefty.

He stood beside her as she sank back into the chair.

"Are you happy?" said Lefty.

"Oh, yes!"

"Homesick," said Lefty. "But then, you only been married for six months, and you'll get over that. How's the kid?"

"Who?"

"I mean Daniel Crossett," said Lefty with a grin.

"Oh!" said Jenny. "Of course he's well."

"And happy?"

"I think so. He says he is. I hope he is, Lefty!"

The brown outlaw grinned again.

"It's a sad business, the first couple of years," said Lefty. "I never could quite make up my mind to go through with it. On account of the first couple of years, I mean. But are you gunna fit in here, Jenny?"

"The place seems big enough to hold me," said Jenny with a flash of her old self.

"Aye," said Lefty, nodding. "And give you a little time—you'll be big enough to hold it; I just looked in. Everybody's well? I'd better be going, Jenny!"

She barred the way.

"Dan would lose his mind if he thought you'd been here and gone without——"

"Of course he would, Heaven bless him! But why should I stay? If I see him, it'll make me want to hang on here. To talk over old days, y'understand. And I can't hang on. I'm taking a vacation, Jenny. When I come back from across the pond, I'll drop in, maybe the kid will be at home that day."

"Oh, Lefty," said the girl, "if you'll give up that life, Dan will do everything in the world for you! It would only be a joy to him to give you such a business that——"

"Would it compare with the mountains that I own and the cities out yonder?" said Lefty. "No, Jenny. I know what he would want to do. But a fish has got to have water; and a bird has got to have air. I couldn't live on money that was given to me. I got to earn my way, Jenny. And lately I been striking it pretty rich!"

He took her hands. His voice changed a little.

"Give the kid luck from me. Tell him that he took half the height off the mountains and half the pay out of gold when he left me. So long, Jenny!"

He stepped noiselessly across the rug. Some one came up the hall; Lefty vanished into a corner shadow, paused, and then was gone behind the back of the maid who just then entered the spacious room with her shimmering tea tray.

And Jenny did not follow.

She knew that there was no use in it, and afterward she sat behind the little tea table and looked again across the black arms of the forest which grew, every stick, on Crosset land, and across the white, cold hills, and into the thin gray of the sky where the sun never could be bright with the brightness which she knew.

"Shall I turn the lights on, madam?" asked the maid.

"No, no," said Jenny. "I'd rather have it dark!"